HEATHER BLACKWOOD

THE
CLOCKWORK
CATHEDRAL

A TIME CORPS NOVEL

CHAPTER 1

"**I**'M ALREADY ON MY WAY home," said Felicia Sanchez, switching her mobile phone from one ear to the other and leaning back in her seat on the bus. "And I have a huge paper to work on tonight. I can't go back to the hospital."

"But you promised," said her housemate, Doug, over the phone.

His voice was nearly drowned out by the roar of the bus engine as it pulled away from the curb. The last of the boarding passengers took their seats and an elderly woman sat down beside Felicia. Doug had been looking forward to Comic-Con for months, and his Dr. Horrible costume would be nothing without the lab coat she had borrowed from her fellow medical student. She had remembered to get the coat, but then had left it in her locker at the hospital.

"Can't I get it tomorrow?" she asked.

"I leave for Comic-Con first thing in the morning."

The air outside the bus window seemed to shimmer, like the waves of air rising over burning pavement on a hot day. But it was a cool February evening in New Orleans. The air moved at her eye-level, blurring her view of the cars on the other side of the street. Didn't air only move in that manner when viewed against a horizon?

"That's weird," Felicia murmured.

"It's not weird. I have to carpool and the drive to Houston will take most of the day."

"No, not that. Never mind."

"So you'll go back and get the lab coat? I'll make a mushroom and spinach quiche for dinner. And I'll even whip up a batch of oatmeal raisin cookies. Then you won't have to cook dinner and you can work on your paper all night."

Felicia sighed. Doug was a bit eccentric, but still a good housemate. He was quiet and always on time with his share of the rent and utilities. He had even been patient with her when she tried to play a multiplayer online game with him and couldn't get the hang of shape shifting and casting spells simultaneously. On top of that, he occasionally packed her a lunch when he was preparing his own. She owed him, and she had made a promise.

"Fine. I'll head back at the next stop."

"Thank you! I'll get started on dinner."

She hung up and noticed a fluttering paper sign tacked onto a telephone pole announcing a Civil War reenactment this week. That meant more tourists cramming into the city on top of those already arriving for Mardi Gras.

Felicia checked her texts. One of her sisters asked for details on Felicia's flight to Los Angeles. In two weeks, Felicia would be the maid of honor in her wedding in Los Angeles, where their family lived. Felicia would have to call her later and give her the flight details so someone could pick her up at the airport.

Her mother had also sent a text saying that her father's biopsy had shown a small skin growth to be benign. Felicia texted back that she was happy to hear it. The warm glow of happiness faded a little as she checked her voice mail and listened to a message from her ex-boyfriend. She would have to think about whether or not she wanted to call him back. She deleted the message.

She checked her e-mail and must have made a little noise of delighted surprise, because the elderly woman beside her glanced over. It was an e-mail from Brazil, from a doctor who specialized in an experimental treatment for a rare form of bone cancer. Nathan, her three-year-old nephew, was receiving treatment in Los Angeles, and his prognosis was not good. Felicia hadn't informed her sister, fearing that Nathan might not be a good candidate. But the doctor stated that he was happy to learn more about the case, and that Nathan might benefit from the treatment.

Clutching her phone to her chest, she bit her lower lip. There was hope yet. She would e-mail the doctor when she got home and give him more complete information, including her sister's phone number and e-mail address.

Out the window, fewer than six feet away, a man rode on horseback. She wanted to yell to him to watch out, that he would get hit by the oncoming cars, but he and his horse seemed to be having an ordinary ride. His demeanor was relaxed, although his back was poker straight and he kept his eyes forward. He was dressed in some kind of nineteenth century clothing with a top hat, breeches and leather boots. He must either be one of the historical recreationists who made a living giving tours of the city or one of the tourists who came for the Civil War reenactment. But what he was doing on a horse in the middle of the street?

"What's that fellow doing there?" asked the elderly woman next to her.

"Doesn't seem safe to me," said Felicia. When she turned back to the window, the man was gone. The woman beside her was rummaging through her shopping bag and had not noticed his disappearance.

The next stop would be at St. Charles Avenue in the Garden District. Felicia would get off, cross the street and take the next bus back to Tulane University Hospital. It was now completely dark, and her stomach growled. Doug's mushroom and spinach quiche sounded better and better.

As the bus approached its stop, Felicia rose, excused

herself as she squeezed past the older woman and moved toward the front of the bus. She gripped the overhead railing, steadying herself as the bus slowed. The air in front of the bus shimmered, and she saw the man on the horse through the front window of the bus. He was directly in the bus's path.

"What the hell?" yelled the bus driver, slamming on the brakes. A few passengers cried out in surprise.

The horse shied and reared up, and the rider gave a shout as he leaned in and held tight to keep from being thrown. The horse bolted toward the sidewalk, the bumper of the bus missing it by inches. Felicia only had a moment of relief until the bus lurched hard, throwing her to her hands and knees. Some of the other passengers screamed.

Felicia pulled herself to her feet, hanging on to the back of a seat. It felt as if the bus had hit something, but nothing had been in front of them, she was certain of it. The bus was now stopped and the air was shimmering in multiple places outside, as if a handful of pebbles had been tossed into a puddle and ripples were circling outward. The blaring car horns mixed with shouts and the high-pitched scream of a terrified horse. The animal tore down the sidewalk, its reins dangling and its saddle empty. Felicia spotted the rider lying on the pavement.

"Open the door!" she commanded. The door swung open and Felicia jumped out. She knelt at the man's side. He was conscious and trying to sit up.

"Are you all right?" Felicia said.

He nodded and rubbed at his back. "I'm sure I'll be fine in a bit."

He had a strong Southern accent. She wanted to examine him for injuries, but he was already climbing to his feet. She offered him a hand up, and he stared at her in bewilderment for a moment before waving her away. He located his top hat and situated it atop his head.

The bus was gone now, and in its place was an old-fashioned vehicle, the type that tourists liked to ride. It looked something like a stagecoach, but was much longer and was painted green with gold trim. Fancy gold script on the side read: *Jackson Square, St. Charles Line.* A seat for the driver was high on the front of the vehicle, and the driver himself scrambled down. Four horses were hitched to the front, and their restless movement caused the vehicle to roll forward a few inches. Felicia noted that the spindly wagon wheels were larger in the back than the front, and its side windows had no glass but were open to the warm, mid-morning air.

Mid-morning air? But it was evening. Nevertheless, the sun was shining overhead and the streets bustled with activity. She felt dizzy and grabbed at a lamppost, noting vaguely that it was topped with an antique-looking gaslight.

"An omnibus accident!" shouted a man behind her.

"I've sent a boy already for the ambulance."

"Get out of the way!" shouted a heavyset man with a bushy gray moustache and muttonchops.

"He's a doctor," cried a woman. "Let him through!"

People poured out of the, what had the man called it? An omnibus? The man with the muttonchops and moustache knelt and examined an injured woman.

Felicia knew she had to help. She was only a medical student, but she was of more use than the strangely dressed bystanders who stood around talking among themselves. She felt dizzy again and her stomach heaved. She swallowed hard and took a deep breath, determined not to vomit. She must have taken a blow to the head when she fell down on the bus. But she didn't remember feeling any pain at the time. And her head didn't hurt now either. But the nausea, dizziness and optical disorientation making evening look like mid-morning had to be a symptom of some sort of head injury.

Historical recreationists poured from the omnibus. A woman in full skirts fanned herself and a man with a top hat offered his arm to her. A few other passengers were lying or sitting on the ground, but most were standing.

The back of the omnibus looked like it had been hit by a ...well, a bus. But where was her bus? And where was anyone who wasn't in a historical costume?

Rows of beautiful Garden District houses lined the street. The wrought iron gate of the one directly across the street squeaked open. A tall man in suspenders and striped brown trousers stopped and took in the scene. He was hatless, and his hair was wild, as if he had just gotten out of bed. He strode across the street toward her.

"Are you all right, miss?" he said. He had an Irish accent. She looked down to see he was holding her by the elbow. She didn't remember him moving to touch her. Did she look like she was going to pass out?

"Why don't you rest for a moment, lass?" he said. "You should come over across the street where there aren't so many people." She felt too dizzy and sick to protest. She allowed him to guide her to a quiet spot near a thick fence of brick and black iron in front of his house. She sat down and leaned against the fence, cradling her head in her hands. The world spun madly and the feeling of nausea overwhelmed her. Worse than that, there were people injured, and she was unable to help them.

"Don't go anywhere," the man said, pointing a finger at her. He took a long look at her, then spun and rushed toward the crowd.

CHAPTER 2

SEAMUS CONNOR LEFT THE WORST injured to the doctor and the ambulance workers who had just arrived. Thankfully, only two people needed to be loaded into the ambulance, both of whom were conscious. Once they were on board, the ambulance driver cracked a whip and a team of horses pulled them in the direction of the hospital.

Seamus would never forgive himself if anyone had been seriously hurt, or God forbid, killed. He was fairly sure that the accident was his fault and he shot a glance at the woman leaning against his front fence. Good, she was still there.

Only a few injured people remained, most of whom were standing. Seamus helped an older man to rise and take his adult son's arm. He watched them walk down the street to await the next omnibus to complete their trip home.

For a moment, he felt a twinge of shame at appearing outdoors hatless and in just shirtsleeves with no jacket. In other circumstances, someone would have mentioned it. Surely his housekeeper, Mrs. Washington, would do so when he returned. At least he had managed to put on some shoes before leaving the house.

But his state of undress was nothing compared to the woman who was sitting with her head in her hands. She was wearing some kind of tight men's trousers, like workmen's pants, made from dark blue denim. They hugged her lower body scandalously, and he forced his eyes away, only to find himself unable to look away. Her jacket appeared to be some kind of purple cotton, with a long serrated metal line down the front and a hood at the back. Other than the hood, which hung down behind her, she was without any sort of head covering. On her feet were the strangest, narrowest shoes he had ever seen. They were made of purple canvas and what looked like white rubber. He had never seen rubber so white before. And how did her feet fit into such shoes?

She raised her head to look at him and he reached up to tip his hat, but upon finding he had none, flashed a grin at her. After ensuring that everyone around him was on their feet, he crossed the street to her. She rose without taking his offered hand.

"We should get you inside," he said. He didn't know where exactly she was from, but it wasn't here. First of all, she needed some decent clothing. Then, he wanted to ask her questions. Perhaps he would ask the questions first.

"Where am I?" she asked, squinting up at him. Her eyes were a light shade of brown, almost amber. They looked too light in contrast with her skin and deep brown hair.

"St. Charles Street. My house is just there," he pointed behind her. "Come inside and rest for a spell."

She looked past him and he could tell she was deciding. Then she swayed on her feet and he grabbed her arm to steady her.

She pushed her hair behind her ear. "Just for a few minutes. Until I feel a little better."

He lifted her leather handbag from the ground and handed it to her. At least the bag looked ordinary enough.

"I'm sorry, miss," he said. "But in the commotion I've forgotten my manners. I'm Seamus Connor."

"Felicia Sanchez." She offered her hand to him sideways, but he took it anyway and bowed over it properly. She gave him a confused look and neglected to curtsey. He had no hat to tip, so perhaps they were even. Sanchez was a Spanish name. Perhaps she was from Spain, or maybe Mexico, judging by her looks.

He held open the front gate for her and took her arm to lead her up the front brick pathway. She seemed steadier on her feet now, though she was looking at his house as if she had never seen one like it.

"I like your house," she said. "You've done a nice job keeping it up. Not everyone does."

"Thank you. I've only had it a few years."

Seamus was proud of his home. It was a newer house and was built in the same manner as many other homes in the Garden District. He had changed the color from plain white to cream and had painted the shutters dark green. The front door was the same shade of green and boasted a shiny brass knocker and a matching filigreed mail slot. Two covered galleries ran along the front of both stories, framed by thick white columns and wrought iron railings that matched the fencing that enclosed the yard. The upper gallery was a pleasant place to sit on hot summer days. In the evening, he opened up the long windows at the front and back of the house, allowing the cool evening breeze to chase out the heat. When he worked in his upstairs laboratory, he loved listening to the rustling of the neighbors' oak trees as the breeze blew through their leaves.

"My housekeeper planted the star magnolias and oakleaf hydrangea over there," he said.

"They're lovely. Are you from Ireland? You sound Irish," Miss Sanchez said.

"That I am."

He hoped she wouldn't ask him questions about his home and why he had left. He hated to lie, on principle. But he did it often enough that it came naturally. Most people were content if he told them he was from Dublin and left it at that. After the famine, so many immigrants had flooded into New Orleans that he was easily dismissed without people wondering why he had left his homeland. A more pressing question was why he lived in the Garden District rather than with the other immigrants in the Irish Channel neighborhood along the uptown riverfront. Miss Sanchez, thankfully, did not press the issue.

She allowed him to hold the door for her and lead her through the hall to the back of the house. The kitchen had a table off to one side and he offered her a seat. She seemed amused as he pulled out her chair. Did she not expect an Irishman to have manners? Many didn't like his kind and thought his people were little more than barbarous white savages. Many Irish had trouble finding jobs, and he knew he was more than fortunate to have a professorship at Tulane where there had only ever been one other Irishman on staff. He tried not to think of the other man.

He put a kettle of water on and from the corner of his eye, saw Miss Sanchez rub her temples.

"Are you feeling all right, then?" he asked.

"I still feel dizzy and sick to my stomach."

Was that one of the symptoms? He wanted to ask her where exactly she was from, but how did one broach such a subject?

"I'm making some tea," he said. "Are you hungry? I can make you a sandwich. I think I have some things around here."

"No thanks. I couldn't eat right now."

He rummaged through the cabinets for the teapot and cups. Now, where did Mrs. Washington keep them? He was about to ring for her, but he wanted to be alone with Miss Sanchez a little while longer. She looked around the room like she had never seen an ordinary kitchen before and seemed fascinated with the pump next to the sink. The thought crossed his mind that she might not be the full shilling, and that she had somehow wandered onto the omnibus from some mental asylum. But no, he was fairly sure he knew otherwise.

"So," he said, scooping tea leaves into the strainer and setting it in the teapot. "Are you Castillian? A Spaniard?"

"Excuse me?"

She looked as if he had said something improper. He needed to clarify. "Your surname is Sanchez. Are you a Spaniard?"

"You can drop the historical recreationist act, buddy."

"Recreationist?"

"Aren't they having a Civil War reenactment or something this week? Is that why you're here?"

"Civil War?" The words chilled him. "What do you mean?"

She sat back and crossed her arms. "Yeah, there's a Civil War coming. Didn't you know? In 1861. You might want to head back to Ireland."

He turned back to the teacups and set them on a tray. His heart thumped hard in his chest, and not just at the prospect of a possible war. He took the kettle from the stove and poured hot water into the teapot.

"So, where are you from, then?" he asked.

"I'm from LA and I'm going to medical school at Tulane."

He had never heard of a city or street called Ellay. Her accent was American, certainly, but was not what he was accustomed to hearing in New Orleans, even with its blend of races and languages. And how could a woman, and a Spaniard, or whatever she was, go to school at Tulane? All his students were white and male.

"That's a coincidence," he said. "I teach at Tulane."

"In the History department?"

"No. Physics and Mechanics. Why would you think I was a History professor?"

The woman shook her head and smiled to herself. She looked better when she smiled. It was much better than the pained and nauseated expression from before or the angry way she had looked at him when he asked if she was a Spaniard.

Oh, but this was exciting. This was more than exciting, this was a miracle. He found himself smiling at her as he offered her a cup of tea.

"I am so glad you are here," he said.

"Thanks." She blew on the tea. He saw that she held the cup in both hands, as if to warm herself, not in the proper ladylike manner which Southern women were taught. But then, judging by the woman's clothing and remarks, she lived in barbarous times.

"I thought I heard voices down here," said Mrs. Washington from the kitchen doorway.

Seamus leaped up to make introductions. "Miss Sanchez, this is my housekeeper, Mrs. Washington. Mrs. Washington, Miss Sanchez." The women nodded to each other and Mrs. Washington eyed the teapot with a displeased expression.

"What, am I not allowed to make tea in my own home?" Seamus asked.

"Not when you run off with it and lose the teapot half the time." But her eyes were warm as she said it.

"I need something to drink when I work and think. And whiskey is no good for either, I assure you."

Mrs. Washington shook her head and set to tidying the kitchen, which Seamus had not thought of as messy. But as she bustled about, he realized that the morning dishes had yet to be done and the place wasn't exactly ready for a guest.

"I'm afraid this is my fault," said Seamus, turning back to Miss Sanchez. "See, I was working on the peroxide engine, but I couldn't open the engine core without destroying it. They have it set up that way, you see. Not fair play, if you ask me. But no one did. So anyhow, I was using a sonic mapping machine. That's my own, you understand. And I was bouncing zed waves off the inside and recording it. I have a device that records the images on thin sheets of aluminium. And I think there was an accident."

Miss Sanchez rubbed her eyes. He knew that she didn't understand a word he was saying. He would put it simply.

"I think you came through from another time. Or another place. Or both."

CHAPTER 3

FELICIA ONLY HALF LISTENED AS Seamus Connor rambled on about some machine up in his laboratory and an accident and how he thought it was all his fault. He said she had come through to his time in 1857. He talked too fast, with too many hand gestures, and though he seemed friendly enough, he must be either mentally ill or entirely too caught up in the whole historical reenactment thing. Probably the latter. She had done a psych rotation, and this man didn't seem mentally ill.

She noticed that the more excited he got, the stronger his Irish accent became. And when he really got going, she had the feeling that he was talking more to himself than to her.

"Tell me where you're from," he said.

"I already told you. I'm from LA."

"And where is that, exactly?"

Fine. She could play along until she felt better. Then she'd take the bus back to the hospital to get Doug's lab coat, go home, and then call her sister to put her in contact with the Brazilian doctor.

"Los Angeles, California," she said. "Do you know where California is?"

"I'm not mentally impaired," he said, looking at her as if she might be.

Right. It was 1857. And California had become a state around the time of the gold rush, in 1849. She remembered that from history class.

"And what year is it for you?" His unblinking stare was unnerving. She told him what year it was.

"Ha!" he shouted. He leapt up and paced back and forth. "Early twenty-first century! Incredible! Do you know how incredible this is?"

She shook her head, but had to smile at his exuberance. He seemed so happy.

"Of course you don't know. You think we're—what did you call it? Recreationists?"

He muttered to himself, occasionally spinning and pacing to the other end of the kitchen. Felicia sipped her tea. It seemed to be helping to settle her stomach.

Seamus Connor was tall and lean and his movements had a herky-jerky quality that made him look a little out of place in his own body. She had heard the term Black Irish before, and wondered if he fell into that category. His hair was black and curly and stuck up crazily. His eyes, which had an impish gleam, especially when he became excited, were blue. She guessed him to be in his mid-twenties, about her age. But when he smiled, he looked younger.

Mrs. Washington, a middle-aged African-American woman, wiped her hands on a dish towel. Felicia didn't understand it. If she were going to play at historical recreation, she sure as heck wouldn't choose to be a black maid in the pre-Civil War South. Maybe this was one of those bed and breakfasts where people paid to stay and Mrs. Washington was the owner. That would explain it.

"Oh! I left something on!" cried Seamus. He leapt to his feet and tore out of the kitchen.

"Must have left something going in his laboratory," said Mrs. Washington. "He does that. A miracle the house hasn't burned to the ground." She got a pained look, as if she regretted saying such a thing.

"Are you hungry? Can I get you anything?" Mrs. Washington asked.

"No, thank you."

Felicia found that her stomach had settled, mostly, and that she no longer felt dizzy. She finished her tea and set it down next to Seamus's half-finished cup.

"What on earth are you wearing?" said Mrs. Washington, catching her first look at Felicia's jeans under the table. "Stand up, dear."

Felicia did so. "I need to be going anyway. Thank you for the tea."

"You can't go out like that. How did you get here wearing that?"

"There was a bus accident. With an omnibus. And I was on the bus." It sounded garbled when she put it that way, but those were the facts.

"And no one stopped you?" Mrs. Washington's voice had softened, as if she were speaking to a little girl.

"I ride the bus daily."

"Of course you do. Why don't you sit down? I'll see if I have a slice of cake somewhere." She turned to the pantry and then spun around. "Did the Professor see you in those? See you proper, I mean?"

"He's the one who invited me in."

"And then he went on and on about his machines. If it was any man other than the Professor ..." She shook her head. "Well, at least he gave you something to drink. I'll give him that."

There was a knock at the back kitchen door. Mrs. Washington opened it and let a boy inside. He was around ten years old and was wearing a striped railroad-style cap and a worn wool jacket over a dirty white shirt and suspenders. His gray pants looked a size too small. His hair was a mousy brown and his cheeks looked a few shades too dark, as if he needed a bath. He hugged a paper-wrapped package to his chest.

"Morning, Mrs. Washington."

"Come on in, Henry. Miss Sanchez, this is Henry. Henry, Miss Sanchez."

15

"How do you do, Miss Sanchez?"

The boy had a Southern accent and he touched the brim of his hat.

"Very well, thank you." Felicia couldn't remember the last time anyone had been formally introduced to her, and now it had happened twice.

"You can set it down on the table," said Mrs. Washington to the boy.

"No, ma'am. The Professor wanted it personally delivered."

Mrs. Washington heaved a sigh and went to fetch Seamus. Felicia looked up to find the boy watching her. He blushed and looked at the floor.

"Do you live near here?" she asked.

"No, ma'am. I live over near Jackson Square."

"Where do you go to school?" Felicia asked.

Henry shrugged and stared at a woodcut scene of a cow and milkmaid on the wall.

"My old friend Henry!" bellowed Seamus as he burst into the kitchen. "What do you have for me today, lad?"

"Books you ordered."

"Excellent. Excellent."

Seamus set to tearing off the paper and looked through the books. Felicia saw that they were old-fashioned but were in excellent condition.

"I suppose you want your pay, eh?" Seamus beamed at Henry.

"If you don't mind too much."

Felicia noticed that Henry had relaxed and had not called Seamus "sir." Seamus dug through one pocket, then another, and handed him a few coins. Henry tucked them into a trouser pocket.

"Anything else you need me to do, Professor?" Henry asked. "Mrs. Washington?" He looked hopefully from one to the other.

"Sorry, Henry. Nothing today," said Mrs. Washington.

Henry looked at Felicia. "Ma'am?"

"No, thank you."

"Hold on a moment," said Seamus. "I have an errand for you. I need you to go get Miss Sanchez a few dresses and have them delivered here."

The boy's eyebrows shot up. "You want me to go to the lady's dress shop?"

"Unless you think they have dresses at my haberdashery." Seamus grinned.

"I suppose not."

"Do you think you can guess her size?"

Henry looked Felicia up and down with the cool detachment of scientific appraisal.

"Yeah. I can make a good guess," Henry said.

"Good boy. Go now and get a few things. Bring me back any money that's left over."

Seamus pulled out a billfold and peeled off a few bills. Henry's eyes were round as he took the money, folded it carefully, and put it into an interior pocket of his jacket. Felicia noted how he kept it separate from the money he had taken from Seamus a few moments ago.

The room dipped and spun. Felicia grabbed for the table. Seamus was beside her in an instant and helped her back into her seat.

"Now, no fainting on me, agreed?"

"Agreed," she whispered.

He poured her more tea and she took the cup, but did not drink, wrapping her hands around it for warmth.

Mrs. Washington let Henry out the back door and closed it. "Anything else you need, Professor?" she asked. "I have some work to finish upstairs."

"No, we don't need anything," he said. Mrs. Washington left and the kitchen door swung shut behind her.

"I need to get home," said Felicia.

"You need to rest. Your home doesn't exactly exist yet."

"Look, I've had fun with you guys and your dress-up. I understand. I really do. My housemate dresses up for conventions, and he gets completely into whatever role he's playing. But it's time I go home now. I have some important calls to make and a paper to write."

"A paper?"

"I have a school paper to write tonight. For the university."

"Right. Where you are a medical student. You are studying to be a doctor." He said it triumphantly, as if he was having a great epiphany. It was endearing and irritating at the same time.

"Yes. I'm going to be a doctor."

"A twenty-first-century woman doctor who is not a Spaniard."

"The preferred term for me is Latina, thanks. I know the Victorians weren't very politically correct, but still."

"Victorians." He said the word slowly. "Victoria is the Queen of England."

"Very good, Professor."

Felicia had an idea. She would call Doug and ask him to come get her. He didn't own a car, but he could ride the bus and accompany her home. Under other circumstances, she might have asked Seamus or Mrs. Washington to drive her, but she didn't want to put them out further or cope with their oddities. She pulled out her phone, but it had no reception.

"What is that?" Seamus put out a hand to touch it as if he couldn't resist. Then he hesitated.

"It's a phone. A wondrous phone from the twenty-first century. But I don't have any reception. Can I use your phone?"

"Phone?"

She sighed. It was going to be a long night. Or day. Whichever it was.

CHAPTER 4

HAZEL DUBOIS SHOVED HER HANDS into her trouser pockets for warmth as she jumped out of the omnibus. She turned a corner in the direction of the dress shop that was next door to the Professor's haberdashery in the French Quarter. The Professor's money was tucked in her jacket pocket and she had a good idea of Miss Sanchez's height and build. The errand would be an easy one.

She almost paused, but forced herself forward when she saw three older boys leaning against a building up ahead. They were sharing a smoke and commenting on passersby. One of them was drinking from a dark glass bottle and another shouted something she could not make out, but a couple passing by glanced at them and hurried along.

Hazel sized up the boys in an instant. They were as poor as she was, lean, hungry-looking and weary beyond their years. Street children then, though they were in their teens. Perhaps too old for St. Aggie's, or they had broken the rules once too often. She racked her brain to see if she could remember seeing any of them before. She knew many of the children around the area, but these ones were unknown. They were young enough to not care about getting into trouble, and old enough to do serious damage in a fight with a younger boy. Or a girl.

She thought she recognized one of them, but didn't want to get closer. She had the Professor's money as well as her own, and she could not risk any kind of confrontation. Crossing the street was the best option. Even if it drew their attention, she would have a head start if she needed to run.

She crossed, jogging to make it across in time before a steam-powered carriage chugged and hissed past her, smoke puffing from a shiny brass exhaust pipe on top. It was beautiful with curtained windows and polished black paneling. The people inside were finely dressed and sat up tall and straight, seeing and being seen. Only the wealthy could afford such a conveyance. The working class and the poor made do with horses, mules or their own two feet. Some who worked with the dangerous machinery in the manufactories didn't even have the latter.

She kept her eyes down, moving quickly but steadily along the sidewalk.

"Hey, Henry!" shouted one of the boys. "Where you off to in such a hurry?"

One of them knew her. She didn't slow, but raised a hand in greeting. Now that she was closer, she recognized the boy. She had met him when she had been new on the streets, right after she had run away. What was his name? She remembered it was something Cajun-sounding, and that he was not raised in the city. She would not stop to speak with him, even if he asked her to. Boys in groups could get rowdy, too curious about what she might be doing, where she might be going, or what might be in her pockets.

Thankfully, the boy did not call again, and she turned down the next street. The music shop sat on the corner, and she promised herself that after her errand for the Professor, she would allow herself to look in the window. The coins in her trouser pocket weighed against her hip, but she needed them for other things, like food. Her eyes lingered on the music shop's window display, but she kept her feet moving.

The dress shop had a new shingle out, painted apricot and white with the picture of a woman's profile wearing a fancy feathered hat. Hazel paused for a moment. She still did not want a hat like that. Not yet. She was eleven, and knew that in a few years, she would supposedly be overcome with the desire for flouncy dresses and rouge and feathered hats. It was difficult to imagine.

Her trousers were too snug around her hips, and she knew they looked it. She was underweight, as were all of the street children, so she knew it was not luxurious eating that was causing the change. She was suddenly self-conscious, wondering if she looked as scandalous as Miss Sanchez had in her tight trousers. Her cheeks felt warm, and a slow shame curled around her heart. She pushed it, and the image of the person it conjured, out of her mind.

Instead, she thought of her violin, tucked away in the abandoned building where she would spend the night. It was the only hope she had of making a decent life for herself. She knew that time was running out before she would look like Miss Sanchez.

The dress shop display held lace-trimmed parasols and a variety of dancing slippers. One pale blue dress looked nice enough. It had a modest neckline and not too many flounces and ribbons. She thought that some day, she might like to have something like that. Maybe a simple dress, with soft fabric and no giant hoop skirt that took up half the room.

But she had business to attend to, and what boy would be seen staring into a dress shop window? She opened the door and pulled off her cap.

Half an hour later, she left with her jacket pocket lighter and the hope that she had given the dressmaker enough information to make Miss Sanchez a few decent dresses. Fortunately, the Professor's friend was of medium build, and many of the styles had bodices that laced up, so knowing her general size was enough to get a dress that would fit her. As for height, Hazel had noted that the top of her own head had fallen just under the level of Miss Sanchez's chin. Easy enough.

The shopkeeper had said to return in an hour, as she had one dress almost finished. Another customer of similar size had ordered it but then changed her mind. Hazel could bring that one to the Professor and Miss Sanchez today. The others would be delivered later.

She was pleased with herself, and more importantly, the Professor would be pleased with her. She liked the Mad Irishman, as some of the townspeople called him. He paid well and was kind to her. He didn't ask her about where she lived or what she did during the daytime. And sometimes Mrs. Washington gave her milk and a sandwich or some bread and butter and even let her sit at the kitchen table. Some people were decent, real decent.

Now, time for the music shop. Hazel thought about simply lingering outside the shop window, but today was too good a day to waste. She would go inside, even if she could not afford anything. But she had to plan it a bit. She had to be patient.

A wooden stand holding an open book of piano music sat in the display window. She did not play piano, but looking it over, she could hear the notes in her head. It was a sprightly piece made for dancing. She wondered if she could adapt it for violin somehow.

She waited until a middle-class couple went into the shop, and then followed. The proprietor would help them, and perhaps leave her alone long enough for her to have some time to herself.

The inside of the shop smelled wonderful, of old paper and rosin and polished wood. Violins, violas, a cittern, a bass and a single cello hung along the wall on one side, while various brass instruments hung along the other. Percussion instruments lined the back wall. She studied the violins, mentally picking which one she wanted to own some day.

A thought occurred to her in that moment. She had held enough money in her pocket an hour ago to buy any of these violins. She could have done it, stolen the Professor's money and done what she liked with it. She was ashamed that the thought had even crossed her mind. The Professor trusted her, and she was proud of that. Besides, from a purely businesslike perspective, stealing this money would mean less of it in the days to come. The Professor and Mrs. Washington's coins had fed her many a night.

Yes, she had done the right thing.

The proprietor of the music shop spoke with the couple, though he shot a series of looks at her as he retrieved something from a shelf. She had seen him before when she had come into the shop a few weeks ago, but he had been absorbed with other customers and she had slipped out before he could speak with her. She glanced at the work table behind the counter and saw an unstringed viola. A broken bridge lay to one side. She studied it for a few moments.

Hazel found the sheet music for violin and thumbed through the booklets. She knew a number of the pieces already, but found one she did not. She flipped it open and scanned it, then went over it slowly, committing it to memory.

Her former music teacher, the man who had instructed her in her life before coming to New Orleans, had praised her for her ability to read music as easily as others read words and to commit whole pieces to memory quickly. It was her only talent, and she needed new pieces to play for the strangers who dropped coins in her open violin case when she played on the street.

The bell over the door jingled as the couple left. She was not finished memorizing the piece, but she was close.

"Well, boy, what are you doing in here?" The proprietor moved to stand close to her, but not too close, as if he was cautious around such a wild creature. His work apron was grimy, but his hands and face were clean. It was a broad face, and with his snub nose and rosy cheeks. She thought it might be a merry face under the right circumstances. He had thinning orange hair, with gray at the temples. Hazel glanced at his hands. They were large and he had short, thick fingers. She wondered how many of the instruments he could play.

"Just looking at the sheet music, sir. I play the violin."

"Oh, sure you do. What, begging on the streets?"

Hazel flushed hot. It was exactly what she did.

"And a pickpocket too, I'd wager." He put his hands on his hips.

"I most certainly am not!"

"Aw, sure. One like you, living honest?"

"I never stole a thing. I play violin and if people want to give me a coin or two, that's their right and their business. And I do some deliveries for them that are too busy to do it themselves."

"Deliveries. I can imagine what sorts of things someone like you delivers."

She glared at him.

"I think you ought to leave," he said.

"I'm a paying customer. Same as anyone."

"Then what are you going to buy? I can't sit and watch you. I have work to do."

"Fixing that viola back there?" She tipped her head at the instrument behind the counter. "You had to replace the bridge, I see. But the new bridge you replaced it with is cracked. A real thin crack, but there all the same. You can barely see it. It'll split in a day or two once the strings are tightened. Then your customer will be upset."

"What are you talking about?" He went to look at the viola, and Hazel was gratified that he had believed her at all.

She went behind the counter with him and pointed to a tiny hairline crack.

"You're right," the man murmured, then looked at her, evaluating. "And you know about instruments?"

"Only strings. I can't do repairs though. Although I did fix a collapsed bridge once. It wasn't broken. But I know you have to loosen all the strings, put the bridge back in place, then tighten the outer strings first until they hold the bridge. Then you tighten the inner strings and retune it."

"Not bad."

"Thank you, sir."

"So you are a paying customer, eh?"

She drew herself up and met his eyes. "That's right."

He busied himself behind the counter and Hazel returned to the sheet music. She found a thin booklet with three Hayden pieces for violin, including a serenade with a single high note that sounded over and over, like a plaintive cry. It was beautiful, and it was a penny cheaper than the others.

"I think you need more baroque pieces," she said. "You have plenty of Renaissance and pieces from the last few decades. There's a big gap though. Not much baroque."

The owner nodded, as if considering it, but Hazel wondered if he was just humoring her. The sheet music cost three cents, much more than she wanted to pay. But she was an equal to this man, a working person. She took the booklet to the counter, pulled out three pennies and set them on the counter one by one. The proprietor opened the register and dropped them in. She folded the booklet and put it in her jacket pocket.

"So why don't you live at St. Aggie's?" he asked.

He was talking about the orphanage that the sisters ran. It was attached to a convent school, and the sisters educated the orphans and made sure they had enough to eat, most of the time anyway. Some of the children who were injured by the machines in the manufactories lived there as well, ones that were no longer of any use to their masters. It was crowded, and children were sent away if they misbehaved too often. At this time of day, she should be at the convent school.

She turned to leave. There was no way she could tell this man why she could never go to the orphanage, or to the school. A warm bed and enough to eat were a powerful incentive. But she knew what would happen if she ever went there. No, she would find another way.

Then she noticed something. The shop owner had moved stiffly, as if he had an injury or was stiff with age. Two weeks' worth of dust coated the instruments and shelves and a broom lay on the floor in a back corner, as if it had been dropped and not picked up. A cane leaned up against a wall, the tip of it worn from use.

She had an idea. It was bold, but nothing ventured, nothing gained, as her late father used to say.

"You had an assistant, didn't you?" she asked. "And he left a few weeks ago?"

The man grew wary. "You know him?"

"No, but I can see the place hasn't been dusted in a few weeks and that you need someone to help you. I can tune instruments and clean the shop. I can also make deliveries."

Surprisingly, the man seemed to be mulling it over.

"Come back later. I'll think about it."

CHAPTER 5

FELICIA NEEDED TO GET HOME. She was not well yet, but she felt a little better. A slow-building headache was starting to throb in the back of her skull, but at least her nausea and dizziness were under control.

"I'm sorry my house doesn't have the phone you are looking for," said Seamus. "But I can ask Henry to deliver a letter for you when he returns."

"No, that's fine." She checked her mobile phone again, but it still had no reception. Maybe if she stepped outside she would have better luck.

Seamus's house was beautiful and historically authentic as far as she could tell. But why would anyone choose to build a house with no phone? Perhaps for the same reason they had a large black wood-burning stove and no refrigerator.

"I need to get going. Thank you for everything. I really appreciate it," Felicia said, rising.

"No, please," said Seamus. "You need to stay here. At least until Henry comes back with some decent clothing."

"I'm sorry, I have things to do."

Seamus seemed to be considering something. "I'll get you some writing paper. Then you can make out a note and by that time, Henry will be back."

The man was nothing if not persistent. But her repeated attempts to excuse herself had been met with offers of more tea, food, even lodging for the night. His Southern hospitality, or perhaps his Irish hospitality, had crossed a line into being unsettling.

"Sure," she said. "Why don't you get me some paper and a pen and I'll write a note to my housemate."

"Wait right there," he said, taking one last look at her.

The moment his footfalls on the stairs faded, Felicia slung her purse over her shoulder and made for the front door. The front hallway of the house was pleasant and uncluttered. There were only two paintings, one of a horse and rider and the other of a verdant landscape. They were set off from the pale green patterned wallpaper by heavy wood frames. A marble-topped table with clawed feet stood near the front door with a blue and white vase of fresh daisies on top. That must be Mrs. Washington's touch, as Seamus, with his wild hair and Attention Deficit Disorder, didn't seem the type to think of such things.

Light poured in through a frosted half-circle window over the front door. It lit the entryway with warmth and Felicia stole a glance backward. The house was lovely, and the people had been kind to her. It was impolite to run off without saying a polite good-bye. Her grandmother would be ashamed. She pulled her hand from the doorknob, but then remembered the phone call she had to make to her sister, Doug's lab coat, her long bus ride and the paper she had to write and thought better of it. She would drop by next week and thank them properly.

She rushed outside, through the squeaky gate and once she had walked a good ways down St. Charles Street, she checked her phone. It still had no reception. Also, the top of the screen should show the time. Instead, it displayed a series of dashes.

"Stupid thing," she jammed it back into her purse.

It was daylight, and judging by the sun, mid-morning. But she knew it had been evening when she had been riding the bus. It was all completely wrong. She had to clear her head. Maybe she had become so disoriented after the accident that hours had passed without her being aware. The sunlight stabbed painfully into her brain, forcing her to squint. She might have an aspirin floating around the bottom of her purse, but she didn't want to stop and search for it.

She had two choices. She could catch the next bus to the hospital, get Doug's lab coat and ride back home. Or she could call Doug, get him to come meet her, go get the lab coat together, then ride the bus home together. Her head hurt, but she thought she was well enough to make the trip on her own.

This was St. Charles Street, a major thoroughfare, and if she walked down far enough, she would find a bus stop. She crossed Jackson Avenue and Josephine Street, but the streets, though paved, were devoid of cars and had no street signs. She must have taken a wrong turn into an unfamiliar neighborhood and ended up where the historical recreationists had taken over. She spotted some other people, all dressed in Victorian clothing. Women wore trimmed bonnets and large bell-shaped skirts. Some had matching parasols and cape-like coats draped around their shoulders. Men had long coats over waistcoats and they wore either top hats or bowlers. Many had walking sticks. A group of boys ran past her, all dressed in caps, suspenders and rough pants. They looked like something out of a Dickens novel.

She checked again for a street sign, but could find none. She was disoriented, but was sure that Martin Luther King Boulevard would be coming up. She knew there had to be a bus stop nearby. She hurried down the sidewalk, which was wooden and must be under construction, and paused at a corner to let a mule-drawn cart filled with barrels and crates cross in front of her.

Up ahead was what looked like a restaurant. But as she drew closer, she saw that it had wooden doors instead of glass and apparently no name. Only a simple wooden sign was nailed over the door with the word Pub painted in large, white letters. A dark layer of grime covered the windows. A few men leaned against the building, one with dark blood crusted under his nose. His feet slid slowly out in front of him, and his back scraped the wall until his rear end rested on the ground. One of the other men laughed at him and the bloody man gave a drunken wave.

Felicia gave them a wide berth, but something else was bothering her. These men looked like recreationists, drunken though they may be, but the other buildings looked wrong also. She did not see a single ordinary street sign, no streetlights, no regular shops and no cars. Carts and horse-drawn carriages clattered past. Could she have stumbled into an area under renovation? That did not make sense either.

She turned at what sounded like the roar of a large truck coming up the street behind her. But it was no truck. Instead, a vehicle that looked almost like a carriage puffed up the street. There were people inside, but it had no horses pulling it. It did have a driver who sat in the place a carriage driver would, up high in the front where he steered with a small horizontal wheel at the end of a long straight rod. The vehicle's engine ground and chugged and a pipe near the back puffed black smoke into the air. The body of the vehicle was made of metal painted a rich burgundy and as it drew closer, she saw that the seats matched the exterior. Two women and two men were inside, chatting among themselves. More recreationists.

"Hey, pretty girl. How you doing today?" asked one of the drunken men who had moved up close behind her.

"Fine, thank you," she turned to leave, but a hand gripped her wrist with more strength than she would anticipate from an inebriated person. He pulled her toward the pub.

"Let's have a drink or two."

"Let go!" She twisted her arm in and down, toward the space between his index finger and thumb, just as her brother had taught her, wrenching her arm free. He reached for her arm again, but she leapt back.

"Now, I just want to have a talk," he said. "Working girl like you is up for a little talk, I'm sure."

"I'm not. I have to be going."

"What kind of jodhpurs you got on, anyway? Never seen none like those."

She spun and another man loomed up in front of her. She put up her hands to keep from crashing into his chest, and he grabbed her arms. She pushed her weight into the man, throwing him off balance enough for her to yank herself free.

"You back the hell off," she said, preparing to knee him in the crotch if he made another move.

"Now that's not very polite."

"You must excuse her. She'll be coming with me," said a familiar voice.

Seamus Connor stood beside them, this time wearing a brown top hat and a matching long brown frock coat over a trim waistcoat and the striped trousers he had worn earlier. Felicia had only a moment to note that he looked quite the proper gentleman when one of the men gave him a hard shove. Seamus moved quickly and deliberately, grasping the man's arm, bending him over, as if folding him in half, until the man knelt doubled over on the ground.

"Now, apologize to the lady," Seamus said.

"Filthy paddy son of a whore."

The man cried out as Seamus did something to his arm. "That's no way to talk about my mother either."

The man tried to yank himself free, and Seamus only released him as the other man, the one with the blood under his nose, took a clumsy swing at him.

The altercation lasted only moments, and Felicia remembered her brother telling her once that fights usually end within ten or fifteen seconds. She only had time to note two things. One, that the two men who had harassed her were far too drunk to put up any kind of real fight. And two, that Seamus had done this before. He seemed to be enjoying it.

Once both men were staggering back to the wall, Seamus adjusted his hat, removed his coat and slipped it over her shoulders.

"You should put this on," he said.

On Seamus, the frock coat hung to just above his knees, but on her it came to mid-calf. It was warm from his body and smelled of pipe tobacco and something else, something like old books.

"You're taking away the view!" yelled one of the men, but Seamus took Felicia's elbow and led her away. She yanked her arm free and continued down the street.

"I expect you are feeling disoriented. Am I right?" He looked as if he wanted to be right.

"I just need to find the bus stop."

"Still trying to get home. Or was it to the hospital where you work?"

"Hospital first, then home, thank you."

"I need to show you something first."

"That's quite all right. Thank you for your help back there." She went to remove the coat and return it to him, but he pulled it back over her shoulders.

"Leave it for now. I'll walk with you."

She drew a few stares as they continued, and a few people who looked her up and down seemed to be studying her feet. She noticed that the people had shoes with front portions that were too large, almost cartoonish. Even Seamus had shoes that seemed like the toe box was much too wide.

They passed a boy selling newspapers and Seamus gave him a coin. He took a paper but did not open it. Rather he folded it in half and tucked it under one arm.

Felicia felt herself being watched. A man reading the Picayune stood behind the newspaper stand. Only, he wasn't reading it but was looking over the top of it at her. He wore all black, in the same style that Seamus wore, except that he wore a long duster that came to his calves.

He was neither tall nor short, stocky nor thin, handsome nor homely. The word "medium" came to Felicia's mind. Even the man's hair and eyes were a medium shade of brown.

He caught her looking at him, touched the brim of his hat and returned to his paper.

"We need to catch a cab," said Seamus.

"There don't seem to be any busses running today. Only the horse-drawn carriages that the tourists like to rent."

"Busses? Do you mean omnibuses? I think we should take a private coach. I think you've drawn enough attention for one day."

This part of the street was busier, with more mule-drawn carts and another motorized carriage. Seamus put two fingers to his mouth and gave a sharp whistle. A horse-drawn coach stopped in front of them. It was a functional solid black, scuffed in places with worn, metal-rimmed wheels.

"Tulane University Hospital," said Felicia to the driver. He raised his eyebrows and glanced at Seamus who gave a quick nod and handed her into the coach. Seamus took the seat next to her, setting the newspaper and his hat on the seat between them.

"Did you see the steam carriage?" he asked.

"That big thing that came down the road right before you showed up? Yes, I saw it."

"I was a ways off, but it looked like you had never seen one before."

"I saw a video of something like that at the Burning Man festival, but other than that, no."

"Your people burn men?" Seamus looked like he was trying to suppress an expression of horror.

"No, the desert art festival. No one gets hurt. Never mind."

She looked out the window toward the opposite side of the street.

"You seem intelligent enough," Seamus said, stretching out his legs and crossing his ankles.

"Enough for what?" She glared at him. Who was he to say such a thing?

"To trust the evidence of your senses."

"This should be Martin Luther King Boulevard," she murmured, spying her first street sign. It hung from what looked like a primitive stop light, with green and red wooden panels that mechanically slid into a viewing window. The coach stopped at the red.

"It's not. It's Melpomene Street," Seamus said.

"Both ways?"

"Yes," his mouth quirked in a grin. "Both ways."

The street to the north should have been Martin Luther King Boulevard, while the part running south of St. Charles should have been Melpomene.

Seamus watched the streets go by. Felicia's headache was getting worse, but she planned on taking a couple of painkiller tablets from the hospital staff lounge. The coach turned down the familiar streets toward the hospital, but her headache must be interfering with her vision. No, that didn't make medical sense. If she had a migraine, seeing auras around things would be normal, but not this.

The world was different. Every street and every shop looked different. The burrito restaurant where she often bought lunch, Mel's Coffee Shop, Pyewocket's Books, all were gone. In their places were strange shops with old-fashioned people moving in and out.

They were getting close to the hospital now, and Felicia felt herself shaking. A thought, a horrifying thought, was taking shape in her mind. Seamus rapped the roof of the carriage with his knuckles and it pulled to a stop. He opened the door and jumped out, turning to offer his hand. She took it, but did not look at him. She heard Seamus say something to the driver and the coach stayed where it was.

This was all wrong. The hospital was too small, only two stories high. There were no darkened glass windows or concrete walls. The usual automatic sliding glass doors and covered entryway were replaced by two simple wooden doors, one of which had been propped open. Inside, a few people moved about, but she could tell that all of them were in the wrong clothing.

She backed up, bumping into Seamus. She understood now. Though she resisted, the thought was fully formed.

"Pardon me," he murmured. "Are you all right?"

Felicia nodded and climbed into the coach. Seamus handed her the newspaper, but she just set it in her lap. Her insides twisted, but not with nausea.

"I've gone insane," she said. "That's the most logical answer. I'm delusional."

"No, you're not. And I think you're handling it very well. Most young ladies of my acquaintance would be fainting or crying by now." He was studying her. "Take a look at the paper."

She flipped it open. It was much smaller than the normal Picayune, only ten or twelve sheets thick. The headline said something about the East India Company. Her eyes snapped to the date. February 17, 1857.

"I don't believe this," she said. "I'm going nuts."

"You're not, as you say, 'nuts.' Let's look at it scientifically. You're a doctor, correct?"

She nodded. "Well, almost."

"So when you look at a patient, you look at the symptoms, the evidence, then draw a conclusion."

She nodded again.

"You use the evidence of your senses to determine what is true, what is occurring, what is reality."

Felicia looked at the newspaper again. Maybe this was a dream. She silently read the headline, "Local Shipping Magnate Accuses East India Company of Piracy." She read it a second time, knowing that one can never read the same words twice in a dream. The words stayed the same.

"So there you are!" said Seamus, grinning. "You see?

The evidence is nearly incontrovertible! Well, not in a true scientific sense, as you can't verify reality. But never mind that. You observe things, just as I do or any of the other people out there on the street do. We have a shared experience of reality, perceived together."

He rubbed his hands together and rattled on, asking questions without waiting for answers. Felicia was vaguely aware that the coach was heading south and she rubbed her temples.

Seamus stopped his chatter and became serious. "Is your head hurting you?"

"It's probably dehydration."

"Or coming through some kind of portal into a different time." He was thrilled by all this. Felicia wanted to smack him.

"Dehydration," she insisted.

"Then we're headed in the right direction. Now tell me all about your world." His eager expression made him a bit unnerving. She was in an enclosed space with a madman. Or she herself was mad. Or both.

She answered a few questions, and Seamus seemed to be storing the information for future use. As they passed Jackson Square, he rapped on the ceiling again and the coach stopped.

"I'm going to get you a lime water from this restaurant. You stay here."

"I can come in."

"Not dressed like that. Just wait a minute."

He rushed into a shop with small round tables out front, some filled with diners. Felicia glanced out at Jackson Square, but it blurred and swirled. She leaned back in her seat, waiting for the wave of dizziness to pass.

The door to the coach opened and Seamus offered her a glass of water with a lime wedge and a sprig of mint. It was a real glass, made of actual glass, not a to-go cup. She took a sip and he climbed in beside her.

"Thank you," she said.

"Nare a bother. We can wait while you finish it. Take your time."

She did. And as she sipped and answered Seamus's questions, her headache seemed to lessen a little. The driver appeared at the window.

"Look, I don't know what you two are up to in there, and I don't care to. But we need to get moving. I got to make a living."

Seamus spoke with him, gave him more money and the cabby muttered something. The coach heaved as he climbed back into his seat.

"If I fell through into another time, why here?" Felicia asked. "Why this time?"

"I told you. It was by accident. I was studying a machine and I think I made a bags of the whole thing. I made a hole, a pathway. And you came through. Isn't that marvelous?"

CHAPTER 6

FELICIA EXAMINED HER REFLECTION IN front of the full-length oval mirror in one of Seamus's unused guest rooms. She didn't look too bad, considering how things were going. Night had become day, and reality had changed completely. She was either insane, or she had moved backwards through time. As Seamus had pointed out, the evidence of her senses confirmed that she was in a different world. And yet, if she were delusional, how would she know that he and the rest of the world were not simply concoctions of her own disturbed brain? But, no. She knew better.

By the time she and Seamus had returned from Jackson Square, Henry had already delivered a few boxes. Inside were most of the things Felicia was currently wearing, including the slate-gray dress and matching fitted jacket. But Henry had neglected to bring everything she would need, perhaps assuming she would have underclothes. Mrs. Washington had supplied the remaining items from some long-forgotten wardrobe in a spare room.

Felicia turned to the side to get a better view of herself. The dress was simple and unassuming, reminding her more of a stiff-backed governesses than a Southern lady. She wore a black corset over her clothing, which was not how she remembered women wearing them in pictures from the Civil War era. It was tight and made bending over nearly impossible, but combined with the basque waistline, it did create a nice hourglass shape to her figure. Her large domed skirt had a few ruffles and flounces, but not so many that she felt like a cake topper.

It had taken far too long to get into the outfit, and Mrs. Washington had muttered under her breath that Felicia had to be mentally incapable because she needed so much help. The corset laced in the front, and the older woman had shown Felicia how to get it on properly and how to layer the crinolines, white cotton pantaloons, stockings and other underthings that a woman needed. After that, Mrs. Washington had gotten to work on her hair, shaking her head occasionally and remarking that it was a wonder Felicia hadn't been arrested in her wild state.

Now, with her hair pinned and her clothing arranged, she looked the proper lady. Perhaps she could see the appeal in doing historical recreation. Playing dress-up could be fun. But this wasn't playing. This all felt real. The people felt as real as the people in her world. She had read the paper, seen the French Quarter, smelled the scent of the river, the food, and unfortunately, some of the people. Everything was vivid and complete.

There was a soft knock at the door.

"There was one other thing Henry had for you," said Mrs. Washington.

She held a pair of gray shoes that matched the dress. Unfortunately, like the shoes she had seen on everyone else, they were too wide in the toe. Felicia took them and looked them over, sliding her hand inside, feeling if there was some kind of stuffing in the toe. There wasn't.

"There's nothing wrong with them." Mrs. Washington put her hands on her hips.

"Oh, they're lovely. But I don't think they'll fit me."

Felicia lifted the hem of her dress and pushed her foot out. Mrs. Washington glanced down, but didn't seem surprised.

"I saw that earlier. Did something happen to you? An accident?" she asked, all traces of annoyance gone. She had a look of genuine concern. "Did you have those shoes specially made?"

"I was born this way," Felicia said, and then thought better of saying anything more. This was too late in history for witch burnings, but if her memory of history was correct, physical deformities were more frowned upon in this time than in her own.

"I have to go make up a lunch tray, as the Professor likes it at noon sharp. But first, may I ask you a question?" said Mrs. Washington.

"Sure."

"Where is your family? I trust the Professor. I'm his employee and will do as he says. But this is too strange. He's never brought home a feral girl before. Was your family unkind to you? Did they hurt you?" She glanced down at Felicia's feet.

"Oh, no. No one hurt me. My family is in California and they are good people. But I'm going to be staying with the Professor until I can get back home."

"It's not proper, a single woman like yourself in a house with a man, even if it is the Professor. He'd never be unkind to any woman or put you in a bad situation, but people will talk."

"If anyone asks, you can say we're cousins."

Mrs. Washington crooked an eyebrow and looked like she was going to laugh.

"Distant cousins. By marriage," Felicia amended.

The housekeeper shook her head, chuckling as she closed the door behind her. Oh yes, a white man having a brown-skinned cousin wouldn't be doing the Professor any social favors, Felicia thought. Well, if what he said was true, and he was the cause of the time hole or whatever it was, then he would have to live with the consequences.

She left her room, went in search of Seamus's laboratory and found it at the end of the hall. The door was open and light poured in through the floor-length windows that looked out over the front of the house.

The room was a disaster.

A desk stood between the two windows, facing the center of the room. But the only way Felicia could identify it as a desk was because she could see the sides. The top was completely covered in papers of all sizes, from large butcher paper rolls to tiny slips that were in piles so high that many had fallen and scattered on the patterned rug like autumn leaves. Glass and silver paperweights teetered on stacks of documents. Piles of books, some open and stained, were stacked on the desk and on the surrounding work tables. Other books were jammed into bookshelves willy-nilly. A few ink pots, both open and closed, sat here and there.

Wiring and tubing, some on spools and some in cut pieces, were scattered over the tables, along with metal and wooden boxes and a variety of mechanical objects in varying states of either completion or disassembly, she couldn't tell. Felicia drew in a breath at seeing what looked like a mechanical arm and a head on one table. Nearby was a clock face attached to something too large to be a clock mechanism and something covered with so much oil and grime that it was unidentifiable. A set of tiny drawers hung over one table, overflowing with gears, screws, bolts, nuts and knobs of various sizes.

A large tack board covered one wall, but only a tiny bit of brown corkwood peeked out around notes and sheets of paper, most of them pinned one on top of the other. Another wall held a blackboard filled with scribbles, equations, diagrams and swirled erasure marks. Beside the blackboard stood a stately grandfather clock, its pendulum swinging gently side to side. It was the only orderly thing in the place.

In front of the clock, Seamus knelt over a spherical machine on a stand. It would have come up to his thighs, had he been standing. The bottom portion of the sphere was intact, but the top cover sat to one side. He wrote something in a leather-bound book.

Felicia cleared her throat and Seamus stood.

"Ah, good to see you, er, all taken care of." He looked over her outfit with approval and Felicia felt like she should do a little spin. Instead, she made a little curtsey, feeling silly, but it made Seamus smile all the wider. "You look lovely."

A pile of crumpled papers surrounded his feet and he shoved them out of the way with the side of his foot.

"Sorry it's a bit of a mess. I don't entertain guests up here often. Well, not ever, to tell you the truth."

"Poor Mrs. Washington must have a heart attack every time she comes in here."

"Oh, she stopped coming up here years ago. We've both been much happier since."

"I can imagine. What's that you're working on?"

She moved forward, conscious of the width of her skirts and careful not to knock anything over. Not that it would make any difference.

"This is the McCullen Peroxide Engine. Very efficient, very clean and very expensive."

She moved forward and looked down into the contraption. To her eyes, it was a mass of gears, wires and cogs. It appeared to be off, as it was not moving or making any sound.

"See this bit here?" He pointed inside to a small metal box. "This is the fuel core. Inside that box is a piece that the McCullen Manufactory doesn't want anyone to see. They have men they call concierges who come to your house to replace the fuel cores when they run out. The people who purchased the machines aren't even allowed to be in the room when they replace it. The concierges come, they replace it, take the old one, and they leave. For a healthy fee, naturally."

"And you're trying to take it apart and see what's inside?"

"Of course! How can I resist something like that? A locked box, a machine so efficient that it produces no smoke, no exhaust of any kind? And they're fairly rare because they're so expensive."

"So how did you afford one?"

He shrugged one shoulder. "Saved my money up." Felicia got the feeling that there was more to the story.

"So what are these engines for?" she asked.

"They can run sewing machines, vehicles similar to the ones you saw earlier on the street, you can even heat your house. Depends on what size you order. They're all custom-made by the McCullen Manufactory on Canal Street."

"This McCullen guy must be a rich man."

"Yes." Seamus's single word was loaded with enough bitterness to make Felicia take a good long look at him.

"You know him then?" she asked.

"Yes. I know him."

The grandfather clock chimed noon and there was a soft knock at the laboratory door, which stood ajar. Mrs. Washington stood at the threshold, and Seamus took a tray from her. There were two plates with beef sandwiches, two teacups and a steaming teapot. After sweeping papers and books aside on a work table, Seamus set the tray down. He scanned the room as if looking for something.

"I'll find it later," he said to Mrs. Washington, who sighed and left. "She wants yesterday's tray. Now, where was I?" He spun around. "The machine. So as I was saying, I was making a sonic map of the interior using this." He gestured to a machine with a metal sheet curling from one elongated roller onto another. Thin scratches zigzagged across its surface. "And what do you think happened?"

"I have no idea."

"You came through! I heard the crash of the omnibus and ran to the window. I saw the shimmers, and then there you were."

"And this machine caused it."

"Well, the machine plus the signal amplification device that I was using along with my sonic mapping machine.

43

My theory is that I created instability roughly one-eighth of a mile wide and you slipped through."

"So recreate it. Do it again, and I'll go back home."

"I can't. I've been trying to do it, but something about it isn't working. I'm recreating the same circumstances, but no luck."

Her stomach dropped and she wrapped her arms around her midsection. She was displaced, lost, and her entire life depended upon this disheveled man recreating an accident.

Seamus slid a pencil behind his ear, picked up his notebook and flipped through. She brought his plate to him and set it on top of a stack of books, perhaps a little harder than necessary. He grabbed the sandwich and took a bite. Felicia poured the tea and ate standing at a work table, but found that she had little appetite. Seamus was humming a little tune as he worked, and anger surged through her. He had brought her here, against her will. He had tried to help her, true, but only because he had little choice. And through it all, he had treated her as some kind of exciting oddity, a scientific anomaly to be questioned and studied. He was not even sure he could get her home at all.

"It's urgent that I get back home," she said. "And not just for my own sake. I have people depending on me."

"Your patients?"

"My nephew. He's in the hospital and his immune system is gravely compromised. He has a form of bone cancer, and there's a doctor, a Brazilian doctor, who has a treatment that might help him. But I didn't tell my sister about it. I was scared she'd get her hopes up, only to have them crushed. The doctor e-mailed me before I left and said that my nephew is a good candidate for treatment. If I don't put them in contact with one another, he'll continue to deteriorate and then he'll die."

She knew that Seamus wouldn't know what e-mail

was, and was about to explain when he asked, "How old is your nephew?"

She was taken aback by the question. It seemed the least important detail.

"He's three."

Seamus nodded, looking at his sandwich and then set it down.

"And the lad will die without this medicine from this doctor in Brazil?"

"Most likely."

"I once had nephews. Nieces as well. I lost a nephew once." For the first time, he was not fidgeting with restless energy. He wasn't even looking at her.

"I'm sorry," she said.

"It's not something I would wish on anyone. No child ought to die. And none will, not if I can help it. I'll get you home. I promise. For his sake, and your own."

"What can I do to help?"

"Nothing really. Maybe find yesterday's lunch tray for Mrs. Washington."

She didn't like the suggestion, but the inside of the machine was a mystery to her, and she knew that staying out of his way was most likely the most helpful thing she could do. She found the lunch tray, eventually, and took it downstairs. When she returned, she found a newspaper from a few days before. While Seamus took apart the device, Felicia read an editorial.

The author was scathing in his criticism of President Benjamin Pierce who was supposedly placating the East India Company. She thought that President Pierce had a different first name, but she must have been mistaken. The East India Company was squeezing out Southern trade ships as they tried to establish profitable trade routes with the Caribbean. Local trade magnates in New Orleans were starting to accuse the Company of hiring mercenary pirates to waylay their ships and steal their goods. The East India Company then sold them and profited. Allegedly.

Below that, another article accused the East India Company of providing aerial and sea-based warships and munitions to both the Indian and the British sides of the current uprising in India. The article made a brief mention that the East India Company had done the same with the Russians and British during the recently ended Crimean War.

"Seamus?" He seemed a little startled at the familiar address, and Felicia remembered that both Mrs. Washington and Henry had called him Professor. Seamus did not correct her, so she went on. "I thought the East India Company was just for trading spices and silk and things with Asia and India. I didn't think they had warships."

"Oh yes, they are quite a military power. Loyal to the British Crown and operating at Her Majesty's pleasure, but some people have a question or two about that. The East India Company invented airships. So though the Company doesn't own the American airship manufacturers, as owners of almost all of the patents, they make a profit from them."

"They never had airships in the history I learned."

"Well, north of the Mason Dixon, there are a number of airship companies. The South has riverboats and large sailing ships as their preferred method of getting goods or people from here to there."

"Let me guess, there's lots of rivalry and tension between the North and South."

"Oh yes. Even before I came to this country a few years ago, tensions ran high. And they're only getting worse."

"I know I mentioned it before, but there is a Civil War coming in 1861. You might want to go back to Ireland. The South is going to lose."

He looked at her, a mix of apprehension and concern on his face. She watched him take a deep breath.

"I cannot go back. My fortunes are therefore yoked with those of my adopted homeland. But wait! I'm missing the most important point. There were no Company warships or airships of any sort in your world, correct?"

"Correct."

"Hmm." He ran his hand through his hair. "That complicates things."

"How so?"

He just grunted and kept working at the inside of the machine. Felicia flipped through the newspaper. Social pages showed the latest styles and who was marrying whom. There were a few advertisements in the back, and she blanched when she saw that there would be a slave auction in a month's time. Accompanying the notice was an ink drawing of a black woman with a patterned rag wrapped around her head. Her skin was inked solid black and the whites of her eyes and her full lips were exaggerated ridiculously.

Felicia closed the paper and sat silently for a minute. She looked down and realized that she was crushing the paper in her fist. She smoothed it and set it aside. The Civil War would end the evil practice of slavery, she reminded herself. Only a little longer. But in those intervening years, how many more people would suffer?

"Almost got it," muttered Seamus. She moved beside him and looked into the machine. He had managed to open the small box. From it, he pulled a small glass tube, filled with a glowing pale blue liquid. It was partially embedded in a mechanism with three wires leading into the tube. The entire thing was no larger than a matchbox.

"It's not the peroxide, if that's what you're thinking," he said. She wasn't, but she didn't say so.

"The peroxide is in here," he said. A large glass tube of translucent whitish blue liquid sat on the work table. "The engine is a marvel. If I didn't hate McCullen so much, I might just shake his hand. See, it uses silver, just a small amount, as a catalyst with the peroxide. The silver adds to the cost of the thing, of course. The reaction between the peroxide and the silver frees an extra oxygen atom and produces water and heat. That means it can be used to generate steam to power a machine. It also generates a small amount of electricity which is used for auxiliary systems."

"But if the peroxide is there, what's that little glass tube with the wires?"

"I have no idea. But I ran all the calculations, and there is no possible way that these engines produce the power they do solely using the peroxide and the silver. They have to have another power source. See, I think the peroxide system is a dummy, a thing to cover up what is really supplying the power."

"And your dislike for this McCullen person has nothing to do with it."

"How could you say such a thing? My observations are purely professional. And I'm the one who invented the peroxide engine, so I ought to know how it works."

"If you invented it, then why is McCullen selling the engines?"

"Because he found a way to make them put out more power than they should. Now, that's interesting." He squinted down into the machine into the hole where the small box had been detached. "A transmitter. Aww, McCullen, you crazy old bastard. Only you."

"A transmitter?" Felicia looked where Seamus pointed.

"It, er," he waved his hand in the air, "it sends messages, signals, though the aether to another machine that receives them. Another thing McCullen and I were working on. That one was his idea."

"So it sends radio waves."

She almost laughed at the astonished look on his face.

"They do have radios in my time," she said.

"Right. Of course."

"So who is it signaling, and why?"

"It's signaling that we took apart the machine and opened up the proprietary piece that no one is allowed to see."

"So what happens when they receive the signal?"

"My guess? They come pay us a visit."

CHAPTER 7

H AZEL DUBOIS CLUTCHED A CRUMPLED paper bag close
to her body. Inside were the remains of a baguette
and a half-empty bottle of milk. She slid silently
into the alleyway, climbed over a shaky pile of discarded
bricks and wood planks and slipped into the window of
her abandoned building. It wasn't truly her building, she
thought. There were other children who lived here, as the
place was large and mostly free of drafts and roof leaks.
As of yesterday, two boys lived there with her, each of
them in a separate room of the old paper factory.

She had already consumed most of the baguette and
milk, not wanting to have to share with the two boys. She
often shared her gains, as did they, but this time she had
been too hungry to wait. And if she wanted to make the
Professor's money last as long as possible, she needed to
keep things to herself.

Hazel passed through the lower story where the main
machinery had once produced giant rolls of paper. The
looming machines, what was left of them, rusted silently
in the gloom. She climbed the rotting wooden stairs to the
upper story where there once had been offices. Most of the
furniture was long gone, but there were boxes, shelving
and a few discarded items that she and the other children
sometimes found useful.

Hopefully, she could slip into her room and hide the
bread and milk. In a few hours, she planned to finish off
both. Going to sleep with a full stomach would feel just
like heaven.

She stopped at the top of the stairs at the sound of someone moving in her room. The person must have heard her also, because he opened the door. It was Alistair, one of the boys staying there. His eyes fixed on the paper bag.

"What you got there?" he asked.

Alistair was taller than she was, though he was a year younger. He was brutish, lanky and uneducated. But he was decent enough company, and he had shared pork pies and sweet buns on the occasions when he could get them. Hazel never asked if he had stolen or bought them. If he had purchased them, it would have been with pickpocketed money anyway. It was better not to know.

"What are you doing in my room?" Hazel demanded.

"I can't believe what happened! Toby cleaned me out and left. I was wondering if he did the same to you, and turns out he did." He shoved the door the rest of the way open with his foot and let Hazel pass by him.

Toby had been the other boy who stayed with them. He had only been there two weeks and had seemed a decent sort. But street children stealing from other street children was not unheard of. It was a crime punishable by a severe beating, so Toby would make sure to steer clear of Hazel and Alistair in the future. After stealing for a living long enough, Hazel supposed it got into your blood. She wondered how long it would be before she succumbed and took up Alistair's offer to teach her to pickpocket.

Hazel's bedroll and an old coat she used as a pillow sat in the corner, though it looked like someone had pulled them up and then tossed them back down. She set the milk and baguette on top of the blanket.

"Go ahead and have it," she said. She couldn't hide the bread and milk now, and seeing how Alistair's eyes never left the bag, she knew he hadn't eaten that day. He sat on the blanket and dug in.

Hazel crouched and looked inside a box she used to store her few belongings. Everything she owned was either on her person or in the box. Everything except her violin, of course. The box was empty.

Her stomach sank. Toby had taken her only dress, the one she had been wearing when she ran away. She knew she couldn't wear it, not out where she might be recognized, but it had been a last link to being a girl. Naturally, Toby did not hope to wear the dress himself, but he would sell it to a rag and scrap man for a few coins. Also missing was her pair of girl's shoes which would meet the same fate as her dress. A small box in which she had kept a few tin toy soldiers was gone. So was a single men's leather glove she had found, too large for her hand, but warm enough on cold nights.

Alistair was watching her. "I went out to the river, as usual," he said through a mouthful of bread. "And when I got back, Toby had gone. He didn't take everything, but he got that pair of shoes I found and the china cup."

Along with being a pickpocket, Alistair scavenged along the river bank. Sometimes, he found something like a china cup, a coin or two, or other things that could be cleaned and salvaged. His china cup had sat on a table beside his door. Propped behind it had been a worn and much-folded holy card of the Blessed Virgin and a burned out stub of a candle, like a little shrine.

Hazel wanted to check on the violin, to make sure that Toby had not found it. It would be worth more than a few coins, she knew that. She had always been careful to hide it when no one was around or to sleep with it clutched to her. The fewer people who knew about it, the better. She would have to wait until Alistair was gone before she checked on it.

She rose, and a few of the coins in her pocket, the ones she had hoped to secret away, clinked against one another. Alistair's mouth stopped mid-chew and he stared at her.

"You got some money!" he said around the bread.

"I was going to share it."

"Were not. You were going to keep it."

She pulled out the coins and slapped them onto the top of a crate that sometimes served as a table. The children usually ate sitting on the rotting floorboards, but occasionally they'd pull up boxes and eat at the table when there was enough to share. It made all of them sad to do it, perhaps because it reminded them of better times at other tables. Hazel never analyzed the feeling too closely.

Oddly, the lid of the crate was ajar. She scooped up the coins and slid the lid aside. Inside, thrown in a heap were her shoes, her dress and the box with the tin soldiers. She didn't see the glove, but it could be buried somewhere underneath.

"You bilge rat!" she said, spinning to face Alistair. "You were robbing me when I came home!"

"Was not!"

Hazel raced to Alistair's room, and sure enough, the china cup was in its place in front of the holy card. The Virgin Mary's eyes were raised and her palms were pressed together in prayer.

"Hard times make a monkey eat pepper, cher," Alistair said from behind her with an evil smile. He popped the last bite of her bread into his mouth and wiped his lips with his sleeve.

"You were going to wait until I left again and then take everything, weren't you?"

"A man's gotta eat. I can't be taking care of a tagalong little snip like you."

"I paid my way! I brought you that food just now."

Alistair was unmoved. "Just tell me where the fiddle is, and I'll go."

"Go to hell."

He grabbed her arm and twisted, pulling it expertly behind her. She yelped. "You've been keeping it somewhere here," he hissed into her ear. "I know you have it. But you hid it clever. Did you think I was stupid? It's worth money and here I am going hungry while you have that thing hid somewhere."

She yanked and managed to kick her foot backward like a mule, hitting his shin. He grunted and shoved her away. She spun around to face him and he hit her hard in the mouth. Pain shot through her lip and a moment later she tasted blood. She blinked hard.

"Now tell me where it is," he said. "Either I take it and go, or I beat you senseless, search for it, take it and go. Take your pick."

"You're a thief."

He laughed. "What of it? What am I supposed to do, starve?" But she saw him glance at the holy card as he said it. She knew he had been raised by a devout family, but then, that meant little. Her own family had been religious.

"Why can't you go home? Or to the sisters? What happened?" she asked.

If she could distract him long enough, remind him of their common plight, maybe he would calm down. She could give him the coins and ask him to go get more food and bring it back. While he was gone, she'd grab her violin and run.

"Nothing happened!" he yelled and slammed her against the wall. Her head rang from the impact. "Now where is that fiddle?"

"It's in my room. Hidden though. Under the floorboard under my bed." She looked at the floor, hoping he would believe the sincerity of her words. She did not need to fake the fear and the pain that made her voice tremble.

"There now," he said, sweeping invisible dust from the shoulders of her jacket and pulling it straight. He turned and left.

The moment Hazel was sure he was searching her room, she tore down the hall in the opposite direction. She had been on the streets long enough to know that children stole from each other. And she knew the habits of those other children. They tended to hole up in one spot, concealing all their little treasures in one place which was usually the same one where they slept. It was human nature. She had not kept the violin as long as she had by giving in to human nature.

She rushed into an old storage room, now covered in dust, rat droppings and cobwebs. Up high was a piece of wall board that was not nailed in properly. She reached up on tiptoes and pulled at it.

"Where in hell is it?" bellowed Alistair down the hall.

Should she answer him, go and pretend to help him? No, that was folly. Her only chance was to run. She stayed silent. He didn't know which room she was in. That would buy her some time.

The wall board was stuck, and she dug her fingers in. A splinter stabbed her, but she pried harder. She wrenched the board off as she heard Alistair pounding back to his room to look for her.

She took the extra moment to set the board down carefully instead of throwing it to the floor where it would make a racket. Inside the hole, she saw the neck of her scuffed violin case. She pulled it up and out and ran. She tore down the stairs and was at the window when she heard Alistair stomping up behind her.

She didn't look back, but jumped out the window, staggered over the pile of bricks and wood planks and sprinted into the night.

CHAPTER 8

"THEY'RE HERE," SAID MISS SANCHEZ from her spot in front of the laboratory window. "Two men are coming up the front walk."

Seamus glanced up for just an instant before reminding himself that he had to work fast. He rooted through drawers and boxes until he found a part that would suit his purpose. He slipped it into the place that had been occupied by the glowing blue tube of liquid and the tiny mechanism and rushed to put the peroxide engine back together.

He had already asked Mrs. Washington to delay anyone who came from the McCullen Manufactory, but the men could always insist upon seeing him and there would be little the housekeeper could do to stop them.

"Is there anything I can do to help?" asked Miss Sanchez. She came up beside him, glancing anxiously at the interior of the engine. He slid in another piece and snapped it into place.

"You can hide this," he said, handing her the small glass tube with its attached mechanism.

He heard a clinking sound from Miss Sanchez's vicinity, but couldn't stop and look up. Already, he heard footsteps and voices in the hallway. Mrs. Washington sounded agitated. Seamus shoved the spherical cover over the engine, and got in two of the four screws before Mrs. Washington knocked on the door.

"I told you he's busy and cannot be disturbed. I wouldn't

be surprised if he stepped out and isn't even here," Seamus heard Mrs. Washington say on the other side of the door. She was giving him the opportunity to slip out through one of the floor-length windows to the upper gallery of the house. He could move across and enter into another room or simply wait outside. But he knew what he needed to do. He dropped the last two screws into his pocket.

Miss Sanchez stood with her back against the far work table. She had the guilty look of someone who had just hidden something important. Well, he knew he would not have such a look. He had spent enough time gambling at taverns and on riverboats to know that, when he had to, he could make his face and mannerisms display whatever he wished.

He tugged down the bottom of his waistcoat, gave Miss Sanchez what he hoped was a reassuring nod, and opened the door.

Outside stood two men, both of them middle-aged, though one was significantly taller than the other. The larger man was completely bald but had a fine, thick black moustache and beard. The short one had wire-rimmed glasses perched on a hooked nose. He carried a black leather case with the words *McCullen's Manufactory of Fine Engines* in metallic lettering on the side. It was an expensive case, and both men wore suits that did not come from a working-class shop. Their hats, which they had removed indoors and held, would cost Seamus a week's wage. Well-paid visitors from McCullen's shop could be nothing but the infamous concierges.

"Hello, gentlemen," Seamus said. "Did you wish to see me?"

Mrs. Washington moved off behind them, throwing a glance back. She made eye contact with Seamus, and he saw her mouth the words, "I'm sorry," before she retreated to the other end of the hall. Seamus knew that she would wait there to show the men out or to fetch him anything he might require. The dear woman was not going to force him to ring for her and cause a delay if he needed her. At that moment, he was grateful enough to kiss her.

"Mr. McCullen sent us to ask you how your new engine is performing. He is committed to the absolute satisfaction of each and every customer," said the shorter man.

"Oh, fine. Fine," said Seamus. "The engine is just what I needed. Thank you for stopping by."

He wanted to bid them good day and close the door, but the shorter man had already stepped through the doorway. The larger man followed, pushing the door all the way open and standing against it with his arms crossed.

"Hello, miss," said the shorter man, and Miss Sanchez gave a curtsey and inclined her head. It looked awkward, but considering that the poor woman had been raised in a world lacking in decent manners, it was the best he could hope for.

"Allow me to introduce Miss Sanchez," said Seamus. "I apologize, but I did not catch your names."

"I am Mr. Gouedard," said the smaller man. "And this is Mr. Kemp." He motioned toward the man at the door who gave a nod.

Mr. Gouedard walked to the machine and took in the disarray of papers and parts around it. Seamus had gotten all the parts, except for the tube, back into the machine. So this man would see none of the engine parts lying about.

"How is it performing?" asked Mr. Gouedard, blinking at him through his spectacles. They magnified his eyes, giving him an owlish appearance.

"Works like a charm. I apologize for not offering refreshments, but I need to be getting back to my work. Gentlemen." He moved toward the door.

"Mr. Connor, we at the McCullen Manufactory want to ensure that each and every engine we sell is of superior quality and performance. I see that you have taken this one apart." He indicated the places where the two missing screws should have been.

"Well, see, I was having a bit of bother with it. But nothing too terrible. It was just making a little noise. Got it all repaired right as rain now."

"You should have called us."

"It was just a loose casing on one of the motivators making a rattling sound. I got it all sorted."

Mr. Gouedard set his case on the floor beside the machine and opened it. Inside were various tools, small mechanical objects, and something with rubber tubing protruding from it like octopus tentacles. "We can't have an engine misfunctioning, can we?" he said. He pulled out a screwdriver and worked on removing the casing.

"Excuse me, gentlemen," said Miss Sanchez, moving beside Mr. Gouedard. "But if this engine is Mr. Connor's property, then he should be allowed to decide what happens to it. Didn't he purchase it from you?"

Mr. Gouedard looked at Miss Sanchez as if he had not seen her before. "Technically, yes. But the legal documents Mr. Conner signed when he took possession of the engine clearly state that the McCullen manufactory retains certain rights to the machine. Mr. Connor keeps ownership under certain circumstances and the Manufactory regains ownership in others."

"What kind of legal nonsense is that?" Miss Sanchez said. Seamus pulled her aside.

"They're well within their rights," he whispered.

"So you are essentially renting the machine."

"In a sense."

"But you're listed as the owner, right?"

"I own it as long as it functions. But if the Manufactory needs to repair it, they take possession. They also take possession of the used fuel cores. There are other times they can take ownership as well. It's all legal."

Miss Sanchez gave a delicate snort and he saw that she

was looking at a crumpled newspaper on the work table. "Legal, right."

"Mr. Connor," said Mr. Gouedard, placing his tools and testing mechanisms back into his case. "The engine is not functioning at all. Mr. Kemp and I will be taking it back to the manufactory. It should be repaired within a few weeks."

Seamus heard Miss Sanchez gasp.

"I'll be needing it sooner than that," said Seamus. "In fact, I need a functioning machine immediately."

"If you have any concerns, you are welcome to speak with Mr. McCullen. As I understand it, you are acquaintances?"

It took effort to keep his reaction in check, but he managed it. He and Mr. McCullen were more than acquaintances. They had once been cellmates.

"I believe I will do just that."

Mr. Kemp went outside and returned with what looked like a trunk with wheels. The two men lifted the machine into the trunk, secured it in packing material, and fastened the leather straps. They rolled it through the hall, carried it down the stairs and loaded it into a waiting steam carriage. Seamus watched from the window as the carriage drove down the street, a trail of steam puffing out of its shining brass exhaust pipe.

"You have to talk to this McCullen person," said Miss Sanchez, from beside him. The window was narrow, so she had to stand close to him to see out. Her shoulder touched his upper arm. "Without that machine, there's no way to get me home."

"I assure you that I will be paying a call on him."

"Look, they're back," said Miss Sanchez. A steam carriage with the McCullen name painted on the side pulled to a stop in front of the house.

"No, that's a different one." Seamus snatched up a bag and started cramming things into it. "Where is the tube I gave you?"

Miss Sanchez opened an empty teapot and pulled it out. A drop of cold amber liquid clung to the bottom.

"Are you mad, woman?" He took it, wiped it with his pocket handkerchief and slipped it into his pocket.

"You said to hide it."

"Hide it, not ruin it. Now help me or get out of the way."

She blinked in shock at his harsh tone. He was immediately contrite. He had to remember not to lose his temper with the feral woman. She couldn't help her ignorance.

"Those men downstairs," he said more gently. "They're the ones who were summoned by the radio signal. The first two really were regular concierges who were checking on me. McCullen probably sent them special and told them I'd likely take the thing apart. He was right, of course. He knows me. But those two men below are certain that I've been mucking about with it. And that's against the legal terms in the contract. Even if they hadn't been summoned by the radio signal, the first two men would eventually inform the legal team of my misconduct."

The front door knocker rapped three times. The upper gallery blocked his view of the men below, but also their view of him. He pulled up the window and climbed out onto the gallery. He put his finger beside his nose to indicate that Miss Sanchez should remain silent. She followed him, struggling for far too long to get her skirts through the window frame. She managed it, eventually, and turned to slide the window shut.

Seamus led her across the gallery to his bedroom window. He hated the idea of a neighbor witnessing Miss Sanchez entering his bedchamber, but there was nothing for it. He slipped into the room first and listened at the door while Miss Sanchez maneuvered herself through the window. It was no wonder she struggled with the dress if she had spent her entire life in those workmen's trousers.

Once Seamus was certain that Mrs. Washington had

let the men inside his laboratory, he led Miss Sanchez into the hall and down a back staircase which was plain and dark. The door to Mrs. Washington's room was ajar, allowing a glimpse of the multi-colored quilt that covered her bed and the oil lamp she kept on a table with some writing paper. Miss Sanchez peeked inside as if she were in a museum.

How lost she was in this world. At first, he had been excited by the idea of meeting a person from the future. But now that she was in his house, living alongside him, she was no longer an intriguing phenomenon, but a living person. She was even more out of place here than he had been coming from Ireland to America. This world was entirely alien to her and she could never live a normal life in it.

More importantly, a life depended upon her return, and if she was trapped forever, that death would hang upon him. It wouldn't be the first life he was responsible for ending, but this was an innocent and a child.

He had been powerless to save the children during the famine, those within his family and in his village. And he had been powerless to prevent the death of his tiny nephew. Perhaps that had been why he had made that fateful choice when he was eighteen. Perhaps it had been a way to have a shred of agency, of control, in a cruel and uncaring world. And in that instant, with that choice, his life had changed forever. He had lost everything, his family, his friends, his homeland. Had it been only seven years? It seemed like so much longer, lifetimes longer.

But he was no longer a penniless farm boy. He would get Miss Sanchez home, safe into the arms of her family. He could bring her to her nephew's bedside, ensure that he got the medicine he required. This time, things would be different. The child would live. The family would be reunited.

"We need to hurry," he whispered. He led Miss Sanchez into the back garden.

The yard was filled with magnolias and crepe myrtle, and Seamus had purchased a white wooden table with matching chairs so he could sit outside and enjoy a pipe and a drink. It helped him think. The garden was a little overgrown, but he rather liked it that way. They passed the garden shed, opened the back gate and hurried down the alleyway that ran behind his row of houses and those of his back neighbors.

"Where are we going?" asked Miss Sanchez once they were far away from the house.

"Somewhere I can get a better look at this device," he said. "I need more time with it so we can figure out how to get you home."

CHAPTER 9

A S SHE DESCENDED FROM THE coach, Felicia understood why Southern women of old always took men's hands when exiting a carriage. All her attention was focused on getting out without tripping over her skirts and falling ass over teakettle. Seamus leapt down from the coach and set down his bag. He turned to offer his hand, which she gratefully accepted. The width of her skirts prevented her from seeing the collapsible metal step, so she moved slowly. Once she was safely down, Seamus paid the driver.

They were once again at Jackson Square. Now that she wasn't so dizzy, Felicia was able to take it all in. St. Louis Cathedral faced the Mississippi with a square grassy area between them. The cathedral had three gray slate-topped steeples, two on the sides and one in the center. The building was built in layered stories, almost like a rectangular cake, with the bottom three layers the same size and the fourth just large enough to support the tallest middle steeple. This steeple was topped with a metal cross. Each story of the building had decorative Roman columns at intervals and multiple narrow, round-topped cutouts, like doors. In Felicia's world, the cutouts were simply indentations in the façade of the building. But here, each cutout looked like it had a seam down the center, as if it could open.

The shining white clock face at the center of the building was larger than she remembered, with huge bronze hands and gleaming bronze numbers. The front doors to the cathedral were large and wooden, with black iron handles. Stone steps led up to the entrance instead of concrete, and there were no hand railings.

Four brick pathways led from the center of the grassy square to each edge. At the intersection of the paths rose a shining bronze statue of Jackson astride a rearing horse. No sharp-tipped iron fence surrounded it, as in her day. And no fence surrounded the square, giving it a more open feel. The square seemed to include more space this way, as if it also encompassed part of the Mississippi and the Café du Monde at the far corner.

Seeing the Café du Monde serving up sugar-sprinkled beignets and coffee made Felicia feel like she was in more familiar territory. Though on closer inspection, she saw that only white people were seated at the tables at the front of the shop. There was a window near the back where a black man was making a purchase.

The Mississippi was just as muddy and wide as she recalled. An enormous white paddle-wheeled riverboat and a flat-topped barge moved upstream.

Seamus picked up his bag. "We'll be heading into the cathedral. There's a door out back in St. Anthony's garden that we can use."

"Why not just go in the front?"

"There is a room upstairs that I can use to get a better look at our little treasure," he said, patting his pocket.

A boy played violin near the cathedral steps, his case was open in front of him, empty except for a single coin. He tipped his face up into the sunlight, his eyes closed, and Felicia recognized him.

"Look, it's Henry," she said.

"Ah! That's excellent. There's something I need to ask of him."

They stood a few yards away from Henry as he played his piece, a slow, mournful song that somehow made

Felicia think of a mother losing a son in a war, though she couldn't say why she felt that way. Something about the lilts and the sorrowful long notes and the way Henry played. It was as if it had too much of a person imbued into it.

Felicia had listened to violin music before and she had seen people playing guitar or drums out around Jackson Square. But something about being so close to this boy, seeing his expression and the tremble of his fingers on the strings made it different. Were people able to play like that without knowing great pain? She hoped so, but part of her knew differently. The boy didn't go to school, had no money, and now that she looked closer, she saw that his lip was swollen and red. It had not been so earlier in the kitchen.

Seamus looked away, into the distance at nothing in particular. Something flickered in his eyes. When Seamus noticed Felicia studying him, his face changed and he gave her a little nod. She knew that he had not wanted her to see him like that. She had invaded his privacy somehow.

Another man stood nearby, apparently lost in thought. He had an upturned nose and Felicia caught a glimpse of graying orange hair under his bowler. He looked like he was waiting for something.

Henry finished and opened his eyes. He looked at the single coin with disappointment. When Seamus's shadow passed over the violin case, Henry looked up. The boy's face lit up, and Felicia understood how fond of Seamus he was. Seamus handed him a coin.

"Thank you," Henry said and pocketed it. He also took the coin from the violin case. He attached the bow inside the lid of the case, laid the violin in gently and closed the lid. Only one of the latches was working, and he fastened it. He did not use the case's handle, but held the case like one would a baby, cradled against his body.

"You play beautifully," said Felicia. Henry looked at the

ground and thanked her. Felicia wished she had money to give him. Now that she had accepted that he was no historical recreationist, she wanted to feed him and see that he was washed up and she wanted to give him a warm, soft bed to sleep in. That must be her maternal instinct talking. It was different from the feeling she had when she worked on a patient. It was less clinical and came from a quieter, deeper place.

Seamus pulled Henry aside and bent down in a discussion with him. Seamus gave him a few bills and Henry nodded vigorously. Then he patted Henry's shoulder and offered his arm to Felicia.

Henry pulled the brim of his cap. "Good-bye, Miss Sanchez. See you in a bit."

As Felicia and Seamus moved away, Felicia saw a man approach Henry. It was the orange-haired man who had been standing nearby.

"Where did you send Henry?" Felicia asked.

"There are a few things I'll be needing," said Seamus.

"Like what?"

"A few items from my laboratory and my study that we didn't have time to get. Mrs. Washington can help him."

"Don't you worry about him?"

"Henry? No. He's tough as old boot leather. Clever too."

Seamus took her around the cathedral to the back and held the wooden gate open for her. An ivy-covered fence with gates on either side surrounded St. Anthony's garden. Birds hopped in the branches of an oak tree that shaded half the garden. Marigolds surrounded a white marble statue of some robed saint, presumably St. Anthony.

The clock face on the back of the cathedral was smaller than the one on the front. Felicia noticed that the doorway-shaped cutouts on this side of the building had no seams.

Seamus rapped on the door, and a few moments later a barefoot man in a rope-belted brown monk's robe answered.

"Brother Stephen, good afternoon. I would like to introduce Miss Sanchez," said Seamus.

The brother nodded but did not speak. Felicia wondered if he had taken some kind of vow of silence and unsure if she should curtsey or say something, she settled on giving him a smile. Brother Stephen held the door open and she and Seamus passed inside. A staircase rose immediately on their right, lit only by the sunlight filtering in from the windows to the garden. Seamus led the way upstairs and Brother Stephen vanished through a downstairs doorway.

She followed Seamus down a dark hallway and through a door to the left. The room appeared to be a storage room and workshop. A single table sat under the room's only window and a decent amount of light shone through the small, grimy panes.

Stacked among the boxes of various sizes along the walls were a number of life-sized mannequins. No, she thought. On closer inspection she saw the seams and joints. Then she spotted one figure that was half apart, its interior components exposed. These were mechanical people in varying stages of completion.

A mechanical man lay in one corner. He had a bushy beard, no shoes, and wore ragged brown robes. His skin was metal, but painted in a fleshy color and his glass eyes looked to one side. On the work table sat two arms and a head. Part of the head's face had been removed, but the part that remained looked like the face of a young woman with pale pink lips. A wig, long and brown, sat in a tangle to one side. Felicia thought she had seen similar body pieces in Seamus's home laboratory.

Seamus stood with his back to the window, arms crossed and watching her with the air of a proud father.

A torso of another man lay on the floor to one side. The man's body was thin, with ribs protruding and a large red wound on one side. The wound was actually a long slit in the surface of the cover, and she crouched down to see that there was some kind of mechanism behind it with a red cloth rolled up inside.

She thought of the seams in the cutouts on the front of the cathedral and thought she understood what these were. They were mechanical people in the form of religious figures.

"This is extraordinary," she said.

"Thank you."

"You built these?"

"Some of them. I work with Brother Joe and together we get them ready for the high holy days."

"And they come out of the front of the cathedral, right? Like one of those expensive cuckoo clocks that have bobbing goats and German girls swirling around with beer mugs?"

"Goats? I'd love to see one of those clocks. But to answer your question, yes, there is an automaton display."

"Automatons," Felicia said the word with a chill. It somehow made the mechanical people a little frightening, as if they were more alive. She noticed that some of the boxes were long and human sized, like coffins. "We never had anything like this in my world."

"No? What did you have? Something more complicated?"

"We never had automatons of any kind. Well, we have cuckoo clocks and the little animatronic people at amusement parks. But nothing like this. And certainly not at a church."

"So no widespread use of automatons in your world, correct?"

"Right."

He nodded to himself, as if confirming something. "I'm sure you already realize this, but you are not in your world's past." His voice was gentle, and he was watching her in the same way he had when they had driven by the hospital where she worked, as if she might cry or faint.

"I'm getting that. It must be some kind of alternative universe or something," she said.

"Alternative universe? What an interesting phrase."

"I saw it on a TV show with my housemate. He watches a lot of shows like that." She was about to explain what TV was, knowing that Seamus would be interested, but he had already taken out the little blue tube with its attached mechanism and set it on the table. He opened a nearby box and selected what looked like a jeweler's loop from a boxed set. He positioned it over his eye.

Felicia examined the other automatons, trying to guess who they were. The torso of Christ was easy, and she guessed that the bearded man in rags was supposed to be John the Baptist. As to the half-faced woman, she couldn't guess, but no Catholic automaton display would be complete without an appearance by the Virgin Mary. Felicia herself wasn't Catholic, but her grandmother was. She tried to think. It was February, so Ash Wednesday would be the next holy day.

A few items of clothing, both men's and women's, hung on a rack to one side of the room and she sorted through them, noting that some of them were of very fine quality. Slaves and children on the streets wore clothing worse than the automatons.

"Professor?" Felicia said, reminding herself of the proper form of address. "Henry was hurt. Did you see?"

"Hmm?" Seamus glanced up from the mechanism, which was now in pieces. He held a silver spring in a tiny pair of tweezers.

"He had a fat lip, as if someone had hit him."

Seamus looked troubled for an instant, and then shrugged. "Henry is a tough lad, and lads fight. He'll be fine."

"Where does he live?"

"No idea. I sent for him at St. Aggie's once. That's the orphanage run by the sisters. But he doesn't live there."

"So he lives on the streets."

"Presumably," Seamus said.

"And you have a big warm house and don't let him stay with you?"

He didn't answer for so long that Felicia thought he wasn't going to.

"Miss Sanchez, may I ask you a question?"

"Yes."

"Are there homeless children in your world? Starving children?"

"Well, yes."

"And how many live with you?"

"Well, I'm a student, and I can barely feed myself and pay rent and tuition. And there are government agencies that provide foster care and food vouchers."

"I see," he said, and did not look up from his work. "And yet, you said there are still children in need."

"Yeah, but they live in other countries mostly. There's not much I can do personally for them. We don't have them running around alone and homeless. And we also don't have slavery anymore."

"I am glad to hear it. But that is not the world in which you now live."

"I've seen that clearly. Tell me something. Is Mrs. Washington your slave?"

"Of course not," he said. "She is a free person of color, as her parents were before her."

"So you pay her."

"Yes. She is my employee."

Felicia was about to ask how much he paid her, but realized that she had no idea what a fair or unfair wage would be, nor would she know if a white servant would make more than a black one. It was almost a certainty, she thought.

She moved beside Seamus and looked out through the window. Below was Pere Antoine Alley, no wider than a single carriage. Two black women were passing, carrying baskets with patterned cotton cloths covering the tops. They both wore long skirts and were chatting.

"Are you an abolitionist?" She said it softly, both wanting to know and dreading the answer.

"I am not."

Felicia noticed that his hands had stopped moving, but he had not looked up at her to answer. She moved away to examine a box near the door. As she pushed aside the straw inside, she noticed that her hands were shaking.

"Why not?" she asked.

He raised his head to look out the window, out over the top of the neighboring building. After a while, he returned to his work. She knew he had heard her.

"So you are okay with slavery?" she asked. "You don't mind people being bought and sold like animals? Beaten and abused?" she asked.

He set the piece into a little vice attached to the edge of the table and spun the arm until it was secure. "No, I'm not, as you say, 'okay' with it."

"Then if you don't support it, you're an abolitionist."

"Not everyone who dislikes the institution is an abolitionist," he said. "Least of all here."

"So you say nothing then. And it gets work done, right? You can keep your job at Tulane. And you can sit back in your nice house and let hungry children run your errands for pennies."

Seamus spun around so quickly and fixed her with a glare so fierce that she took a step backwards. He seemed to fill the room, and she was suddenly aware of his size. He was tall and strong, but his usual distracted manner made him seem boyish and harmless. Now he looked every inch the man who had folded the ruffians in half when she had been accosted in front of the pub.

"You know next to nothing about me, Miss Sanchez. I did not invent the institution of slavery, nor have I ever owned a slave. There are starving children, women on the streets, war, disease and death. I take it those are a constant in any time. I have seen neighbors and friends die because of the potato blight. I've watched my sister bury her only daughter. She didn't speak for a month. I've seen brother turn on brother for half a loaf of bread and sisters fight over whose child would receive a few spoonfuls of milk. And as for Henry, don't you think I have asked Mrs. Washington to give him a sandwich or something to eat as often as she can? And don't you think I pay him a little more than is warranted for his services?"

"But he lives on the streets!" she shouted.

A man came in through the door. Like the other brother, he wore a brown monk's robe. He was short and stout, his rope belt tied up under his overhanging stomach. He looked from one to the other of them.

"Hello, Brother Joe," said Seamus. In an instant, he seemed to return to his normal size, complete with disarming grin. "I needed to come up here to work on something. May I introduce my cousin, Miss Sanchez." He moved closer to Felicia and touched her elbow. It was just the right amount of physical proximity between cousins, and just the right tone of voice to introduce her. Felicia suddenly understood something. When the concierges had come and now with Brother Joe, Seamus had proven to be an excellent liar.

Brother Joe pressed his lips together in disapproval. "I can see the resemblance," he said. "Or hear it anyway, clear down the stairs."

"I'm sorry for that," said Seamus. "Friendly disagreement. But forget about that. I need your help. Could you take a look at something for me?"

"Now you know I don't understand these things like you, Mr. Connor," said Brother Joe, fitting one of the jeweler's loops in front of his eye. The men bent their heads together and spoke to each other in low tones.

Felicia returned to studying the automatons, and pushed open one of the larger boxes. Inside was a male automaton in elaborate Roman clothing. This must be Pontius Pilate. His glass eyes stared skyward, frozen in time.

CHAPTER 10

HAZEL ENTERED THE PROFESSOR'S YARD through the back gate and stowed her violin behind the trunk of one of the crepe myrtles. Mrs. Washington answered the kitchen door.

"Hello, Henry."

"The Professor sent me," Hazel said after glancing into the kitchen behind Mrs. Washington to make sure no one was there. "He needs a few things."

Mrs. Washington let her in and closed the door. "What sort of things?"

"He wanted me to bring some money," said Hazel. "He told me where to find it in his study. He said you'd know which book. And he also wanted an invitation from his desk. The desk in the study, not the laboratory."

"Well thank heaven for that. You wouldn't find a thing in that laboratory. Now wait a moment. What sort of invitation?"

Hazel shrugged. "I don't know. Something about a party. He said it was the only invitation that would be on the desk."

Mrs. Washington looked thoughtful and Hazel knew she was wondering what sort of party was so important that the Professor would want an invitation while hiding out from the men from the McCullen Manufactory. Both of them knew that the Professor enjoyed music and dancing, but he wasn't such a bon vivant that he would insist on attending if it was imprudent to do so.

"Mrs. Washington? Why are the men from the manufactory trying to find the Professor?"

The older woman glanced at the door, as if someone would appear and listen in. "The Professor was working on the machine that he bought. And those men don't like it one bit. They don't want it taken apart, so the Professor had to go on and do it."

"Yeah, that's his way."

"Where is the Professor now? And is Miss Sanchez with him?" asked Mrs. Washington.

"They're both at the cathedral with the brothers. The Professor told me to bring the things to him there."

Mrs. Washington led Hazel up the back staircase and into the Professor's study. "The men left a bit ago, but said they'd be back. I don't know when that will be, so we should try to hurry," she said.

The study was messy, but not nearly as bad as the laboratory usually was. Mrs. Washington and Hazel both rifled through the papers and envelopes on the desk. Hazel felt a moment of warmth inside, standing together with Mrs. Washington, both of them reading and sorting, stacking the papers between them.

"Here it is," said Mrs. Washington. She handed Hazel the envelope. It was high-quality paper, heavy and smooth with embossed lettering.

"It's from that McCullen fellow. I thought the Professor hated him," said Hazel.

"He does. I'm surprised he didn't burn the invitation the day he got it. But mad as he is, the Professor sometimes surprises you by having reasons for what he does. Well, most of what he does."

The envelope was open already, and Hazel slid out the invitation. The script was very fancy and she had to concentrate to make out the words.

"It's to a mummy party," Hazel said, wrinkling her nose. "What is that?"

Mrs. Washington took the invitation, as if to verify, though Hazel knew that the woman believed her.

The housekeeper shook her head. "They get a mummy straight from Egypt. And then they unwrap the pitiful thing."

"That sounds horrible."

Mrs. Washington did not criticize the behavior of the white people who chose to engage in such things, but the disgusted look on her face made her feelings plain enough to Hazel. "It's for the day after tomorrow," she said.

"Do you think the Professor will be away from the house that long?"

"I hope not." Mrs. Washington placed the invitation back into the envelope and gave it to Hazel. "Now for the money." She moved to the bookshelf, pulled out a brown and gold volume and flipped it open to reveal a cut-out rectangle inside. She took the stack of bills and hesitated a moment before handing it to Hazel. The girl noticed the hesitation.

"Don't be worried," Hazel said. "I promise to take it straight to him and not steal a penny."

"I know you will. It's just a good bit of money. It's not safe to carry so much. Do you want me to go with you?"

"Naw, I'll be fine."

Mrs. Washington didn't look so certain of that. They descended to the kitchen and Mrs. Washington went to the pantry. Hazel waited. She wasn't about to leave so long as there was a chance at getting something to eat.

"Did the Professor say you had to come back to the cathedral right away?" said Mrs. Washington, her voice muffled behind the pantry door.

"No, I can take a while." Hazel leaned forward to catch a glimpse of whatever Mrs. Washington was going to offer her.

"You can bring supper with you then," said Mrs. Washington. She brought out a metal pail and proceeded to fill it with bread, sliced meats, a wedge of cheese, three small sweet cakes and a large mason jar of iced tea. She tucked a checkered napkin over the top, poking the edges down around the contents until she was satisfied that they wouldn't rattle.

"Take that to the Professor and Miss Sanchez. Those poor brothers can barely afford to take care of themselves. No sense adding more mouths to feed. And you make sure to eat some too."

"Thank you, Mrs. Washington," said Hazel. She let Mrs. Washington hold the door for her and, after retrieving her violin, gave a wave to the housekeeper who was watching her through the kitchen window.

It was only mid-afternoon, and she wasn't hungry yet. The food in the pail would keep until suppertime. She headed down the alley and toward the cathedral.

By the time she knocked on the back door of the cathedral, she thought she would be ready to eat, if the Professor and Miss Sanchez wanted to eat right away. And if she was very fortunate, the brothers might offer her something to eat as well. She remembered the half baguette and bottle of milk that Alistair had eaten, and she felt a flash of anger. Still, she would be eating twice in one day, three times if the brothers had anything, and that wasn't too bad.

Brother Stephen answered the door, recognized her and let her in.

"Afternoon, Brother," she said and removed her cap. Her hair was getting too long, and she worried that it might make her look feminine. She needed to remember to set aside a little money for a visit to a cheap barber. Either that, or she could purchase some scissors and do it herself. Looking a bit rough wouldn't hurt any.

As she climbed the stairs, she thought of the night she had cut her hair, the night she had run away. It had been more difficult to cut it than she would have thought. Her hair had been in a single light brown braid down her back, and she had worked the scissors over and over at nape of her neck. Each slice of the scissors cut a few more of the hairs, until the heavy rope of hair had fallen to the floor. She remembered looking at it through her tears, and she had almost left it there. But then she gathered her wits. Leaving it would let her aunt and uncle know that she had cut it. She had picked it up and had thrown it in a rubbish can as she raced down the dark street, her arms filled with her violin and her small black dog, Mandy.

The door to the work room was ajar, and Hazel saw Miss Sanchez sitting on a crate while Brother Joe and the Professor worked on something at the table. Miss Sanchez looked nice in her dress, and Hazel felt a flush of pride in knowing that she had been part of obtaining it. The woman's dark hair was pinned up properly now.

"Hello, Henry," said Miss Sanchez. She seemed genuinely pleased to see her. She patted the crate next to her.

"Mrs. Washington sent some supper," Hazel said. She was about to mention the other things, but she didn't know if the Professor wanted Brother Joe to know about the money or the invitation. Hazel took a seat next to Miss Sanchez and set her violin behind her. The room was too small for four people to move about comfortably, and she didn't want to risk someone kicking the instrument.

The Professor looked through the contents of the pail and placed the cloth cover back over it. Hazel would have to wait here if she wanted some of it, which meant that she would lose valuable daylight hours that could be spent playing for money in the square. She was contemplating whether she should ask for some of the food now, come back inside every half hour or skip playing altogether when she realized that the Professor had asked her something.

"Did you get the money and invitation?" repeated the Professor.

"Sure, sure," Hazel said and pulled out both. The Professor handed the invitation to Miss Sanchez and slipped the money into his jacket pocket.

"Professor?" Hazel asked. "What exactly is a mummy party? Mrs. Washington said that people buy mummies in Egypt and bring them home to take them apart."

Brother Joe turned from the work table and Miss Sanchez looked up from the invitation. She looked like she had never heard of such a thing either.

"They don't take apart the mummy," said the Professor. "They just unwrap it. Sometimes mummies were buried with jewelry or other valuables. It's a bit of a treasure hunt."

"Desecration of the dead, I call it," said Brother Joe. Miss Sanchez looked like she agreed.

Hazel wondered if mummies wore clothing under their wrappings, but imagined that any clothing might be rotted away, leaving the shriveled mummy naked.

"But under the wrappings, do they have—" She stopped herself. She drew in a breath and locked her eyes to the floor. The Professor shifted his weight, and she thought he must be keenly aware that he was in the room with a woman, a child and a man of the cloth.

"Now then." The Professor waggled his eyebrows and rubbed his hands together. "The mummy party is our secondary plan. I will be paying Oren McCullen a visit tomorrow, but if I know him, the likelihood of me getting answers or another engine will be slim. Still, I have to try."

He must be talking about trying to find a replacement engine. She knew he was obsessed with mechanicals and was known to be quite the eccentric by the townsfolk. When they called him the Mad Irishman, it was sometimes with affection, and sometimes not. But why would he go speak with McCullen? It must be very important. Miss Sanchez fiddled with the invitation, and Hazel had a flash of understanding that it had something to do with her.

Brother Joe and the Professor went back to their work,

and Miss Sanchez turned a little toward Hazel.

"Do you want something from the pail, Henry?" she asked. "Are you hungry?"

"No, thank you. I had a little something earlier. But I'll be grateful to have some of it around suppertime."

"Where are you going to stay tonight?"

Hazel froze. How did Miss Sanchez know that she had nowhere to stay? There was no way for her to guess. Brother Joe had never given her any trouble before about not staying at St. Aggie's, but with all three adults, they might insist that she go there tonight.

"It's okay. I might be able to help," said Miss Sanchez very softly, low enough that the men could not hear.

"Okay?" said Hazel. She had never heard this term.

"I mean, it's all right."

Hazel nodded and looked at her hands. If the Professor liked Miss Sanchez, and Miss Sanchez was willing to help her, then perhaps the Professor would let her stay with him. She could imagine living with the Professor, in one of the spare guest rooms. Even in the attic. She could help Mrs. Washington with housework and the Professor could afford to send her to school and maybe she could even have a music teacher again. She imagined sitting at the table with Mrs. Washington and the Professor, eating like a family. Tears stung her eyes, and she turned away so Miss Sanchez would not see. Hazel so wished that she had a kind uncle like the Professor, mad and unpredictable as he was. But no, it was too much to hope for. She had to get the thought out of her mind. She blinked until she was certain that the tears were gone and fiddled with her hat.

"Professor, I have good news." She forced herself to smile brightly. No sense in dwelling on upsetting things. "There was a man down in the square. His name is Mr. Augustus. I'm not sure if you saw him. But he owns a music shop. And he asked if I would be willing to play at the Steamboat Festival. He teaches music on the side, and there are other music teachers, expensive ones, that only the best families can afford. And their students are going to be playing, and he asked if I would play as one of his students."

"Why doesn't he get one of his own students to play?" asked the Professor.

"Who knows? But this is a big chance for me."

The Professor was thinking about it, and he didn't look pleased. Why wouldn't he be happy for her? He knew she made her living with her music, and this was an extraordinary opportunity.

"Professor, it means I could be heard. There are going to be people here from up North and everything. There are conservatories up there, like one in Boston and one in New York that let boys play with them and pay all their expenses if they're talented enough."

"Aw, Henry. It's not that I don't think you're talented. You are. You are one of the finest players I've ever heard, and not just for a lad. You're a fine player compared to grown men. But this man asking you to play and pose as his student, it doesn't seem right."

"That part doesn't matter! What matters is that I have a chance at something better."

"It could be dangerous," said Brother Joe.

"Dangerous? How?" Hazel demanded. She was beyond using her good manners. Why did these people insist on ruining her one good chance at a better life? Would they have her go to St. Aggie's until her uncle found her?

"The engines," said Brother Joe. "The peroxide engines are having problems. They're not safe. I've given extreme unction to a number of people at the hospital who died of injuries caused when they explode."

"What does that have to do with the Steamboat Festival?" Hazel asked.

"The McCullen Manufactory has struck a deal with the largest shipping company in New Orleans. Their new ship will be making her maiden voyage," said Brother Joe. "It will have one of the new peroxide engines, and the Professor and I have been talking. I told him about the injuries I'm seeing and hearing about. We both agree that the engine is unstable and could very well crack or even explode."

"But I won't be on the ship. I'd be on one of the stages," said Hazel.

"Even so," said the Professor, "it's dangerous."

"And living on scraps and sleeping in empty buildings isn't?"

"Now, Henry. Be reasonable."

"I am being reasonable! The music shop owner said he'd be able to write letters of recommendation for me for the Northern conservatories. This is my only chance."

How could she tell them that in a year or so, once she could no longer pass as a boy, there would only be one profession open to her?

"And besides," said the Professor, "the boys who get paid room and board have to work for it. They work peeling potatoes or tending the boilers in the basement. It's not without much hard work."

"I don't care if I have to scrub chamber pots!" Hazel glared at him and hot tears stung her eyes, these ones from anger. Why did she cry when she was angry? So weak and womanish. She jammed her cap on her head and reached for her violin to go downstairs, but Miss Sanchez placed her hand on the case.

"Stay here," she said in a low voice. "You might be able to stay."

Hazel wasn't sure what Miss Sanchez meant, but the woman's eyes darted to the Professor's back. He and Brother Joe were back working at the engine part. If Hazel wanted to stay with the Professor, she had to have better manners. Shouting or storming out would not do.

"Tell me about this Steamboat Festival," said Miss Sanchez.

"What, you haven't heard of it?" asked Hazel. Everyone knew about the annual event. It was an occasion for picnics or strolling, seeing and being seen. Many businesses shut down for the day and their employees had a day off.

"I'm not from here. I live far away."

Well, that much was obvious if Hazel gave it any thought. Even Yankee women didn't dress in men's clothing. And Miss Sanchez's accent was different than any she had heard, and with all the Italian, Irish and German immigrants, along with the Spanish, Mexican, Caribbean newcomers, African slaves and free people of color, she had heard quite a few.

"Well, they have a big fair every year," Hazel said. "The businesses around here put up booths selling food or iced drinks or hats or toys. All kinds of things. Everything you can imagine. And there are games like races and the ring toss. And of course, the steamboat parade, all down the river. All the finest ships go by in a big line, with lights and everything. They have bands play and last year they had a small orchestra for part of it. I stayed and even managed to speak with one of the players afterwards."

"Is this for Mardi Gras?" asked Felicia.

Hazel shook her head. She had heard of Mardi Gras before, but only in a religious context. The Tuesday before Ash Wednesday involved a few small-scale luncheons and family gatherings, but nothing like the Steamboat Festival.

"Mardi Gras will be something different this year," said the Professor. "I heard there will be a parade."

Miss Sanchez suddenly looked distant and far from home. Hazel thought that perhaps she didn't have anywhere to go either. Perhaps that was why she was with the Professor. He had no family in America, though Hazel had heard him mention a family back in Ireland.

"Well, that will have to do," said Brother Joe. He removed a small light blue tube of liquid and attached mechanism from the vise and set it on the work table. The Professor eyed it.

"Looks like I'll be paying a visit to McCullen first thing in the morning. Either I'll get this sorted out, get locked up or they'll find my body in the river." He laughed, but Hazel saw that Miss Sanchez and Brother Joe did not appreciate the joke.

CHAPTER 11

SEAMUS STEPPED BACK AND DUG a handkerchief out of his pocket. With a sigh he wiped his eyes. They had returned to his house around midnight, once he was certain McCullen's men would not return. At least he hoped they had the good grace not to knock on doors in the middle of the night. He glanced out the window, but the street was silent and empty.

The fumes from his latest chemical test burned his eyes and nose, and he needed to stop for a bit. His sleeves were rolled up and his waistcoat was unbuttoned and hanging open. He knew he looked a sight, but if Miss Sanchez was offended, she did not give any indication. She had remained sitting in a nearby chair, flipping through some books and outdated women's magazines that Mrs. Washington had given her.

Mrs. Washington's daughter had worked as a housekeeper for the house's previous residents, and she had departed with the family when they had moved, leaving behind a few odds and ends, including magazines and some old clothing. It had been a lucky thing, as Miss Sanchez had needed more feminine articles than Henry had purchased.

He turned up the two gas lamps on either side of the work table. Miss Sanchez moved the magazine away from her face a few inches, and he realized that she had been struggling to read it. He reminded himself that he was no longer the poor farm boy forced to conserve lamp oil. He could burn both gas lamps as much as he liked, and pay for it easily. And if he ran into financial difficulties, an evening of gambling would resolve the problem. He knew that his head for numbers and probabilities gave him an unfair advantage, but it wasn't as if he were cheating, so he had no qualms about making a few extra dollars. Besides, his acquisition of money was in the name of scientific progress.

Miss Sanchez tossed the magazine aside. "I have an idea. As long as I'm here, I might as well be useful. Do you think Mrs. Washington has any moldy food?"

"I should hope not! Why—"

"Penicillin. You don't have it here, but I can grow it. It's good against infection."

"This mold will become medicine?"

"Only one way to find out. In the morning, I'll ask Mrs. Washington to let me have some stale bread or old cheese. I can try growing it on various organic mediums. I know which mold it is. At least, I think I do. I could use your microscope and set my things up in a warm, dark corner of the laboratory. Maybe over there." She pointed to a corner work table.

"Won't it create a bad smell?"

"Not if I use enclosed containers. Now, let me see."

While she sorted through the things on his table, making room for her project, he suppressed the urge to eject her from the room. It was only a small corner, he reminded himself. And if anyone understood the need for a space to experiment, it was he.

Seamus wiped his eyes and picked up some protective goggles, silently chiding himself for forgetting them. Again. In his enthusiasm for figuring out what exact chemical was inside the faintly glowing blue tube, he had neglected safety procedures. He should know better.

"Are you okay? I mean, all right?" asked Miss Sanchez as he tucked his handkerchief away.

"Yes, I'm all right." Seamus opened a window. The air outside was uncomfortably cool, but it dispersed the fumes. It would not do to have him dizzy or addled while working on such an important project.

"What does the term 'okay' mean?" he asked. "I understand it is a synonym for being all right, but what do the letters stand for?"

Miss Sanchez looked as if she had never thought of it before. "I have no idea. Just one of those terms that evolved over time I suppose. But there's a sign for it too. Like this." She made her index finger and thumb into a circle with the other three fingers sticking up.

Seamus knew a few hand signs of his own, though none of them were suitable for a woman. He decided not to further Miss Sanchez's education in that area.

"So, how is it going?" she asked, watching the smoke rise in a white cloud from his chemical set.

"Not well. I can't figure out what the blasted substance is."

"I took some chemistry as an undergrad. Is there anything I can do to help?"

Seamus almost gave her a condescending look, imagining how silly it was that a young woman could possibly assist him in figuring out something so complex, but he stopped himself. He bit back the quick dismissal he had been about to say and motioned her over.

He explained the tests he had run, seeing what reactions he could get from mixing the glowing blue fluid with other known fluids. Miss Sanchez nodded and stopped him a few times to ask questions. Her understanding was not as complete as his, but then, she had said that she was studying medicine to be a doctor. Perhaps she possessed greater knowledge of tonics and creating medicinal tablets than he did.

"I wish I knew more about science in your time," Miss Sanchez said. "And I wish I'd studied history. The way everyone here speaks seems off. It's not like the 19th century books I had to read in English class. And you talk about atoms, but I'm pretty sure atomic theory didn't exist in 1857."

She bent over his notes, and from this proximity, he could smell her hair, a soft, sweet, almost fruitlike scent. Her hands were small and delicate, and she flipped back and forth through the pages.

"Only a few people understand it," he said. "That, and a few other unique pieces of information I have were the only things that let me keep my professorship after the accident."

"Accident?"

Blast. He had been careless in speaking too freely. The fumes must be affecting his mind. Miss Sanchez was waiting for him to answer, watching him with those eyes that were too light a shade of brown. In the lamplight, they looked almost gold.

He turned to open the window further and Miss Sanchez stepped back. Good. He needed a little space to work.

"There was a little accident," he said. "An explosion in our laboratory at Tulane. No one was killed. But the building seemed to—well, it wasn't entirely all there."

"What do you mean? You blew it up to rubble?"

"Some of it, yes."

"And the rest?"

"Gone. Just gone."

"How could it be gone? Like vaporized or blown to dust?"

"No, it seemed to have gone somewhere else."

"I see."

Seamus nodded, pleased that she understood. He pulled the safety goggles down over his eyes, making sure the cloth padding was pressed securely against his face and the strap was snug.

"You think it went to another time?" she asked.

"I do now. It wasn't only that some parts of the building

were missing. Objects were missing. Files, experiments, whole bookshelves. But things came through to this side also."

"Things? What kind of things?"

"By luck, it was late and McCullen and I were the only people in the building. I thank God for that. And, as neither of us was harmed beyond a few cuts and bruises, we sorted through the debris. It was lucky so much of the building vanished, or we would certainly have been killed when it collapsed. As it was, there was plenty of space and we found a few things. Some files and a radio."

"A radio, in 1857," Miss Sanchez said in wonder. "My God, that could change everything. Imagine a radio in use during the Civil War, coordinating troop movements. Or President Lincoln giving the Gettysburg Address by radio."

"President Lincoln? You mean Ezekiel Lincoln, that man from Illinois?"

"No, his first name was Jacob. Jacob Lincoln. He was president during the Civil War. He insisted that the union be kept together and he wouldn't allow the South to secede."

"Ezekiel Lincoln died right before he would have been elected senator of Illinois," said Seamus. "He was predicted to win, but he got ill suddenly and was dead before the next morning. There was talk of poison."

"But he was supposed to die in the Ford Theater. He was shot."

Seamus thought for a moment, then tore off his goggles and strode across the room. He didn't need anything from that area of the room, but he knew he had to move. It helped him think.

"This is good. Better than good!" he said. Miss Sanchez looked amused and he realized he was grinning at her. "This means that we are completely sure you are from an alternative universe, as you call it. There are more than just differences in technological advances like airships and automatons. I think I could account for those. But something as vastly different as a president—that's big. What's more important is that there might not have to be a Civil War. It's not a certainty, only a possibility!"

"You think it can be stopped?"

"We might not need to. There might be no need to do a thing. The men named Lincoln don't even have the same first name. And even if they are the same man, nothing is certain. If Lincoln was central to it—you did say he was important, correct?"

She nodded.

"Right. So if he's not president, maybe there won't be a war."

"But if there's no Civil War, then the slaves won't be freed. They could be slaves forever. And then there would be no Civil Rights movement, no Martin Luther King Jr." she trailed off.

"You said a street was named for him?"

"Yes. He helped black and white people to integrate. You know, so they could eat together and go to the same schools and get married. This was in the 60s."

"At the same time as the Civil War?"

"No, the 1960s."

"And this is important to you? This integration?"

He saw a flash of anger cross her face, and then her effort to control it. "It's important to everyone. The idea of people being segregated and treated differently based on race is abhorrent to most people. It needs to die out."

"Then what must you think of me?"

She drew back at the directness of his question, but he watched her think it over. She was nothing like the women of his world who would have laughed and fluttered their fans in dismissal. Either that, or they would have bid him a curt good night and sailed from the room, nose in the air.

"I think you are a decent man, though mistaken in your

90

complacency," Felicia began. "Gravely mistaken. But it's not your fault. You are a product of your time, I suppose. You can't help it."

Her tone made Seamus think that she was trying to spare his feelings by being polite. He loathed the feeling it gave him, of being condescended to and pitied. He would rather she rant and rail at him if she didn't like something. Treating him like an ignorant schoolboy galled him.

"First of all, my thoughts and ethics are my own. I can, as you say, help it. I am not some ancient barbarian, ignorant and in need of you to bring me enlightenment. And secondly, I don't like slavery," he said. "If I think about it, I wish it didn't exist. But it's one of many evils in the world."

"Then why don't you oppose it? Why stay quiet? You should be fighting against it."

How could he explain to her what it was like to be a penniless immigrant, so concerned with his own survival that he never thought about slaves or anyone else? It wasn't as if he could help anyone by trying to oppose established practices. One man could do nothing. And even once he was established financially, he was still powerless to help anyone. The best he could do was to keep quiet and out of trouble, and he could barely manage that.

"It's simply the way it is," he said. She was glaring at him now, and he looked out the window, into the dark where gaslights flickered at the top of their lampposts. He felt Miss Sanchez watching him.

"Weren't you raised to think that black people are less than white?" she said. "But you don't treat Mrs. Washington as if she is less than you are. You don't think she's less, do you?"

"Of course not. She's God's child, as am I. As are we all."

"But doesn't it bother you, to see what people endure?"

He had seen plenty of what people endured, but he did not want to burden Miss Sanchez with what he had seen during the famine, in prison, or afterwards in New Orleans. What he had said in anger at the cathedral about the famine was enough.

"Of course human suffering troubles me," he said. "But this is how it has always been. The weak and the strong, the poor and the rich. Your world is like this also, is it not?"

Miss Sanchez sank into a chair looking suddenly exhausted. The clock had chimed two o'clock in the morning a few minutes ago.

"Yes, there is slavery in other parts of my world," she sighed. "Maybe my world isn't much better. There's starvation, war, child prostitution."

The last words sent a surge of fury through Seamus. The evil in the world was real, and he had seen some of it face to face. And its victims were always the small, the poor, the powerless and the weak. Her pain over the subject of slavery and her talk of a world where the institution did not exist made him wonder. If things could be better, different, then there was hope. And maybe that was something.

Miss Sanchez rubbed her eyes. She had such a hopeless look. He squatted next to her chair. "Then you and I must do what we can to improve this one, eh?" he said softly.

"Starting with a good night's sleep," she said and rose. "I'll look in on Henry before I turn in."

Henry was ensconced in a guest room. He had been so grateful to Seamus for allowing him to stay that Seamus had felt ashamed that he had not done so sooner. The boy had always been so cheery and had never asked to stay before, and Seamus had simply assumed he was content in his current state. It had been thoughtless of him.

It made Miss Sanchez happy that the boy was in the house, full of food and sleeping in a real bed. It gave Seamus a little feeling of unexpected contentment to think of Mrs. Washington, Miss Sanchez and Henry all sleeping under his roof together. It was almost like when his brothers and he had shared a bed when he was a boy. When the boys were asleep, one beside him and two with their heads down at the other end of the bed, he would lie awake in the dark, thinking night thoughts. Their slow, even breathing and the warmth of their bodies had been a comfort in the dark. His sisters had been in their bed at the other end of the room, and his parents through a sheet that hung as a divider. He had never felt alone then.

He usually tried not to think of his family. He could never see them again, and as far as he knew, they thought he was dead. He had lost them forever.

And once Miss Sanchez and Henry were gone, his house would be empty once more. The pleasure of their presence was only temporary.

Miss Sanchez popped her head in the door. "Tell me, why do you hate McCullen so much? You said you invented the peroxide engine and he stole it. Is that what it was?"

He nodded. "In a nutshell, yes." He wasn't about to tell her his long and complicated history with Oren McCullen, in Ireland, in Mountjoy Prison, or at Tulane. He would have his fill of the man in the morning.

CHAPTER 12

"THERE YOU ARE! I KNEW you would be coming to pay me a call," said Oren McCullen.

Seamus closed the office door behind him and shook McCullen's hand.

"Of course I had to come by. I have a few things to discuss," said Seamus.

"I thought as much."

McCullen looked genuinely pleased to see him, and looked him up and down in approval. The man was ten years Seamus's senior, which put him in his mid-thirties, shorter than Seamus, but more powerfully built. He was handsome, though he looked more weary than when Seamus had seen him last. He knew better than to think that it had made McCullen softer.

McCullen motioned to a wooden chair and Seamus took it, setting his hat on the empty chair beside him. McCullen took a seat behind his desk, which unlike Seamus's desk, was nearly empty but for a few items which were set neatly at the corners. Seamus remembered the arguments in their shared laboratory at Tulane over where Seamus had put one item or another. McCullen had even teased him after the explosion, saying that now the entire building looked like Seamus's side of the laboratory and that he should feel at home.

"It's good to see you again, Seamus," said McCullen in Irish Gaelic. The sound of his native tongue gave Seamus a surge of startled pleasure which faded as he met McCullen's eyes.

"You miss it?" Seamus asked, also in Gaelic. They both knew what he meant.

"Neither of us can go back, now can we?" said McCullen, his face pained. "Aside from a few of the Irish barmaids and street women, you're the only one I can speak our language with."

Seamus considered denying McCullen the pleasure and insisting on English. But he didn't know how thick the walls were, or if one of McCullen's workers would walk in at any moment. Gaelic would be best.

"So, what do you think of the engine?" asked McCullen. He was watching him too intently, and an idea occurred to Seamus. McCullen cared what he thought. He wanted Seamus's approval and admiration. It had been a personal weakness in his partner, and Seamus wondered how he could use it to his advantage.

"It's marvelous. I took it apart, of course," said Seamus.

"Of course. I knew you would before I allowed you to purchase it."

"Then why did you send me one? And why did you sent your concierges over afterward to take it away?"

McCullen shrugged. "Rules are rules."

"Then you know why I'm here?"

"You want to know how it works, of course. You never could resist a mystery like that. How does the engine work? How did McCullen do it?"

"You did it by stealing my peroxide engine designs." Seamus couldn't help himself. He knew he had to keep McCullen happy if he had any chance of getting an engine and getting Miss Sanchez back home. But the theft of their work violated every ethical principle he held. They might both be former convicts, but they didn't have to be thieves.

"We worked on it together," said McCullen, his voice placid.

"Then you should have brought me in on the project to work on it with you."

"The peroxide engine never could produce enough energy to do what these do and you know it."

"So how did you modify it? What is the substance in that little tube inside and how does it work?" Seamus asked.

McCullen leaned back in his chair and crossed his legs, ankle over knee. He looked like he was about to take a catnap.

"Would you like some brandy?" McCullen asked.

"I don't think I'll be here long enough for that."

"Come, come now Seamus. I know your mother didn't raise you to refuse hospitality, kindly offered."

Seamus was about to tell McCullen that he had never met his mother, nor had any idea how she had raised him to behave, but he stopped himself. "Very well, then. Yes, I would greatly enjoy some."

McCullen opened a cabinet and removed a cut crystal decanter and two matching glasses. He filled them and handed one to Seamus.

"So how did you do it?" Seamus asked. "The peroxide engine worked, but you did more. You went beyond anything we had done before."

McCullen had pleasure in his expression. Seamus was on the right track. McCullen's pride had not changed.

"Perhaps I'm a little bit jealous," said Seamus. "I have no idea what you did, even after looking at it for hours. I couldn't figure it out. But then, I didn't have the entire engine to study, only a piece."

McCullen gave a little one-shouldered shrug, as if to say that what he had done was nothing out of the ordinary. "Tell me what you did to figure it out," said McCullen. He turned a little to the side, but Seamus knew that he had his full attention.

"Well, I tried to make a sonic map using zed waves."

"That aluminium recording device of yours?" asked McCullen.

"The same. And I took it apart. It's the blue tube inside that's the key to the mystery."

Seamus and McCullen sipped their brandy. How many times had they shared a drink together? How many pots of tea had they shared in their laboratory? How many drinks of whiskey before that? And in Mountjoy Prison, how many tin cups of murky water?

Yet here they sat, both prosperous, though McCullen was vastly wealthier than Seamus. Two escaped prisoners, living by their wits. But unlike McCullen with his theft and dangerous machines, Seamus lived a clean life. Well, except for a few extra drinks, a few evenings with dockside women and a few games of cards here and there.

"Ah yes. The blue tube," said McCullen. "And you couldn't understand it or the piece to which it is attached?"

"I told you that I couldn't understand it."

"I always thought you were my equal, old friend."

The remark stung, and Seamus stiffened before forcing his body and face to relax. McCullen knew that he was dying to know about the blue tube, no matter how he acted or what he said.

"If you aren't going to tell me what it is, why did you have me here?" Seamus asked.

"Just a visit."

"Nostalgic for your old friend?" Seamus knew McCullen was up to something. He was glad he had agreed to speak Gaelic. Though he was getting nowhere, perhaps with patience and reminders of his past, McCullen could be softened. It was unlikely, but he had to try. "I doubt you miss my company so much that you'd allow me to dismantle an engine, have your men come to my home and then deny me knowledge of the device just to drink brandy with me."

"You aren't so appealing as all that, no," said McCullen. "Though I've heard you've caught the eye of a lady or two on the riverboats."

"Listening to gossip, McCullen? Like a common fishwife?" Seamus said it lightly, not wanting to genuinely anger him. But he also didn't want his personal life examined too closely.

"I know you can't afford that fine house of yours on a professor's salary. Without the money you make gambling, you'd be living in a different neighborhood, rubbing shoulders with the other stinking Irish flooding into New Orleans."

"You and I once stank a bit," said Seamus, his tone still light. Irish prisons were not known for allowing prisoners to bathe with any regularity. "I wouldn't be too harsh on our countrymen. They want the same as we do. They are just like us."

"No, Seamus. They are not like us." McCullen was dead serious. "Their minds are different than ours."

"If you mean our mechanical talents, then we should be thanking the good Lord for giving us what we have and using it to make things better for those who can't do so for themselves."

"Then we are of an accord," said McCullen. He set down his glass and leaned in. "Come and help me make the world better. Come work with me."

"You mean, on engine design? But you already have a working engine."

Seamus didn't dare mention the explosions, the danger that these engines seemed to present. If he stated that the engines were somehow faulty, McCullen would interpret that to mean they were failures and might throw him out for the insult. He would lose his chance to send Miss Sanchez home.

"True. But you could work for me. As a concierge," said McCullen.

"A concierge? Changing out engine cores and doing maintenance on the devices?"

"It pays well. Better than your professorship."

Seamus thought of the fine clothing that the concierges had worn at his house. But he'd be waltzing in hell before he worked as McCullen's employee.

"I don't need your money."

"Of course not. If you need money, you head to the riverboats. With your way of watching the cards, a few hands of bourre and you have what you need. The legendary good luck of Seamus Connor. Though of course, that's not your real name."

Now they were on dangerous ground. A few words to the wrong people, and Seamus would be in irons on his way back across the ocean. Seamus could, in turn, reveal McCullen's past. They were essentially at an impasse, but money tipped the scales in McCullen's favor. He might have enough money to buy his way out of any difficulties, should Seamus start talking and reveal what he knew. Seamus did not think McCullen would betray him. He had money and power here in New Orleans and it was simply not worth the risk of losing it all.

"I don't like you keeping tabs on me, Oren. Why do you care what I do? You have the engines, wealth beyond the dreams of avarice and my peroxide engine designs. There's nothing more for me to offer you."

But both of them knew it wasn't true. With a pang, Seamus thought of their former friendship, the good times they had spent together. And the bad. He remembered the day he and McCullen had secured a position at Tulane, entirely under false credentials, of course. McCullen had gotten Seamus a position, saying that they came as a team and he wouldn't work without his partner. That night, they had gone back to the room they shared in a drafty boarding house and had drunk an entire bottle of good whiskey. They had laughed and pounded on the wall good-naturedly at the sounds of the street girl next door, plying her trade. Within a week, they had rented better quarters in a better section of town.

McCullen was lonely. He wanted Seamus's friendship again, but on his terms, with Seamus in a subservient position. Well, he could think again.

"I'm not interested, Oren. I wish you well in your endeavors, but I do not want to work in your employ. I will, however, be happy to see you at your party tomorrow evening." Seamus had one more chance to discover what the blue fluid might be and he was going to take it. He got up from his chair.

McCullen likewise rose. "Will you be bringing your pretty lady friend? Miss Sanchez, is it?"

How did he know about Miss Sanchez? He hadn't seen her himself, surely. One of his men must have reported back to him. Seamus couldn't very well tell McCullen that Miss Sanchez was his cousin. The man knew his background too well.

"You do have eyes and ears everywhere," Seamus said, trying to keep a little admiration in his voice.

"Indeed. I would love to make her acquaintance. A Spaniard, is she?"

Seamus would love to see Miss Sanchez give McCullen one of her withering looks for that, but as she was not here, he said, "She's Castillian."

The lie would give her passage into society and would allow her to mingle with wealthy white people. Miss Sanchez had told him that her grandparents were from Mexico, but though Mexican women could mix in some levels of society, they were denied others. A Castillian she would have to be. He would have to delicately inform her of this when he got home. He sensed it would be a touchy subject.

"I am looking forward to making her acquaintance," said McCullen.

CHAPTER 13

FELICIA SAT ON THE EDGE of her bed and stared at the low battery warning on her mobile phone screen. For some reason, she wanted it to keep its charge as long as possible. She knew it was silly to care about it, but she dreaded the screen going black. She couldn't charge it, of course. And in 1857, it was a useless object, even fully charged. Well, the Professor could have fun taking it apart and poking around inside. But other than warping the correct order of technological advancement, the phone was worthless.

She looked through her pictures, stopping at a shot of her nephew. She wanted to memorize his face, and the faces of everyone else she loved. She scrolled through her voice mail list and played the week-old messages from her mother and sister. Their voices comforted her. They meant she belonged somewhere, with people who loved her in a world that made sense. She had family, but also friends, a career, a future. Here, there was nothing. She set the phone on her bedside table.

The gold hands on the small porcelain clock on her dressing table said that it was almost noon. Seamus was punctual about lunchtime, always wanting it served in his laboratory at noon sharp. She had noticed that he didn't much care when breakfast or supper were served and seemed surprised when she or Mrs. Washington summoned him for those meals. But lunchtime mattered to him.

Felicia had been in Seamus's house for two days and she wondered about the Professor. He had a complete lack of organizational skills both in his laboratory and on his person. His clothes and person were clean, but his pockets were stuffed with odd bits of things and his hair was often a wild mess. He had a habit of pacing and gesticulating when he was agitated or had an idea. But he also would descend into brooding silences, deep in thought. She hoped he was thinking of how the McCullen machine could get her home and left him alone at those times.

Perhaps the reason the Professor liked lunch to be exactly on time was to have a predictable way to break his day into parts. She wondered if he was the type of person who would forget to eat if not reminded. He seemed to forget most other things if they were not the object of his immediate focus.

He had gone to the university the previous day after his visit to McCullen and had gone again this morning. He had classes to teach, and Felicia wished she could have gone along to listen. But a woman in class would have stood out too much, even if she posed as his cousin.

At first when she had come, she wondered if she was delusional, but after waking in Seamus's guest bedroom two days in a row, she had to accept that she had arrived in the past. It was the past in a world that was much like her own, but differing in key respects. Lincoln was dead. Whether his name was Jacob or Ezekiel, he was gone. It bothered her more than she thought it ought to. It wasn't as if she had known him personally. She had seen pictures of him in her school books with his serious but friendly face and his stovepipe hat. He would now be no more than a footnote in a history book. No elementary schools or streets would be named after him. And he would not be in office to keep the country together or to free the slaves, bloody though the struggle would be.

She had to get back to her own world. She knew that

without the Professor figuring out what had brought her here and how to get her back, her chances were slim. No, they were less than slim. She would never get back and her nephew would die. She would never see anyone she loved again. Trapped in a strange past with no money, no family and no way to make a living, she would be like a piece of debris, cast up by the tide. She had no family connections and no friends. Aside from Mrs. Washington, Henry and the Professor, she didn't know a single soul.

She couldn't think of that. She needed to focus. She had done a rotation in the Emergency Room and she remembered the level of focus necessary to keep a calm and organized mind while working on a patient. The rest of the world faded away at those times. Right now, she had to focus on getting home, and the Professor was the only key. She had to be practical and keep her mind on things over which she did have some measure of control.

Item one, lunch. She could join the Professor in his laboratory for lunch and see how his progress was coming along. He had been in the laboratory all day, even asking for breakfast to be sent up. She knew he must have slept at some point, but she didn't know when that would have been. He seemed to live in his laboratory. She could see if there was anything she could get him that would speed the process. While there, she would check on her penicillin experiment.

Item two, Henry. The boy could read and write and seemed reasonably educated for the time period. Though she didn't know much about nineteenth-century education, she knew he should be able to read and write. He did. He also knew a little Latin, which impressed her, and apparently Henry had asked Seamus questions over the months of their acquaintance as he knew a fair amount of science. Felicia wanted to make sure that before she left for home, Henry was taken care of.

Item three, she needed to figure out what to wear for

this evening's mummy party. Her other dresses from the dressmaker had arrived in boxes and Mrs. Washington had hung them in her wardrobe. She felt odd having anyone handle her clothing and she was uncomfortable with the idea of a servant, but Mrs. Washington seemed to take her duties in stride, and Felicia deeply appreciated her help.

All of her new dresses were ordinary day dresses, suitable for wearing at home or into town. Two hat boxes with bonnets sat on top of the wardrobe and she had enough stockings and underthings to last between wash days. But she had nothing suitable for a party.

She glanced at the clock again. There was no more time to muse over clothing. Felicia went downstairs and met Mrs. Washington in the kitchen. After loading a tray with two covered bowls of gumbo, two hunks of bread and two glasses of tea, she headed upstairs. She knocked on the laboratory door at noon, careful not to unbalance her tray, and Seamus admitted her. He pulled two chairs together.

"Tell me about Mardi Gras," Felicia said after a sip of cold tea. "In my world, it's a huge party."

"Not much to tell. This year, there will be a parade through the Quarter, ending with the automaton display at the cathedral. What is it like in your world?"

"Well, there's drinking. Lots of drinking. There is the parade, of course, but it's huge in my world. There are lights and dancers and music. People on the floats throw beads and trinkets for people to catch. Women flash their—um. They try to get beads. It's just a huge party. People come from all over the world to see it."

Seamus seemed like he was going to ask her a question, but then Henry opened the laboratory door.

"A package came for you, Miss Sanchez," he said.

Felicia noticed that the boy glanced at the food, but did not seem overly interested. Mrs. Washington was keeping him fed. Between the two women, he wouldn't stay scrawny for long.

Seamus looked worried. "From whom is this package?"

"Didn't say," said Henry. But he had an apprehensive look. Felicia wondered who would be sending her a package.

"Well, let's take a look then," Felicia said and stood. She had been eating with her bowl in her lap and her tea glass on a tiny empty spot on the desk. She gathered them up and set them on the tray which was resting on the floor near her feet. It was no wonder Mrs. Washington refused to enter the laboratory and would only stand in the doorway. She couldn't imagine trying to clean such a place.

When they arrived downstairs, Mrs. Washington was standing over the package in the front parlor. It was set on a low table and she eyed it as if it might be dangerous. She looked up when the Professor, Henry and Felicia entered.

"Came a few minutes ago," she said.

The box was large, silver and tied with a huge green silk bow. The ribbon looked expensive, though Felicia thought that all ribbons in this time period might be made of nicer quality stuff than the ones she bought at the after-Christmas clearance sales.

She untied the ribbon and lifted the lid. After pushing aside wads of tissue paper, she froze. Inside was a mound of burgundy fabric, but that was not what had startled her. A card resting atop the shining cloth said, "For the lovely Miss Sanchez." It had no signature at the bottom.

Felicia lifted the card and looked at it. Of course, the handwriting was not familiar. She flipped it over, but the back was blank.

"It's from McCullen," said Seamus darkly.

"You recognize his handwriting?" asked Mrs. Washington.

"Yes."

Felicia lifted the dress from the box. Mrs. Washington looked it over and nodded in approval. Felicia didn't need to browse through an outdated fashion magazine to know that this dress was fine and expensive. The burgundy satin hung in heavy flounces around the skirt and a few embroidered embellishments decorated the bodice. The waist looked too small, but Felicia hoped that it was due to the enormity of the skirt.

She held it up to her shoulders and the hem swept the floor. That was good. She could wear her sneakers with it and they wouldn't be noticed. It would not do to be tripping in pretty but clunky dress slippers.

"You're going to look lovely," said Mrs. Washington.

Even Henry was not immune to the dress's charms. He held his hands over his mouth, but removed them to say, "It'll be real nice on you, Miss Sanchez. Real nice."

Seamus scowled. He rifled through the tissue paper, tossing it in crumpled handfuls to the floor. Mrs. Washington did not stoop to pick them up. Seamus found nothing and glared at the empty box. He muttered something Felicia could not make out. It didn't sound like English.

"Tonight is our chance to get the plans for the engine," he said. "This makes you conspicuous."

"Won't other women be in similar dresses? Should I wear one of the ones I already have?" Felicia was confused. Her impression had been that the mummy party was a formal event.

"Yes. Yes, they'll be in similar dresses. It's just that people will look at you in that."

Mrs. Washington had a little smirk on her face, but the instant Seamus looked up, her face became bland.

"Henry," said Seamus, drawing the boy aside. "Tell me what the delivery man looked like."

Henry told him and Mrs. Washington leaned over to whisper in Felicia's ear.

"He's unhappy that you're going to draw people's eye."

Felicia had never thought of herself as any sort of great beauty. Then she caught on. She was the Castilian cousin, and would probably be the only woman in the room who wasn't white. Yes, that would draw attention to her. They were hoping to obtain the plans for the engine, and blending in would be crucial.

Seamus started pacing and muttering. Henry met Felicia's eyes and gave a little shrug as if to say, "That's the Professor."

"It's a good thing McCullen sent the dress, isn't it?" Felicia asked. "I needed something to wear, and this solves the problem. My skin color is going to draw attention no matter what I wear."

"That is not what bothers me," said Seamus.

"Then what?"

"McCullen is up to something."

CHAPTER 14

"HENRY, WE'RE GOING TO NEED you tonight," said the Professor.

Hazel stood frozen. The Professor was in a foul mood, but she couldn't figure out exactly why. Of course, the hated McCullen sending Miss Sanchez a dress had bothered him. But if he had wanted to get her a fancy dress himself, then why hadn't he? And he must have known that Miss Sanchez would attract attention at the mummy party. How could she not, with her dark hair and pretty eyes. Hazel thought they almost looked like cat eyes. A woman of her complexion would always stand out, especially if she were beautiful.

"I do not want to involve you, but I may have no choice," said the Professor. They stood at the foot of the staircase, the Professor in his evening clothes, a white shirt with black pants, a teal and gold patterned waistcoat and black coat with tails. His top hat sat on the claw-footed table next to the door. Hazel thought he looked handsome. Even his hair was orderly, with just a touch of pomade to keep it from becoming its usual wild mess. Mrs. Washington was helping Miss Sanchez to get dressed and fix her hair upstairs.

"It's the only way we can get Miss Sanchez home," said the Professor.

"Why can't she take an airship or a boat?"

"She just can't," said the Professor. He was looking over Hazel's shoulder, distracted by his own thoughts.

"Just tell me what to do, Professor. And I'll do it," Hazel said.

"I know you will, lad." The Professor rumpled her hair fondly. "But this is a little dangerous is all."

"I'm not afraid."

But Hazel was afraid, especially when the Professor gave her the look he was giving her now, an evaluating look, as if judging if she were up to the task.

"I know McCullen well," he said. "He liked his desk near his bed, as he always had ideas right when he was falling asleep. So he'd jump up and work on something, sometimes staying up all night. When he became obsessed with something, he would only take breaks to eat or sleep. Sometimes not even that."

"That sounds like you."

The Professor's look told Hazel that she had better not point out similarities between McCullen and the Professor again.

"My point," said the Professor, "is that his desk is likely to be in his bedroom. Or if not, in a room close by."

"McCullen is rich. So wouldn't he have a proper study?"

"It's possible. We'll have to see when we get there. I'll find a way to let you in, then you'll stay with me. We'll find the plans and get out. If needed, I can slip you the plans and you can bring them back here."

"What plans?"

"For the engine. The McCullen engine."

"And we need the plans to get Miss Sanchez home?"

The Professor did not answer, as he was looking up the stairs. Miss Sanchez descended carefully, holding the railing with one hand and her skirts with the other. Henry caught a glimpse of a purple shoe beneath her crinolines. The deep burgundy color of the dress suited her coloring, and now that it was on, she looked like one of the fancy ladies Hazel had seen going to a ball once. She had only seen them as they went from their carriages to the front door, but each one had been a differently colored frilled blossom.

Seamus gave a curt nod and turned to grab his hat. Hazel knew the Professor had been taught manners, but instead of being polite, he was adjusting his hat and ignoring the lady.

"You look very nice, Miss Sanchez," Hazel said.

"Thank you, Henry. I don't know if I'll be able to breathe, but as my mother said, you have to suffer for beauty."

Hazel's mother had said the same thing on more than one occasion. Hazel remembered sitting on her mother's bed, watching her lace her corset or pin up her hair. She sometimes let Hazel use the powder puff to put a little powder on her nose, though she always told Hazel that she was pretty enough without it. But her mother was dead, and her aunt had been a very different sort of woman.

The Professor seemed to recover his manners and offered his arm to Miss Sanchez. After a moment's hesitation, she took it.

"Come along, Henry," the Professor said over his shoulder.

Hazel pulled the door closed and trotted behind them down the front walk. A hired carriage waited at the curb. The Professor handed Miss Sanchez into the carriage and then climbed in himself. Hazel scrambled in behind him and sat down just as the carriage jerked forward.

The Professor looked Hazel up and down. She hoped that her usual street clothes would be sufficient for their visit to McCullen.

"Miss Sanchez will have to stay downstairs," he said. "People would notice if she leaves for any length of time."

Hazel looked at Miss Sanchez, who nodded reluctant agreement.

"I don't like this idea. What if Henry gets caught?" said Miss Sanchez.

"I know, but I can think of no other way," the Professor said.

Miss Sanchez sighed. "You'll be careful, won't you?" she asked Hazel.

"Oh yes. I'm very fast, and I can hide well."

In fact, she could hide in plain sight, she thought.

Her stomach churned as the carriage stopped a block away from the McCullen house. The Professor made sure she knew which house it was and she headed for the back garden gate. Once she found the right house, she hoisted herself up enough to peek over the fence. The grounds were extensive and lavish, and the back of the house had a glass-domed conservatory attached. She mentally plotted a path from the garden gate to the back door that might allow her to get into the house without being seen. But she wouldn't move until the Professor came for her. She found a spot near the fence and waited.

CHAPTER 15

FELICIA WANTED TO TAKE A deep breath to steady her nerves, but could not. A different sort of corset was required with an evening dress than with her everyday dresses. This one had to be worn under the dress and laced from the back. Mrs. Washington had laced Felicia in far more tightly than was comfortable. It was no wonder that women in old stories were always fainting. They could barely breathe.

Mrs. Washington had assured her that it was necessary for an event like this. And after looking in the mirror, Felicia had agreed that her waist looked very small, though she wondered if her lower ribs would be permanently deformed. She had a horrible moment when she thought of her ribs snapping and perforating her internal organs, but knew that it was impossible. Probably.

The carriage stopped at the end of a line of three other carriages that waited on the curved stone driveway of the McCullen home. The three-story mansion was magnificent. There must have been fifty gaslights and lanterns hung along the first story and along the sides of the driveway. They looked like stars, or maybe candles, casting a golden glow over the yard. Even the front entrance was lined with metal luminaries.

The house was immaculately landscaped, with perfectly trimmed topiaries and brick-bordered planters. The huge double front doors were both propped open with white urns and servants in crisp uniforms stood on either side.

They left the carriage and Seamus offered her his arm. They climbed the stairs to the entrance. A man stood to one side with a book open in one hand. This must be the bouncer, Felicia thought. In her time, he would have had a clipboard.

"Mr. Connor and Miss Sanchez," said Seamus. The man gave a little nod and they passed.

A long blue runner with silver trim ran over the marble floor, leading into a grand circular room where a curving staircase rose to the upper story. The ceiling was domed with elaborate white molding. Felicia wished she could stay there, taking in the beauty of the place, but she moved on to the double doors on the left, where a few couples were already chatting.

The adjoining room had a few tables set up. Felicia judged the number of guests to be around forty, about evenly split between men and women.

Seamus brought her punch in a crystal glass and saw to it that she was seated at a table near the farthest edge of the group where people chatted and nibbled hors d'oeuvres.

"Will you be all right alone?" Seamus asked.

"Of course," she said. But she wondered. She knew next to nothing about the social mores of the era, though she had noticed that, as predicted, she was the only non-white person in the room. Aside from the black servants who circulated with trays of food, that is. "Go on. Henry is waiting."

She had never been to a house like this, lit by so many flickering gaslights and smelling of a mixture of savory food and the ladies' perfumes. The art on the walls had to be original, as she supposed that mass production of prints hadn't yet begun. Even the guests' dresses and suits had to be individually made. The only formal events she had attended were her high school prom, and the hospital staff holiday party. Management had rented a ballroom at the

Marriott on Canal Street and she had bought a cocktail dress at Macy's especially for the occasion. Nothing in her experience could have prepared her for this.

A couple introduced themselves as Mr. and Mrs. Still and sat down at her table. The woman was young and friendly looking, with gold hair in pincurls. Her husband was a little older and was balding. Felicia introduced herself and took a glass of champagne from a servant's passing tray. There was no harm in keeping her hands busy and her glass of punch was empty.

"How do you know our host?" asked Mrs. Still. She leaned forward eagerly, her curls quivering.

"I'm here with Mr. Connor," she said. "He is an acquaintance of Mr. McCullen."

"And how do you know Mr. Connor?"

The woman was fishing for information, Felicia realized. Mrs. Still was trying to place her in her taxonomy of complex social relationships in New Orleans high society. She wanted to know Felicia's connections and place.

"I'm his distant cousin. From Spain," she said.

"Oh, did you hear that?" Mrs. Still turned to her husband. "She's from Spain!" The woman was inordinately delighted with the revelation. "Where in Spain? We were in Spain during a tour of Europe two years ago."

"Well, my parents are Castillian, but I was raised in the United States." She hoped she would not be required to have any knowledge of Castille. She spoke Spanish, though anyone actually from Spain would hear the difference immediately.

"Are you as scared as I am to see the mummy?" Mrs. Still hunched her shoulders up and had an expression of dread, as if the mummy might come alive and attack the guests.

"It is frightening," said Felicia, becoming serious. "But we'll have to be brave, won't we?"

Mrs. Still nodded soberly and Mr. Still gave a silent chuckle that his wife did not notice.

A man was approaching them, smiling and saying a few words to guests along the way. He was good looking, in his mid-thirties with sandy brown hair and an air of self-assurance. He was of medium height and strong build, and Felicia noticed a few of the ladies giving him an appraising look. His eyes locked on hers and she stiffened involuntarily when he did not look away. She knew he had been looking for her.

"Miss Sanchez, I presume?" he said once he reached her table. "I would wait for Mr. Connor to introduce us properly, but it appears he has left you all on your lonesome. I am Oren McCullen."

He took her hand and bowed over it, but thankfully did not kiss it. McCullen's Irish accent was much fainter than the Professor's, almost imperceptible. She wondered if he was intentionally trying to lose his accent. He wouldn't be the first immigrant to do so.

"Pleased to meet you," she said.

"You look a vision in that dress."

Felicia gave the man credit for keeping his eyes on her face instead of looking her up and down. She was about to thank him for sending the dress, not wanting to be ungrateful. But something about Mr. and Mrs. Still listening to the two of them prevented her.

A servant at the far end of the room rang a bell.

"Time for the unwrapping," said McCullen. "There will be a late supper afterward, followed by dancing until very late. Or very early, I suppose. I hope you will allow me the pleasure of one dance?"

How could she refuse? "I would be happy to."

"As Mr. Connor isn't here, you must allow me to be your escort for the unwrapping. These things can sometimes be a little much for a lady."

Felicia had seen far worse things than mummies in the emergency room. And unlike the mummies, which were centuries dead, the people she had seen had still been alive. Most of them anyway.

McCullen offered his arm. She took it, wondering silently if a woman was ever allowed to walk anywhere without a man to hang on to. A door at the far end of the room led to a sitting room. Couches and chairs must have been pulled in from other areas of the house, as the room was filled with enough seating for the guests, some of whom were already finding their seats.

At the front of the room was a sarcophagus. It wasn't as elaborate as the ones Felicia had seen in museums or on TV. For a sarcophagus, she supposed it was quite ordinary. It was rectangular and carvings of grapevines snaked up the sides, but no three dimensional figure rose from the lid to indicate what the mummy might have looked like in life. She wondered if the sarcophagus was perhaps a modern creation and the mummy had been placed into it by the person who had stolen it from its resting place.

McCullen seated her between Mrs. Still and himself. He left her to speak with some of the guests.

Mrs. Still leaned over. "Do you suppose the mummy is a man or a woman?"

"I couldn't guess."

"I think we'll find out soon!" Mrs. Still whispered.

It wouldn't be long now. They were going to completely unwrap the mummy and expose the poor naked thing to everyone's scrutiny. Felicia was not squeamish about either death or nudity, but she did believe that the dead, even the long dead, should have some dignity.

But there was nothing she could do. Seamus and Henry needed as much time as possible to find the plans, and the longer everyone, including the servants, were downstairs, the better. The Professor had been gone for more than twenty minutes, and she wondered how they were faring. Surely, if they had found the plans, Seamus would have returned to her side.

"Ladies, gentlemen." McCullen stood to one side of the sarcophagus, beaming at the assembly. "Thank you for honoring me by joining me for my little gathering. I hope you are enjoying yourselves."

The crowd made murmurs of appreciation.

"As you know, Krewe Taranis will be hosting a parade on Mardi Gras. It promises to be quite a grand time. But there's something more. I am going to share a little secret with you. Do you promise to keep this to yourselves?"

A few heads nodded. Well, if McCullen wanted everyone in New Orleans to be discussing something by the next morning, this was the way to do it. If the guests knew that they were being used, they didn't seem to mind. A few of them had hungry, eager looks.

"Krewe Taranis has decided that the theme for this year's parade will be Enchanted Egypt." He said the last two words in a low, soft voice and people had to strain to hear him. He waited a few moments for the people near the front to whisper it to people at the back before he continued.

Felicia had heard of the krewes, but not Krewe Taranis. In her day, there had been many krewes. They were groups of people who created the Mardi Gras parade floats. There was always friendly competition between them to see whose floats would be the most beautiful and elaborate. Or the most outrageous. The ideas, of course, did not conflict during Mardi Gras.

Felicia noticed that McCullen hadn't mentioned the automaton display at the cathedral which would follow the parade. Surely he knew that Seamus had created the automatons with Brother Joe. Did their rivalry run so deep that McCullen would stage a whole parade in order to upstage his former colleague?

McCullen motioned to two servants on either side of the room who both came to stand beside the sarcophagus. They stood motionless while McCullen took a seat beside Felicia. Then they each took hold of the sarcophagus lid and pulled it to one side and propped it against the wall.

The guests gasped as the mummy was revealed. As expected, it was wrapped in cloth strips, though Felicia noted that they were much darker than she had imagined they would be. The two servants used scissors to clip away at the wrappings on the head of the mummy. Once it was loosened, a man from among the guests stepped forward. With hesitation, he pulled at the cloth, exposing the mummy's face.

Its skin was gray and desiccated and clung tightly over its protruding cheekbones. Its eyelids were slightly parted, though Felicia could see nothing but darkness beneath them. The eyeballs were probably as rotted and dried up as the rest of the poor thing. Its mouth was stretched open in a silent grimace, lips pulled back from grayish teeth.

After the entire head was revealed, one of the servants removed two small gold hoops from the mummy's shriveled earlobes and handed them to a female servant. The woman showed them to McCullen, who nodded. She then moved around the room, allowing people to examine the jewelry. Finally, she set the earrings on a lacquered tray and stood to one side with it.

Another male guest stood up, and McCullen gave him a nod. He moved to the front and removed the wrapping from the mummy's neck and shoulders, revealing a gold circlet, like a long crescent, with blue stones embedded at intervals. The necklace made the same tour of the room that the earrings had, and her stomach turned. The next person would unwrap the mummy's chest and if her guess was correct, this mummy was female.

A woman rose, smiling with her hand over her mouth and looking repeatedly back at her giggling companions. Once she was face to face with the mummy, she gasped and almost turned away. But she screwed up her courage and pulled at the wrapping with delicate fingers. She allowed a servant with scissors to help her cut away some of the more stubborn pieces of wrapping and the mummy's rotted clothing to reveal the chest and ribcage. The ribs stuck out, as the surrounding flesh had collapsed inward. Dark nipples, like gray eraser heads, stood out against the small rises of the mummy's flattened breasts.

The woman turned to the crowd, her cheeks scarlet. A few of the others gave her light applause. A servant removed a thin gold chain from around the mummy's waist. It made its way around the room.

"Are you not enjoying yourself?" whispered McCullen. He was so close to her that she could smell his cologne, like pine needles. "You look unwell. Do you need some air?" he asked.

Felicia tried to relax and uncrossed her arms. She had been scowling in disgust and knew she ought to be polite and blend in. Mrs. Still touched her hand.

"Amazing, isn't it?" Mrs. Still said, as if they were making a grand archeological discovery together.

"I have never seen anything like it," said Felicia.

McCullen leaned in again. "Do you know what will happen to the jewelry?"

"No, what?" Felicia said.

Once the female servant had placed the waist chain on the lacquered tray, McCullen stood and took the tray. He waited until he had everyone's full attention. "These lovely trinkets, as well as anything else our ancient friend offers us," here he nodded toward the mummy, "will be worn by the Queen of the Mardi Gras."

A group of young women exchanged looks of delight with each other.

"The King will ride on a grand float in the parade," continued McCullen. "On the day of the parade itself, he will select his queen from the many beautiful ladies of our fine city. This lady will have the honor of wearing these invaluable historical artifacts. Or rather, we will all have the honor of seeing her display them to their best advantage."

The young women immediately put their heads together in discussion, glancing now and then at McCullen.

A door at the side of the room opened, and the servant who entered caught McCullen's eye. For a moment, Felicia caught a flash of irritation on McCullen's face, but he quickly recovered the appearance of good humor. He gestured for a volunteer to come and unwrap the next portion of the mummy. He met the servant near the door and listened as the man whispered in his ear. He got a dark look, glanced at Felicia and then left the room.

In the moment the doors opened, she heard a familiar voice.

"Call your men off, Oren, or I'll take care of them myself."

The guests turned toward the door. As another guest began his work on the mummy, Felicia wondered if she could leave without anyone noticing. She was near the front, and there was no way she could manage a stealthy exit. She heard muffled voices through the door, and she shot up from her chair. All eyes were on her as she sailed across the room and pulled open the door.

She found herself in a wide carpeted hallway with sculptures and vases in small alcoves along the walls. Two servants held each of Seamus's arms while McCullen stood up close to him. Henry was nowhere to be seen.

"I offer you a good position in my company, and this is how you repay me? With theft?" said McCullen.

"I didn't take anything." Seamus was not struggling against the two men who held him.

"No?" McCullen looked to one of the servants who shook his head. "So you didn't take anything. But you were rummaging around in my office. What was it that you were looking for?"

McCullen knew exactly what Seamus had been searching for, Felicia thought.

"Ah, Miss Sanchez," said McCullen, as if he and Seamus were having a pleasant chitchat. "I apologize that my former associate has been so rude as to leave a lady without her escort."

"I'm fine on my own."

A roar went up from the guests behind the door, and Felicia imagined that the mummy's genitals must have just been exposed. So much for the idea of prudish Victorians.

"I know you wanted to take something. Just tell me what it is," McCullen said to Seamus.

"Unlike you, old friend, I am not a thief."

"Yes, yes. Not a thief. But you are a murderer." His last word was so low that Felicia almost didn't hear it. But it hung in the air as Seamus glared at McCullen. Then he looked down.

"I will never understand you, Seamus. You still let yourself be tortured by it. After everything."

The door to the mummy unwrapping opened, and a few people came out to see what the commotion in the hallway was about. The door was held open long enough for Seamus to see the gray figure propped up inside the sarcophagus. He took in the naked mummy with a look of disgust. He said something in another language. Felicia guessed it was Irish.

McCullen spun around. "You address me in English in this house."

"You are what you are," Seamus said and paused, "but why did you bring that thing here? It's disgraceful."

"Offended by a nude woman? Now, that's not the Seamus I know." McCullen smirked.

"Not by the nudity or the rotted nature of the thing. But with what you've done to it."

"But that's not all you said, brother."

"The rest I cannot repeat with a lady present," Seamus said.

"Ah yes, your lady friend. Well, after being left alone with strangers, she will have the pleasure of watching you be loaded into the police wagon. They should be here in a few minutes."

McCullen joined his guests while servants herded the remaining people back into the room with the tables, leaving Seamus with the two servants and Felicia.

"What can I do?" she said. Seamus's eyes were narrowed in thought, and she wondered if he had a plan. "Can I call a lawyer? How does it work here?"

"Tell Mrs. Washington. And see to Henry."

The police came quickly and quietly, taking Seamus outside and loading him into the back of a square horse-drawn police wagon. Felicia had heard of paddy wagons, but never thought to see one, let alone one with an actual "paddy" inside. Seamus sat on a bench on one side, and an officer closed the double doors and locked them. A servant came and spoke with the police, presumably giving them the details of Seamus's crime. Felicia wondered if he was the butler, but she had no way of knowing. Felicia remembered that Seamus had admitted to nothing, so perhaps there were no charges that could stick. She could hope.

As the horses pulled the wagon down the curved stone drive, she shivered and rubbed her arms. Seamus was a good liar, she remembered. He might be able to lie his way out of this. Unless this was just another way for McCullen to assert his dominance over Seamus by humiliating him. In that case, it was all for show, and Seamus soon would be home. Luckily, none of the other guests were outside to witness anything. McCullen had enough propriety to keep the upper crust of New Orleans society inside, eating and dancing. Word would spread soon enough, she had no doubt.

"Ma'am, the master asks that you come back inside," said a servant at the door.

The master could shove it, for all she was concerned. "Could you call me a carriage instead? I am not feeling well and I need to go home." She did her best to look miserable, which, under the circumstances was not hard to do. The servant nodded.

A murderer. That's what McCullen had called the Professor. Seamus was a good liar, and could have denied it. She would have believed him over McCullen in an instant. But he hadn't. Which meant one of two things. Either he was careless, which was a possibility, or he might have wanted Felicia to know. The Professor was eccentric, but he would never be careless about confirming something so serious, especially in front of servants. He would only do so for a good reason, and the only one that made sense was that he wanted her to hear it. That meant that he was in more trouble than a simple trespassing violation. He could be wanted for murder.

CHAPTER 16

HAZEL CROUCHED DOWN BEHIND A plant with thick arching stems and enormous, fanlike leaves. If she made herself small and sat near the main stem of the plant, its leaves and those of its brethren would conceal her. It wouldn't work in daylight, of course, but the only illumination in the conservatory was the diffused light of the crescent moon. Unless someone looked closely, she would not be seen.

There were people in the yard behind the McCullen house, and Hazel could not risk a run for the fence. Her heart was still beating hard. The Professor had insisted that she leave at the first sign of trouble. He was very stern about it and had made her give her word.

The two of them had been in McCullen's office, as the man did not have a desk in his bedroom, as the Professor had predicted. The office was the complete opposite of the Professor's, with neatly labeled file drawers, a tidy desk and bookshelves filled in an organized fashion. They had been wrong to assume the tidiness of the room would make it easy to locate plans for the engine.

They had gotten in a good twenty minutes of searching through files and papers before a servant had found them. Hazel heard footsteps a moment before the Professor, and by the time the door handle turned, Hazel had already scurried under the desk.

The Professor talked to the servant for a long time, making a convincing argument on why he should be in the room. But ultimately, the servant insisted that he escort the Professor downstairs. After they left, Hazel waited under the desk. She could leave. That was what the Professor had instructed her to do if he were waylaid. He would want her to obey him. Or she could delay her departure just a bit to try to find the plans. She decided to go through the files. She knew the term "peroxide engine" and she would recognize it if she read it.

Thankfully, the servant had left the gaslight on. The curtains were closed, so anyone in the backyard would not see a light upstairs. She slid a drawer open and tried to remember where she had seen the Professor leave off. About mid-way through the papers, she decided, and started to thumb through them.

She found nothing about a peroxide engine. Absolutely nothing. She had listened to the Professor curse under his breath as he had gone through, and she now did the same.

Flopping down into a chair, she glared at the file cabinets. Why did McCullen have to make the Professor's life so difficult? She knew he had stolen an idea from the Professor, and that it must have been a terrible betrayal for the Professor to harbor such deep anger at him. The Professor could anger quickly, but it was always short-lived. So his longstanding bitterness toward McCullen had to be well-deserved.

The Professor and McCullen had been the closest of friends. That must have been the cruelest cut. Hazel was old enough to know that the worst pain came from those closest to you. And the Professor and McCullen had been close. Not as close as family, but not far from it.

She had a sudden thought. If the Professor was in trouble, someone would be on their way to this very room soon to see if he had stolen anything. There was no clock in the room, so she couldn't possibly know how much time had passed. But every moment brought her closer to someone coming into the room. She had to get out.

She slipped through the door, leaving the gaslight on behind her. A light under the door might draw attention, but if the servant who had found the Professor remembered leaving it on, then her turning it off would indicate that someone else was working with the Professor. She knew with all her heart that the Professor would not give her away. Not even if they beat him or tortured him. So she was obligated to be careful and not do anything to foolishly make her presence known.

Feeling very much the trusted and clever friend of an important person, Hazel slid along the hall and down the back staircase. All of the servants were downstairs as far as she could tell, assisting with the mummy party. Good.

She wished she could see the mummy. Once, when her parents were alive, her father had shown her pictures of Egypt. There had been an illustration of a pyramid with slaves in loincloths toiling under the blazing Egyptian sun. Taller men brandishing whips had stood over them, looking menacing. Those were the overseers, her father had explained. Hazel had never been to a plantation, but she knew that there were slaves and overseers there too.

She snapped to attention as she heard someone approaching. She could not afford to daydream. She slipped into an empty room while the person passed, and then hurried down the hallway. She was in the shadows in the dark downstairs hallway when a couple crossed the hall in front of her. They were moving from the main house into the conservatory. That was the direction she was heading, as it put her closest to the back garden gate.

Thankfully, the couple passed through the conservatory and out the French doors at the back. Once they were gone, Hazel crept into the conservatory, which had more light than the dark hallway. That was comforting, but also left her more open to being seen.

The conservatory was enormous and octagonal, with a domed glass roof and glass walls on all sides except the one attached to the main house. A large round area at the center was paved in gray stones. At its exact center was a three-tiered planter, filled with ivy and other draping greenery. Off to one side of the paved area sat a garden table with two chairs. Orange and lemon trees ringed the area, surrounded by lower, thicker plants. Hazel chose a spot under the plants with the largest leaves and peered through the glass to the outside.

It was warm and moist in the conservatory, and she felt sweaty. She knew that once she calmed down, she would feel cooler. Fear always made her hot. She tried to still her thoughts and focus on being small and unobtrusive.

The couple outside walked slowly, so slowly, to a little bench at one end of the yard. They sat and talked for the longest time. Then another couple emerged from another part of the house and meandered around the yard, then came in through the conservatory. Couples and groups came and went, and still Hazel waited.

Her legs felt cramped, and she had to move from her squatting position to settling herself on the ground. She knew it would get dirt on her trousers and Mrs. Washington might scold her if she ever washed them. She hoped she could stay with the Professor long enough for that to happen.

The crowd thinned, and then she saw two servants check the conservatory and then the yard. She hoped it meant that they were clearing out any remaining guests. Her chance to leave was coming.

A young blonde man with a thin moustache and narrow face came in and sat down at the garden table. He crossed his feet at the ankle and leaned back, crossing his arms. He looked like he was settling in to wait for something. Hazel cursed silently, trying a particularly vulgar phrase she had heard one of the street boys use. It suited the situation, she thought. She would never have said it aloud, but felt justified in thinking it. She came up with other phrases as she waited.

"I am so glad you were able to wait for me," said a silhouetted man in the doorway. The man had a very faint Irish accent. This must be McCullen.

"How could I refuse? I've wanted to join Krewe Taranis for some time."

"Your uncle spoke highly of you," said McCullen. "Tell me what you know about the krewe."

Hazel tried to listen, but her mind drifted as the younger man leaned forward and spoke to McCullen excitedly. The man was clearly enamored of this krewe and with McCullen himself. He rambled on, smiling and nodding in agreement with whatever McCullen said. He reminded Hazel of a puppy, trying to play with an older, grumpier dog.

She snapped to attention at the word, "war."

"Your uncle told you that?" said McCullen.

The young man looked as if he had made a mistake and wanted to take back his words. "Only a little. I figured out the rest myself."

"Very astute. What else have you figured out?"

"I'm not sure, but it looks like Ireland and France might join the South. But then there is Wales."

Even Hazel knew that Wales had one of the most formidable militaries in the world. A war with Wales involved would be bloody and terrible.

"And Buchanan?" asked McCullen softly.

Hazel remembered that Buchanan had won the last presidential election. He would take office in a few weeks.

"I heard he didn't survive. Breckinridge will take his place."

Hazel got a chill. The future president was dead?

"I heard the krewe did Lincoln as well. Is that true?" asked the young man.

Hazel couldn't see McCullen's face now, but she saw the young man draw back a fraction.

McCullen waited a few seconds and then spoke. "The krewe is solely for making floats. Do you understand?"

The young man nodded, looking down at his hands. And at that moment, Hazel felt sorry for him.

CHAPTER 17

"SEAMUS CONNOR, BORN JANUARY 17TH, 1832, Dublin, Ireland, it says." An officer was reading from a file. "Is that correct?"

"Yes, that's what I told the first man who was in here." Seamus sat in a back room of the police station. The room had two chairs, one table and one grimy window. A single gaslight hissed in its bracket on the wall. Thankfully, he had not been placed in a cell. The very idea made his heart pound and his palms sweat.

He had already given his statement, explaining that he had wandered off into McCullen's house out of curiosity, but as he had taken nothing, they could not charge him with theft. He hoped it was only a matter of time before he could leave. He was more than weary of this little display of McCullen's power.

Another man entered and took a seat across the table from Seamus. He was wearing ordinary street clothes with a black duster. Not an officer then. He was of medium build and height with brown hair and eyes. He looked familiar, though Seamus thought he had the sort of face that is so ordinary, there might be hundreds like it in the world.

"My name is Neil Grey. And I believe we have a few things to discuss." Mr. Grey nodded and the officer left them, shutting the solid wooden door behind him. "Coffee?"

"No, thank you."

Something about the man made Seamus relax a fraction. But he couldn't let his fatigue cloud his wits. If Grey wasn't with the police force, he could be in McCullen's employ.

"I know you would like to return home," said Grey. "So I will be brief. I am the consulting detective assigned to a particular case, and you are going to assist me."

"Is that so?" Seamus was in no mood to be bullied further. If this man had the idea that he was easy to control or intimidate, then he was in for disappointment.

"Well, you have a choice, of course," said Mr. Grey. "I cannot force you to assist. But you are uniquely qualified, we need your help, and you need ours."

"Who is the 'we' of which you speak?"

Grey looked pleased, as if Seamus was a child who had learned to tie his shoes. It put Seamus's teeth on edge. Any friendliness he felt toward the man evaporated.

"I work with a private agency," said Mr. Grey. "I was called in because the New Orleans Police Department has found itself in need of our services. The first detective they assigned to this case ended up dead. Now, here is what we have so far." Grey slid a few pages across the table to Seamus. "They are notes on the McCullen peroxide engine. You know of the accidents, I presume?"

"I've heard that some of the engines explode. Something is wrong with them."

"Indeed, something is. And we need your help in finding out what it is," said Grey.

"Who are you working with?"

"The New Orleans Police Department."

"You said you were a consulting detective. Consulting from where?"

Grey pulled out a page and laid it on top. "Would you be so kind as to look at this?"

"If you need me to help, you can meet with me at my house properly instead of trying to convince me in a police station in the middle of the night."

"You've never stood on formalities before, Mr. Connor."

"You know nothing about me. We've never met before."

"Of course not," said Grey. But there was the slightest hint of pleasure in his look, as if they were friends.

"Where do I know you from?" asked Seamus. "You look familiar."

"As you said, we have not met before."

His curiosity got the better of him and Seamus looked over the first page, then through the rest of the file. There was nothing containing information on the blue tube or its role in the machine. There were, however, numerous reports of explosions and injuries.

"You need me to see why the engines are exploding."

"Yes."

"Well, I can save you some trouble. I don't know. As I'm sure McCullen has reported, I purchased an engine, took it apart and couldn't figure out how he's getting such high energy output out of the cursed thing."

"So, you have no idea why they are exploding?"

"None, I can't even figure out how the engines are supposed to work under normal circumstances, let alone what makes them explode. I'm afraid I am no help to you."

"You are too modest, Mr. Connor."

"If I had a way of finding out why people are being harmed by these things, I'd be happy to supply the information. There's no love lost between me and McCullen. But I'm sure you already know that. Tell me, do you have any copies of the plans for the engine?"

"We do not. It is a closely guarded secret," said Grey.

Seamus knew that fact all too well.

"Is there any way to get an engine to dismantle?" Seamus asked.

"Unfortunately, no. The McCullen Company is very selective in choosing customers, an admittedly odd marketing strategy. But effective, in this case. There is far more demand for the engines than can currently be met. The cost of the engines has been driven to astonishing levels."

"Couldn't the police confiscate an engine from someone who already has one?"

"They could, but they won't. The engines all belong to well-to-do families, the explosions have been kept quiet and if you ask me, a few palms in the police department have been greased."

"That's a serious accusation."

"Yes. But I tell you because I need your assistance. You are the inventor of the peroxide engine and you were close with McCullen. You have the best chance of discovering what is happening with these engines."

"This doesn't make sense. Why do you care how the engines work? They injure people. Isn't that enough?"

Mr. Grey had the faintly pleased look again.

Seamus shoved the papers back across the desk. "I'm knackered. I need to go home."

"If you wish, Mr. Doyle."

Seamus froze. Mr. Grey met and held his eyes. There was no malice in Grey's face, none of the triumph that Seamus would expect a person to have who knew his name. This man did not draw pleasure from the power he held. No, he looked, what was it? Almost sad. As if he did not enjoy what he had to do. It was the look his father had worn when he carried a switch to the barn after Seamus had done something wrong.

"My surname name is Connor," Seamus said. If there was any chance of avoiding this, he would take it.

"The police do not know. I have not told them. But I do require your help." Mr. Grey stacked the papers, taking longer than was necessary.

"And if I do not help you?"

Mr. Grey opened his hands in a gesture to say that anything could happen.

CHAPTER 18

"**O**H, THANK HEAVEN!" CRIED MRS. Washington and drew Seamus into her arms. Seamus's housekeeper had never embraced him before, and after a moment of him awkwardly patting her back, she pulled away, muttering an apology.

"It's all right," Seamus said. He pushed the front door closed behind him and secured the lock.

"I was just so worried after Miss Sanchez told me what had happened at that awful man's party," said Mrs. Washington. "I was going to go down to visit the bank in the morning, and then Miss Sanchez was going to go to the law office downtown."

"I don't think that will be necessary anymore," he said.

Felicia stood behind Mrs. Washington, a broad smile on her face. "I take it they released you?"

"More or less," he said. "They didn't charge me with anything, but someone from the police office will be here in the morning."

There was the sound of a knock at the back kitchen door. Seamus went to the kitchen, only to see a short silhouette through the door's wavering glass panes. He opened the door.

"Hey, Professor," said Henry. The boy wiped his feet on the mat and removed his cap. He was filthy with dirt caked all over his trousers, shoes and hands. The boy also had purplish circles under his eyes, but then, it would be dawn in a few hours and he had not slept.

"What happened?" Miss Sanchez asked Henry. "Did you walk all the way home? Alone in the dark?"

"I had enough money to hire a cab."

Miss Sanchez didn't look pleased with the idea of Henry alone at night. Of course, that was the boy's usual state, but Seamus knew that Miss Sanchez disapproved. Now that he thought of it, the idea of Henry alone at night bothered him as well. Strange that it had not concerned him before.

Henry dropped into a chair and rubbed his eyes. "I heard something that McCullen said. It was about a war."

Seamus caught Miss Sanchez's eye. She took a seat across from Henry.

"What did he say?" Miss Sanchez asked.

"He was talking about a krewe. And this younger man was with him. The younger man said something about a war. And France and Ireland might join in. And Wales."

"Wales?" Seamus let out a breath and took a seat. "Let's hope not. What exactly did he say?"

Henry paused as he collected his thoughts. "I'm sorry, Professor. But I didn't listen in very well until they mentioned a war and then those countries. Then they said something about Buchanan. The young man said Buchanan didn't survive, and Breckinridge would take his place."

"Didn't survive what?" Seamus asked.

Henry shook his head. "He didn't say. Just that he didn't survive. And then the younger man said that he had heard that the krewe did someone else. I think the name had an L."

"Lincoln?" asked Miss Sanchez.

"Yeah, that was it. How did you know?"

"Go on, Henry," said Seamus.

"Well, the other man said they did Lincoln also. But McCullen didn't agree or disagree. He just said that the krewe was for making parade floats only."

"This is bad," Miss Sanchez said, glancing at Seamus. "Buchanan was supposed to be president. Then Lincoln."

Henry looked like he was going to correct Miss Sanchez, but Seamus put up a hand and Henry closed his mouth.

"What were Buchanan's policies?" Miss Sanchez asked.

"He opposed slavery in the new states," said Seamus. "Breckinridge believes each state should decide for itself."

Seamus glanced at Mrs. Washington, who was standing across the kitchen. She was busying herself with something, but Seamus knew she was listening. He didn't mind.

"What about the East India Company?" Miss Sanchez asked him.

"The South favored Buchanan because he promised to put limits on the Company's activity in the Caribbean. Well, in American waters anyway. Now, Breckinridge, he's the son of one of the major owners of a Northern airship company. He wanted to raise tariffs on the steamship companies. So the South would pay more, but the North and South would both benefit from the revenue."

"So if Buchanan died, or was killed, and Breckinridge took his place, the North would generally profit?"

"That's about the size of it," said Seamus.

"I wish I knew their first names, to see if they're the same people," she muttered, and Henry gave her an evaluating look. The boy was bright, but Seamus knew there was no way he would figure out what was happening. It was far too strange and unlikely.

Miss Sanchez looked at the corner of the ceiling, deep in thought. Her hair had come down from its pins in places and small tendrils were brushing her shoulders and the back of her neck. She had a pleasant, easy look about her, even if she was still in the hateful gown that McCullen had sent. Even exhausted and weary, she was putting her mind to the problem instead of allowing him to handle it for her.

Seamus pulled off his coat and threw it over the back of his chair. He leaned forward on his elbows and leaned his head in his hands. "This is bad," he muttered.

"What's bad?" asked Henry.

"Pay it no mind, lad," said Seamus, raising his head and forcing himself to sit up. The boy didn't need any more worries on his narrow shoulders. "I'm just worried if Buchanan truly is dead. I hope you heard wrong, or that McCullen was lying. I wouldn't put it past him."

Mrs. Washington was no longer pretending to do any domestic busywork but stood stock still, listening. Seamus decided that enough had been said.

He rose and pushed in his chair. "I think we all could use some sleep. Oh, and Henry." He glanced at the boy's filthy clothing. "Tomorrow, you need to get yourself some new clothes. The ones you have are in need of washing. And you have to look your best on Saturday for the Steamboat Festival."

Henry looked happy, but Seamus thought he saw the boy's eyes moisten. It made him uncomfortable and he turned away. Miss Sanchez gave Seamus a look that said she was not finished speaking with him. Well, she knew where she could find him. After the night he had experienced, he did not think he would get much sleep.

Twenty minutes later, Miss Sanchez was in her nightclothes and sitting in his laboratory. He was getting more used to the woman's strange ways. Her culture allowed women to wear trousers, or even what she described as "shorts," which sounded like little more than underclothes. Both men and women went hatless and the bathing attire they wore to the beach might have just as well been nothing. It reminded him of the tales of the South American and African natives who roamed about, naked and childlike. They were, in a way, innocent. He had said as much, bringing a laugh from Miss Sanchez, who assured him that "innocent" was not a good descriptor of her time.

And now, Miss Sanchez was in a long cotton nightgown with a heavy robe over it. Mrs. Washington must have given it to her, as it was a few sizes too large for her. The slippers on her feet were too bulky as well.

"I know you aren't used to our world," he said. "But here, a woman would not converse with a man in her nightclothes," he said. If somehow he was unable to send her back home, he would have to educate her on proper ladylike behavior.

"Yeah, I figured. But you aren't going to put it in the society column of the paper, so I'm not too worried."

She seemed oblivious to any discomfort that he may experience at her state of undress. He was by no means unfamiliar with the female form, but he found that he liked Miss Sanchez. He supposed, in a way, he respected her. And seeing her like this, well, something was not right about it. He decided to think of her as one of the innocent savages, whether she liked it or not. He found his pipe, took a few pinches of tobacco from a small pouch and packed it. After rummaging through his pockets and a few drawers, he found a box of matches and lit the pipe.

"That'll kill you, you know," said Miss Sanchez.

"What'll kill me?"

"Smoking. It's bad for the lungs."

He looked down at his pipe and then put it between his teeth. He turned to his work table.

Miss Sanchez leaned against the table, either too weary or too uninterested in convincing him to give up the pipe. "The deaths of Lincoln and Buchanan are designed to drive a wedge between the North and the South," she said. "Is that what you are thinking too?"

Savage she may be, but not unintelligent or prevaricating.

"Yes. If, as you say, Lincoln was to keep the union together, these deaths seem as if they would make it more likely for the country to split. Perhaps Lincoln had stated his opinion on this, and it led to his killing."

"What was it that Henry said about Ireland, Wales and France?"

"Well, in a conflict, the British would support the North. Economically, John Company is in competition with the South, so giving them dominance over Southern trade would benefit the British."

"John Company?"

"The East India Company," he explained. Of course, she didn't know the nickname. "France and Ireland will oppose England and will side with the South."

"Sounds like my world. France and Ireland have always had conflict with the English. And what's this about Wales?"

He shook his head. "Wales would ally with England. If Wales comes in, it could be terrible. Their military is one of the strongest in the world."

"Seriously?" She sounded as if she were about to laugh.

"Yes, I would not jest about something like that."

She was silent for a minute and Seamus returned to his work. He pulled together his papers, making an attempt to put all the notes related to the peroxide engine in one place. He was exhausted, but if he organized his materials, he might be able to connect some of the ideas, find a new way of looking at them.

"So, how does one get peroxide for these engines?" Felicia asked, flipping absently through a stack of papers. Seamus took them from her.

"Well, you need electrolysis of an aqueous solution of sulfuric acid or acidic ammonium bisulfate. Then you hydrolize the peroxide sulfate that results."

"Is that all?" Felicia muttered. "Wait. Isn't sulfuric acid dangerous?"

Now, how did she know that? Oh yes, her university education. Her knowledge was so scattershot that these things still surprised him.

"Yes. It's dangerous. Much of what I do is dangerous."

"Like when you murdered someone? Was McCullen telling the truth?"

She was right beside him, and when he straightened up, he found her watching him intently. He hadn't seen her with her hair down since her arrival, and it made her look younger. He was put in mind of a little girl on Christmas Eve, waiting expectantly in her nightgown.

At his hesitation, she looked wary. He understood that she expected him to lie. He wouldn't.

"Yes. I killed someone," he said.

She exhaled, and Seamus realized she had been holding her breath. The poor woman, trapped in a strange world with a man she knew was a murderer. But she was not pulling away from him. She was staying just where she was. How extraordinary. She was not afraid of him.

"And you thought the police knew this?" she asked. "That's why you didn't deny it when McCullen mentioned it?"

"I thought McCullen might have told the police, yes. I thought if you told Mrs. Washington, she would execute a plan that she and I had made. She'd use a letter I have in my safe, withdraw my funds from the bank and hire the best legal counsel I could get."

"I didn't tell her the murder part, only that McCullen had you arrested."

"Thank you." He felt himself relax a bit. McCullen's two servants had overheard their master, but they knew nothing of the details. Servants' gossip without proof was meaningless. As long as McCullen kept silent, he would remain safe.

"Is that how you know McCullen? Did it happen in Ireland?" Felicia asked.

"Yes." He set down the papers and rubbed the bridge of his nose. "I suppose this involves you now, so you ought to know."

"Involves me? How?"

"When I was at the police station, a man named Neil Grey

came in. He knew about my past, and I am now required to assist him in investigating the engine explosions. If I do not, he will expose me. And since finding out how the engines work is the sole path to finding a way to send you back home, it involves you."

"How do you know this Grey man knew your past? Did he have any proof? McCullen might have told him something and he used it against you."

"He knew my name."

"It's not Seamus Connor?"

"Seamus is my Christian name, yes. But I was born with a different surname."

She looked away, and got the thoughtful look she wore sometimes.

"McCullen called you brother. Are you related?" she asked.

Miss Sanchez had not asked him his true name. Either she was not interested, which was next to impossible, or it was something else. She was allowing him his privacy. It placed her in a vulnerable position, knowing he was a murderer, but not knowing his name.

"No. We're not blood," Seamus said. "We're from different parts of Ireland. But we were in prison together."

Miss Sanchez cleared off a chair and sat down, positioning her body so she was facing him, but not directly. She was waiting. He finished with his stack of papers.

"The man I killed was my older sister's husband. He came from the north to help work my father's farm. My brothers and I worked, but we needed an extra hand. He was strong and worked hard. We gave him board and meals. In return, he forced himself on my sister, Branna, and got her with child. I didn't know, nor did my brothers or our father. If we had, the animal would have gone missing and a fresh pile of dug up earth would have appeared a few miles from our farm. I think my sister didn't say anything from shame. I will never know. Whatever happened, they were wed shortly after her pregnancy was discovered.

"Times were bad, as they were. And still are, I presume. In his own home, the man was a drunkard, vicious and cruel. I had gone to their house to bring over some bread our mother had baked. She had enough flour for an extra loaf, and we wanted to make sure Branna had enough to eat while she was with child. Well, I heard yelling, a man's voice and a woman's. Then I heard the unmistakable sound of a flesh hitting flesh, and my sister let out a little cry.

"I didn't bother to knock, but nearly tore the door off its hinges coming in. I was on my brother-in-law before he knew what was happening. My sister screamed for us to stop, but when I saw the blood on her face and her belly swollen with child, something broke free in me. I beat the man until we were both bloodied up and he was on the floor. He wasn't dead. He wasn't even senseless.

"As I stood there panting, tasting my own blood and covered with his and my own, he managed to pull himself to stand. He swore he'd kill me. And he gave a smile that chilled me to the bone. The man, he wasn't human.

"Well, I tried to get Branna to come with me, to return to our father's farm. But she wouldn't. I'll never understand that either."

Remembering his sister, his whole family, made his chest feel tight and heavy. He pulled back the curtain and looked out into the night sky. The reflection of lamplight on the glass prevented him from seeing the sky properly. He yanked open the window, oblivious to the cold.

Miss Sanchez was beside him. "Sometimes, abused women don't want to leave their abusers. It's a common dynamic in an abusive relationship. It's the same with rape victims. They often don't wish to report it because they're ashamed."

He had a stirring of curiosity as to how Miss Sanchez knew these things, but he couldn't bring himself to ask.

"There are so many stars," Felicia whispered. "We don't have that many. I mean, they're there, but we have so much light from the city that we can't see them all."

"Want to go out?"

"In my jammies?" she paused. "Well, why not?" She slipped through the window. It was quick this time, as she did not have large skirts to hinder her. Seamus turned off the light and slipped out onto the upper gallery. In the dark, no one would see them. Miss Sanchez seated herself with her back against the house and her knees drawn up under her chin. She pulled her nightgown and robe down over her legs, covered her feet and wrapped her arms around her legs. Her dark hair hung down her back and over her shoulders. Her face was upturned to the sky. He sat down beside her.

"Are the stars the same?" he asked.

"Yeah, they're the same."

Seamus leaned back and took a deep breath of the chilly night air. It was clear and quiet, and the lights in the houses across the street were out. He liked this time of night, when things were so still. These stars were the same stars that looked down on him when he was a boy. And they were the same from Ireland to New Orleans, from the nineteenth century to the twenty-first. They sat in silence for a few minutes.

"The next night, my mother and two of my sisters left the house," Seamus said. It felt good to speak so quietly in the night. It was like a confessional, here in the dark. But Miss Sanchez was more pleasant company than a priest behind a curtain. "They looked like they were going to a funeral. My brother and I made one of our other sisters tell us what was happening. Branna might be losing the babe. That animal had beaten her again the next night, and she was so thin and frail to begin with. I heard my mother and sisters return long after we were all in bed. Branna was not with them."

"Did she die?"

"No, but she was injured badly. She lost the child, and the blood loss took a toll on her body as well. I knew that animal would kill her, as he had killed my tiny nephew. One of my sisters told me that the child was a boy."

Miss Sanchez put her forehead on her knees.

"I got up in the dark, got my father's hunting rifle and went to my sister's house. I killed him. The police came, naturally. And Branna died of her injuries the next day. But I'll always know that it was me that killed my poor mother."

"She died too?" she whispered.

"No, no. I mean figuratively." He gave a wry smile. "She was yelling and swearing every second the police were at the farm to take me away. She would have beaten them herself if my father hadn't held her back. She's a ferocious woman, my mother. But I know losing me and Branna and her grandson would take a toll. We'd already lost my other sister's daughter. My mother died a little with each one of us. There was so much death, then. Neighbors. Friends."

From the corner of his eye, he saw her raise her arm and wipe at her eyes.

"It's all right, lass. Branna and the baby are with God. And that monster is burning in hell. I've gone to confession. My soul is cleansed."

The words didn't seem to give her much comfort, but then, they'd been little comfort to him either.

"I went to prison after a brief trial. I was guilty, of course. They sent me to Mountjoy Prison. They called it, 'The Joy,' and if there was ever something more misnamed ..." He shook his head. "Well, while inside, I let it be known that I could fix mechanical things. The more useful you were, the better. After a while, I was given a choice. Transport to Tasmania, or life in prison. I decided to take my chances in Van Dieman's Land.

"They transferred me to Spike Island and there I met

Oren McCullen. He worked on machinery with me. He was brilliant, cunning and he had a theoretical understanding of possibilities. By that, I mean, he always knew you could send signals through the aether, like the radio. And he had other ideas, which we worked on together. He arranged it so we were cellmates, and we spent many nights discussing ideas, talking back and forth between our bunks.

"McCullen had friends on the outside. The man had a hatred for the English that I've rarely seen, even from Irishmen who fought them. That's how he ended up in prison, for killing two Englishmen. Well, he had friends who also hated the English. And they had a plan. While being transported from Spike Island to Van Dieman's Land, they would send a boat and break him out. He told only one other person about the plan, his closest friend.

"He said we could take new names, settle in America. So many of our countrymen were flooding in after the famine that we'd hardly be noticed. Some of McCullen's fellows broke us out just off the Spanish coast. We came to New Orleans, and the authorities had no way of knowing where on earth we had gone. After working odd jobs and sharing a stinking little room in a filthy boarding house, we decided to use our heads. Between the two of us, we could figure out almost anything mechanical. And McCullen had a way to charm people. Both of us were decent at lying, and we lied our way into professorships at Tulane. I teach there still."

"But you must be a good professor or they would have fired you by now."

"By 'fired,' I assume you mean dismissed me?"

At her nod, he went on. "I teach well. My students learn. I write books and papers and make a living."

"So it's not really fraud, if you provide the service for which you're paid."

"That's one way to look at it. But I did obtain the position under false pretenses."

Miss Sanchez didn't seem bothered by that. Well, after finding out he was a killer and an escaped prisoner, a little harmless lie, as she would say, was no big deal.

CHAPTER 19

THE NEXT MORNING, HAZEL TOOK the Professor's money and bought three pairs of trousers in a size that would fit her, as well as four shirts, a pair of shoes and a new cap. Once home, she took her old, dirty clothes to Mrs. Washington, who added them to the laundry.

The Professor and Miss Sanchez were talking in the kitchen. Once Hazel was dressed in clean clothing, she hurried down to the kitchen to show the Professor what his money had bought. Another man was with them. They were seated around the kitchen table and the other man was removing his long black coat. He must not have been there for long.

But why was the Professor entertaining a guest in the kitchen rather than in the front parlor, the library or any of the other rooms suitable for such a purpose?

The Professor introduced them. "Mr. Grey, this is Henry Dubois. Henry, Mr. Neil Grey."

Mr. Grey studied her intently, and even after the Professor continued speaking, the man's eyes did not leave Hazel's face. It was as if he were memorizing her features. He looked like he was pleased to see her, and though she detected no hostility from him, it made her uneasy.

"Henry, come see this." The Professor was grim and handed her the newspaper. The headline proclaimed that president elect Buchanan was dead. He had died from eating contaminated food at a banquet.

"It says the food was bad, but does this mean he was poisoned?" Hazel asked.

Mr. Grey gave her an approving look. "Very astute. That is what many people think happened, including me."

"But why do it when so many others would be sickened?" asked Felicia. "Never mind. I get it. Collateral damage."

Hazel had never heard the term before, but she thought she understood the meaning. The Professor continued talking to Mr. Grey and Hazel could tell that Mr. Grey looked away from her with effort. She had been out when Mrs. Washington had served lunch and she went to the stove and took some chicken and vegetable stew and a leftover roll. She brought the bowl and a spoon to the kitchen table and took a seat at the end furthest from the adults.

"The names of the men in the krewe are unknown," said Mr. Grey after giving Hazel a brief glance. He didn't seem to mind her sitting there. "It's not a secret society, per se. More of an informal grouping of men, all wealthy."

"How do you know that if you don't know who they are?" asked the Professor.

"A name will leak now and then. A hired person will say something. But then, naturally, it is hushed up and there is never any evidence that any of the men are members of the krewe. Even proving that the krewe exists is difficult. If McCullen used the word publicly, it was intentional."

"What are their political leanings?" asked Miss Sanchez. "If they're responsible for these two assassinations, then it sounds like they want the South and North to break apart, to become two countries."

Hazel thought it was odd for a woman to be conversing with men in this way, wondering about politics and assassinations. But neither the Professor nor Mr. Grey seemed to find it strange. Something about that was wrong. The Professor was odd, and after the past few days, he was used to Miss Sanchez's blunt speech and ways. But Mr. Grey did not know Miss Sanchez.

Mr. Grey leaned back in his chair. "That's just it. No one

knows their politics. We hear about this assassination and Lincoln, and it sounds like some shady cabal, bending the arc of power to suit the desires of unseen men. But no link has ever been found. No one was convicted of Lincoln's poisoning, and from the way this article is phrased, a few others died with Buchannan. There was a banquet, and some of the food was bad. It looks like bad luck."

"Food poisoning," murmured Miss Sanchez. "I'd like to know the symptoms he exhibited."

"Other reports on the krewe make them sound like they are just rich men, playing cards and drinking brandy," Mr. Grey went on. "A few of them may go hunting together, or they may call on each other. They spend time at their clubs. They bring in young women for entertainment."

Hazel stopped chewing mid-bite and looked up. The Professor stared at Mr. Grey in horror. How could he mention such a thing with a woman and a child in the room? But Miss Sanchez just nodded, as if unsurprised.

"Why are they putting on a Mardi Gras parade then?" asked the Professor. "What purpose could it serve?"

"I think they're doing it to gain the goodwill of the people. McCullen specifically mentioned the krewe, so he wants the name being spoken of about town. Tell me, Miss Sanchez, how did the guests react when McCullen mentioned the krewe?"

Miss Sanchez shrugged. "They just listened. There weren't any shocked reactions or questions. Oh wait. I see. Do you think they already knew about the krewe?"

"Some of them. And many would have heard about it secondhand," said Mr. Grey.

"McCullen wouldn't do this without a good reason," said the Professor. "He wants word around town to be that the krewe puts on parades. The appearance of being a group of silly rich men, playing at secret society would be a good way to put one over on the public. Especially now that more and more people know about the krewe. They want to be known as men who spend too freely, not as men of influence, engaging in secretive deeds. If it weren't for what Henry overheard, we would never suspect that the krewe and these deaths were linked at all."

Mr. Grey glanced at Hazel. "Is there anything you would like to add?"

Hazel shook her head, her mouth full. She hadn't said a word or given any look to draw any attention to herself. Mr. Grey glanced over her clothes, perhaps noting how new and clean they looked.

"Mr. Connor tells me that you will be playing at the Steamboat Festival tomorrow," Mr. Grey said.

She swallowed. "That's right."

A thought occurred to her. Was this man a friend of her aunt and uncle? Is that why he had been studying her face? Would he remember seeing her at one of their dinner parties, playing violin for the guests? She had done it often enough, and more than one person had commented on her ability. She may have been in dresses and braids then, but few people played as well as she did. This was a fact, not arrogance.

She could not afford to be scrutinized at close range. She needed to leave. Hazel put her dishes on the counter under the window and slipped out of the kitchen without saying a proper good-bye. She felt eyes on her back as she left.

The next day, Hazel wiped her violin case clean and rosined her bow. She tuned her violin, twisting the pegs until the sound was right. She would need to do it again at the Steamboat Festival, as the change in temperature and humidity would affect the instrument. But she did it now anyway. It calmed her nerves.

She played a few notes, then let herself fall into playing an entire piece, a short one, as she, Miss Sanchez and the Professor would be leaving soon. Then, she put the violin away and rushed downstairs. Miss Sanchez and the Professor were waiting below.

"Under no circumstances are you to go near that riverboat, do you understand me?" said the Professor.

"Do you really think it might explode?" Hazel asked. The idea sounded far-fetched, but if that man from the police and the Professor both said it was dangerous, she had the good sense to listen.

"Mr. Grey has informed us that odds are good. I'm required to be there, as I have to assist him. Miss Sanchez has offered to help, and as I cannot forbid her," he sounded just the slightest bit bitter at the thought, "she will be there as well. But you, you need to stay safe."

"I'll only be playing for part of the afternoon. Is there anything I can do for the rest of the time?"

Miss Sanchez said, "Just listen to what people say. You have a knack for being invisible, so keep your ears open about the peroxide engine, assassinations or the krewe."

Hazel pulled her cap onto her head and straightened her jacket. She had planned on doing just that.

CHAPTER 20

AFTER PINNING HER HAIR IN a knot at the back of her neck, Felicia tied the ribbons of her straw bonnet under her chin. Thankfully, the bonnet did not obstruct her peripheral vision. The front of the bonnet ended just at her ears, leaving her face and the front of her hair exposed.

Felicia had selected a light yellow cotton dress with a green sash, hoping she was appropriately dressed for the Steamboat Festival. From Henry's description, it would be a day of light-hearted fun. Felicia dearly hoped that would be the case. What were the odds of the McCullen engine exploding at the festival? He didn't seem to be a man who was overly concerned with preventing injury to others. But he would know business. He would not want the public spectacle, including the injuries. It would ruin his company.

Felicia wondered if he knew anything about the shimmering doorway that had taken her from her world to this one. If she spoke to him, perhaps he would provide the information to get her home. But no. Seamus had tried, and had been denied.

McCullen had shown an interest in her. How much of that had been attraction? Not much, she guessed. He only wanted to torment Seamus. And if denying her a way home twisted the knife, then McCullen would do it. He would not give up secrets for her unless it would hurt Seamus.

She thought of her mother and father, her sisters and

brother, her friends, and of her housemate, Doug. Were they worried about her? How long had she been gone? Would the Professor be able to arrange it so she stepped back to the moment, or at least the day, she had left? Somehow, that seemed so unlikely now. A freak accident could not be predictably reproduced.

She needed to focus on the things she could control. Today, her task was to keep an eye on the riverboat that held the McCullen engine. At the first sign of trouble, she would alert one of them. What they would do about it was anyone's guess.

Felicia shrugged on her fitted brown coat, fastened the tortoiseshell buttons and grabbed her small leather handbag. The bag and coat were two other finds from Mrs. Washington. The handbag was probably out of style and the coat was old, but both were still serviceable. She followed Henry and Seamus to the street where Seamus hailed a horse-drawn cab.

The cab took them past Jackson Square and the French Quarter. They rode parallel to the river until they reached an area of grass and hard-packed earth that teemed with activity. The streets around the Festival were crowded with people of all sorts. Most were walking, but Felicia spied two of the steam-driven carriages depositing merrymakers at the spot by the river where they were the most likely to be observed and admired. A few heads turned to watch couples descend from the carriages. The women opened parasols and tipped them back over their shoulders and the men donned hats. The group proceeded to take a long walk around the perimeter of the fairgrounds.

A stage stood at the end of the grounds farthest from the river. A few pavilions sat behind it, presumably dressing rooms or areas for performers to store their belongings. Two sets of booths ran in curving lines toward the river. The effect was that of a rough circle, with the stage at one end and the river at the other. Directly in front of the stage, someone had constructed a wooden dance floor. A few chairs and small tables sat nearby for revelers to rest. In the cleared area at the center of the booths, people reclined on picnic blankets.

Richer and poorer, black and white, the old and the young moved among the booths, playing carnival games, eating sweet rolls, meat pies or fried catfish or sipping hot coffee or iced tea.

Seamus scanned the crowd. He wore an old coat and a scuffed brown bowler hat. He looked like a hundred other men there, completely unremarkable but for his height and his inability to quite hold his body still.

"I need to find Mr. Augustus," said Henry. "That's the man with the music shop." The boy hurried off, clutching his battered violin case to his chest.

A riverboat pulled up to the shore, and within fifteen minutes, two more joined it. All of them were gleaming and white, like floating gingerbread ships with fresh paint like icing covering the wooden trim with its elaborate cut-outs. The largest steamboat had a bright red paddlewheel and two enormous smokestacks with decorative brass caps, each spiked like a royal crown.

"That's the one," said the Professor, pointing. "The Delphia Queen."

Seamus started for it, Felicia following behind. "No," he said, turning on her. "Stay back. The thing is dangerous."

"And you'll do what, stroll and flirt?"

He looked confused, then unhappy. "Understand, I need to get down to the engine room, and it's no place for you. Besides, if McCullen mentioned the two of us to the ship crew, then both of us together are going to tip them off. He knows I want an engine. And the biggest one is sitting right where I can get to it. Best if I go alone."

Felicia hated it, but she had to admit that he was right. Seamus could fake an American accent, tip his bowler down over his eyes and pass for a worker. He could blend in and lie his way inside, while she would stick out like a sore thumb.

"I'm going to keep an eye on Henry," she said. "Oh, and Professor." He turned back. "Good luck."

He gave a playful wink and headed off. Felicia glanced at the stage where a five-piece brass band played. Without any kind of modern sound system, the music was a pleasant background sound instead of blasting to every corner of the festival. She found that she liked it. Henry probably waited backstage, and as she could not go there, she took her time and examined some of the booths.

The games cost a penny each, and she saw that carnival games had not changed all that much in over a century. A burly man threw a stitched leather ball at a stack of milk bottles and a young girl attempted to aim a wooden ring onto a board covered in widely spaced painted wooden pegs. The peg at the center was red, the surrounding pegs orange and the ones around the perimeter yellow. The girl's ring caught on a yellow peg and she sighed in disappointment. A young couple stood side by side at another booth, both of them holding miniature bows and aiming them at paper targets. At a word, they both shot, and the woman giggled as her arrow went wide. The man's arrow hit the target, and he turned to her with false humility, telling her that she had done well. She smiled demurely and he moved closer. No, not much had changed at all.

Felicia bought a cup of hot coffee with the money that Seamus had given her and moved toward the tables set around the dance floor. If she couldn't help Seamus on the Delphia Queen, she would keep an eye on Henry.

A large booth next to the stage was hosted by The Southern Cargo and Trade Company. Pencil drawings of ships fluttered on a cork board while white lettering on a slate promoted Southern shipping as superior to Northern airships in both cost and speed. Of course, airships could go inland, which the slate board failed to mention. On the far side of the stage was a second booth, this one from the Mississippi Cotton Collective. She wasn't interested in seeing their booth and learning about the virtues of slave-picked cotton. Giant banners tacked to the back wall of the stage named The Southern Cargo and Trade Company and the Mississippi Cotton Collective as sponsors of the day's festivities.

Felicia approached the stage, where a new band had taken the place of the previous group. They played a lively tune and she took a seat at one of the tables, surrounded by tired dancers who laughed and chatted, some sipping cool drinks. Others danced, sweaty, exuberant and oblivious to any danger.

She listened to the music and angled her chair so she could glance at the Delphia Queen now and then. She heard no commotion nor saw anyone being hauled off the ship, so Seamus must be all right.

Ten minutes later, he dropped into the seat beside her. "The engine isn't too bad. However, it is exhibiting irregular catalyst uptake, and there's too much smoke."

"Couldn't that be because it's a new ship? A new engine?"

"Could be," he said. "But I don't think that can completely account for it."

The band completed their set and the dancers left the floor. Felicia's coffee had cooled and was sitting in front of her. Seamus took a sip absently, an oddly familiar thing to do. Felicia didn't say anything. A moment later, he realized his error and mumbled an apology. Stage hands brought out chairs and music stands.

"Where is Mr. Grey?" asked Felicia. She had not seen him anywhere. Though he would blend into the crowd, she knew what he looked like and would have spotted him.

"He's around," said Seamus vaguely. "Look," he said. Henry and two other boys walked out on stage and bowed to the crowd.

CHAPTER 21

H AZEL WAS A FEW MINUTES into her last piece when she saw the man. He was standing at the back of the tables, watching her with an unwavering gaze. Her eyes met his, and he gave a little nod. He did not smile, nor did his expression change, but it was enough. How long had her uncle been there, watching her, listening? He had been there without her knowing. The thought terrified her.

The Professor and Miss Sanchez sat off to one side at a small table. Miss Sanchez was watching the performance, but the Professor kept glancing at the Delphia Queen. Hazel so wanted to make both of them proud, to show them that she was good for something other than sneaking about like a common street rat. After the performance, she imagined that Miss Sanchez would have a little smile and the Professor would muss her hair and tell her she had done well.

But Hazel couldn't run to the Professor and Miss Sanchez after the performance. She knew that. She was safe while she was on stage, but if her uncle knew anything about her new life, anything at all, he could find her. So she could not give any indication that she knew the Professor. Her only hope was to run. To vanish behind the stage, maybe find her way into one of the pavilions and slip out under a back flap. Yes, she would run. Her heart pounded and her bow hand trembled. A long note came out with a slight warble.

She focused on the sheet music. Mr. Augustus was off to one side, listening. He would have heard the mistake. This was her big chance, her only chance, and it was going to be ruined because of her uncle. Her anger surged. It wasn't fair.

It had not been fair when her parents had died of the influenza outbreak that swept through the area north of New Orleans. First her mother had sickened, then her father. She had caught the fever also, but after two weeks in bed, she had recovered and found herself alone in the world. Alone but for her little black terrier, Mandy. Her father's brother had a wife, a house and no children, so a neighbor had seen her packed off to the city. Her parents had lived outside of New Orleans and it was a short cart ride into town. Hazel found her uncle's house to be pleasant, a medium-sized house with a large tree to climb and cool places to sit and think. If only he and his wife had been so pleasing.

Aunt Beth was a sad-faced woman of few words. And those she had were often punctuated by sharp pinches, given to the back of Hazel's upper arm whenever she forgot her manners. If she cried out or pulled away, another harder pinch would follow, this one twisting the flesh until Hazel held still to receive her punishment in silence. By the end of the first week, her right arm, the one that was nearest her aunt at the dinner table, was covered in purplish bruises.

Mandy, her little black terrier, trotted behind Hazel everywhere, either in the house or in the yard. She stayed in the yard when Hazel was at school and Hazel brought her inside in the afternoons, let her outside at supper, and brought her in at night. She held Mandy at night, crying into her fur until she could only lay there, staring out the bedroom window at the black sky. Mandy would lick her face and snuggle her head up under Hazel's chin. They slept that way most nights.

One night, Hazel was in bed, her stomach empty because she had been sent to bed with no supper. She had forgotten to put her school shoes away and had left them downstairs. Her aunt's motto was "start as you mean to go on," and she was determined to train Hazel to be a proper and responsible young lady. The offense had to be punished. It was the only way someone like Hazel would learn, and so Hazel had been sent to bed early. She had read a book for a while, then got bored and played her violin as softly as she could so she would not disturb her aunt and uncle and draw further punishment. She picked up her book again, and once it was too dark to read, she cuddled Mandy, whispering to her in the dark until she fell asleep.

A growl from Mandy woke her. Her bedroom door was open and her uncle stood in the doorway. Her eyes were accustomed to the dark, and she saw that he was in his nightclothes. At first she wondered what was wrong, but he didn't look upset. He sat on the edge of the bed and Mandy growled again. Her uncle grabbed the dog by the scruff of her neck and tossed her out the door, closing it noiselessly. Hazel had been too shocked to protest. She remembered him pulling back the blanket and the way his hand had felt as he moved it up her leg.

He had come to her room some nights, doing things she wished she could forget and whispering terrible things in the dark that Hazel only half understood. But she understood enough after that first night. She was not like other people, not like other girls. She was worse, so much worse, something vile and repugnant. Her parents had loved her, but it had only been because they had to. That's the way mothers and fathers were. Mandy was too stupid to know any better, so the dog loved her too. But the truth was that Hazel was a thing apart, a thing with the appearance of a girl, but without the light heart or laughter that her friends at school seemed to possess. Sometimes, she wondered if she had a soul.

After Uncle Andrew left her room, Mandy would always run back in and lick Hazel's face until she could not tell if the wetness on her cheeks was from her tears or the dog's saliva. Then she would breathe in the scent of Mandy's fur and try to sleep and forget. Eventually, the sleep would come.

One night, Mandy whimpered and leapt from the bed as the door opened. She stood in front of the bed and then launched herself at Uncle Andrew, yanking on the cuff of his pajamas. He kicked her, and she skidded across the floor, only to scamper forward and clamp her jaws down on his ankle. Uncle Andrew's hand shot down, grabbing Mandy by the neck, but the agile little dog twisted, sinking her teeth into his hand. He flung her and she hit the wall with a sharp bang. She lay unmoving on the floor.

Hazel ran to her. Mandy shook her head and staggered to her feet, only to fall again. The dog was dazed, but would live. Hazel screamed and flew at her uncle, beating at his stomach and chest. She was screaming words she had never used before. She called him every vile word she could think of. Her uncle caught her wrists in his hands, and twisted to hold both her wrists in one hand. He hit her so hard that her ears rang and she couldn't see straight.

He told her that if she made a sound, he would kill Mandy right then and there. She knew he was not bluffing. His eyes glittered in the dark, and she felt she was falling into those eyes, into the black pit that was the hole where her soul should be.

Uncle Andrew shoved Hazel back on the bed and Mandy gained her feet and leapt up beside her. Mandy sunk her teeth into his wrist, shaking her little head from side to side.

He seemed to move slowly as he grasped the little dog. He twisted the dog's neck, putting his strength into it. Hazel knew from a young age that wringing chicken necks was not as easy as it looked. It took strength. She screamed and tried to pull at his arms. The dull sound of Mandy's neck snapping echoed through the room. Her small body went limp.

Uncle Andrew held up Hazel's little friend. "This is what happens to noisy, bad animals. Do you understand, girl?"

She reached for Mandy, but he jerked the dog away and tossed her to the floor. Her body slid and came to rest under the window. Hazel kept her eyes on the dog as she lay there. The moonlight glinted on Mandy's dead black eyes.

Later, her uncle left and she was alone with her dog. As she knelt and cradled Mandy, she looked up to the sky, where one of the sisters at the convent school always pointed when she talked about heaven. The moon was a few days past full. It was enough light to see outside, if one were to go outside.

She knew Uncle Andrew would come looking for her, so she couldn't pose as an orphan to the sisters who ran the city orphanage. But there was another way. She stole her aunt's sewing scissors and cut off her braid. She carried the braid, her violin and Mandy out the back garden gate. She ran, throwing the braid into a neighbor's rubbish can. She had to decide which way to go. She had to think. She was a child, and a bad one at that, but she knew that there were dangerous people on the streets. People who would harm her. She had to be cautious. Mandy's body had no warmth left, but it did not smell and was not stiff. She knew it would be with time.

Hazel ran until she reached Esplanade Avenue and then followed it until she reached St. Louis Cemetery. If there were criminals lurking, they did not appear that night. The New Orleans water table was too high to bury bodies deep underground, lest a flood send the dead rising again. The cemetery was filled with white crypts, most of them with family names carved over the small doors. They looked like little homes, miniature little mansions housing the bones of generations. She had always liked the look of them. She knew what was inside and that proper little girls didn't like such things, but she couldn't help herself.

One of the tombs had three shallow steps leading to the small door, and Hazel laid Mandy on the topmost step. The name on the tomb had been French, like so many family names in New Orleans, but she could not remember it afterward. Her own ancestors, the Dubois family, had come from France long ago. The tomb seemed like a good place for Mandy. She kissed her dog between her ears, stroked her fur and after a while, turned away.

Hazel now held her violin in the sunlight of the Steamboat Festival, but her hands had steadied. The thought of Mandy did not bring tears to her eyes. She would not cry. Or tremble.

She poured that night and all the other nights before and since into her instrument. It sang for her. It sang her fear, her hurt, her loss of Mandy and of something else she could not name. It sang her last moments of freedom, here in the sunlight, facing the muddy river. The piece was familiar to her, the round-bellied black notes on the page were old friends.

And when she finished playing, her eyes were dry and she felt a new ferocity inside. Anger was a sin, said the sisters at the convent school. But it would serve her today.

She followed her two fellow players off the stage. She watched from the corner of her eye as her uncle moved around to the side and headed for the back of the stage. He would be behind the stage a few moments after she stepped down. She pulled open her jacket and stuffed her violin and bow inside. Before her foot touched the bottom step, she pulled the bottom of the jacket through her belt, making a tight little pouch for the instrument.

"What is that you are doing?" said Mr. Augustus, looking at the bulge. The neck of the violin stuck up near Hazel's ear and the bow stuck up even farther. She kept her eyes straight ahead, and as soon as she saw a clear path, she ran.

She knew her uncle had seen her. She was counting on it. She had a plan.

Thick clouds of black smoke poured from the twin smokestacks of the Delphia Queen, though the ship was docked and the engines should be barely running. The steamboat would be pulling away from the dock at sunset to start her slow cruise downriver. The smaller ships would go first, all of them lit with tiny gaslights. The grandest ship of all, the Delphia Queen, would bring up the rear, a band playing on deck and crowds waving from the riverbanks.

But Hazel thought it a good likelihood that the Delphia Queen would never make her voyage. As she drew closer, she thought that the engine was louder than it ought to have been. Halfway to the ship, she ducked between two game booths. She crept out to look for her uncle. He wasn't there.

She kept low, scanning the crowd. She flinched at a loud crack, a gunshot. In a cleared area near the picnickers, a group of children and few young men were hopping madly, holding burlap sacks up to their waists. People on the sidelines yelled and whistled. A man to one side lowered the starting gun.

Then she spotted her uncle. He was too close, only a few booths away, but he had not seen her. He was looking away from her, toward the stage and then he turned in profile toward the sack race. Hazel bolted.

As she got closer to the steamboat, she noticed that men around it were running from place to place instead of walking calmly. Some were shouting. Something was wrong with the ship, just as the Professor had said. She wanted to run in the other direction, away from any danger, but she had to be brave. She might be small and afraid. She might even be running away. But she had to be brave. Like Mandy, who bit and fought until the end. Mandy had died for her, and Hazel would not allow her friend's sacrifice to be in vain.

Hazel saw a boy lifting a sack of oranges. He turned and headed for the ship. Hazel hefted a potato sack and nearly bent over backwards, trying to balance the weight. She staggered for the ship, headed for one of two gangplanks. The closest gangplank was near the bow of the ship. A second one was down a thin pier that jutted out into the river and ran along the port side of the ship. That gangplank led to the stern of the ship. No one stopped her as she mounted the gangplank and set the sack down against a railing. She couldn't see the boy who had gone before her, and had no idea where he might be so she could not follow.

But she saw Uncle Andrew. He was striding toward the ship, his eyes locked on hers. She looked away and took a step backward, bumping into a man who told her to get to work. She spun and fled around the bow of the ship and tore down the starboard deck, dodging and ducking to avoid the men who were running and yelling around her. For now, the ship was freshly painted and immaculately clean. Once years of crowds had walked over the polished boards and leaned on the railings, the ship would look like the others that moved up and down the river, weary and worn.

"She's burning too hot!" shouted a man close by, startling Hazel. She leapt away and kept going.

"Captain knows!" yelled another.

From her uncle's vantage point on the port side of the ship, she would be invisible until he was on board and circled around the bow, as she had. That was good. She ran hard and almost lost her footing as she turned the hard corner at the stern of the ship. She pulled herself to a stop. The red paddlewheel was still, and this part of the ship was quiet. Hazel crept until she could see both gangplanks and the whole port side of the ship. She adjusted her violin against her body. The feel of it was comforting.

Her uncle stood at the bottom of the far gangplank, pointing at the ship and talking to a man who blocked his way. She couldn't hear her uncle, but she knew he was trying to frighten and intimidate the crew member. The man was slender and young, but Hazel liked him when she saw him point a finger at her uncle and say something that made his eyes bulge in fury.

Uncle Andrew forced himself past the man, ramming the man's shoulder with his own. The crew member made for him, but one of his fellows held him back and said something. Both of them looked up at the ship, evaluating. The engine roared. It seemed to have a low sound that Hazel felt in her feet and stomach and a higher sound that was growing louder. The deep thrumming created waves of vibration that shook the ship. Her uncle vanished around the bow and Hazel made her move.

She pounded down the rear gangplank and ran up the pier, her heart racing. Once she reached the festival area, she tried to lose herself in the crowd. It was difficult, as people moved so slowly and she had to press against people or push her way through. It was impossible to both move quickly and be inconspicuous. Hazel decided for speed. She sprinted for the line of booths and ran behind them, toward the stage. She couldn't take time to look for the Professor or Miss Sanchez. They might worry about her, but she would have to meet them at home.

Behind the booth for Mississippi Cotton Collective was an opening. A group of sweaty boys with hoops and sticks sat on the ground, resting from their game. She would run past them, past the stage, then through the scattered pavilions and be free.

"Hazel!" shouted a man's voice. Before she could think, she had turned. Mr. Grey gestured frantically for her to come toward him. How had he known her name? She ducked past a row of elderly ladies, past the resting boys and sprinted for the stage.

There was an explosion, a flash, and Hazel felt herself flying for an instant before she crashed to the ground, her shoulder and hip taking the brunt of the impact. For an instant, it was strangely silent, and then the world went black.

CHAPTER 22

F ELICIA BRUSHED A STRAY HAIR away with the back of her wrist and looked over the man on the hospital bed. He was one of the people injured when the stage at the Steamboat Festival had exploded. She had heard someone shout that the Delphia Queen's engine had been overheating, and minutes later, an explosion had destroyed the stage. She had not stayed at the festival to see what happened to the steamboat. Instead she helped with the injured and then left for the hospital with the third group of patients, knowing where she would be of the greatest use. She told the paramedics that she was a nurse and jumped into the ambulance before anyone could object. And once she had worked side by side with the Sisters of Mercy here at St. Cecilia's Hospital, no one thought to question her credentials.

The jowly red-faced man in front of her slept, peaceful at last. His arm was in a splint and his cheek, which had a bad laceration, had been stitched. There had been no anesthesia.

Hearing the moaning of the injured and the screams of those in surgery made Felicia feel as if she had aged a decade in the hour she had been at the hospital. The surgeons had naturally ordered her from the room when they performed what passed for surgical procedures in this time. She had not objected. She would never forget those screams, not in a hundred years. They had been muffled by a heavy door, but it made no difference. She would have to ask Seamus if ether had been discovered yet and how to get hold of some. Something had to be done. The current methods were horrific.

Upon her arrival, she had tied a nurse's apron on over her dress. But even with the apron, her dress would be ruined. Blood, mud and other fluids spattered her apron and some had soaked through. It felt wrong to be in unsterile clothing, but she had no alternative. It wasn't as if she could obtain fresh scrubs or latex gloves. She had made sure to wash her hands with harsh lye soap after each patient, and the skin on her hands was tight and dry. The sisters may have looked askance at her for insisting on repeated washings, but she refused to compromise what little protection from infection she could offer her patients.

She spent the next half an hour cleaning and bandaging lacerated hands and faces, removing splinters of wood from flesh and setting broken bones. Thankfully, many of the patients were unconscious for the procedures. As there were no disinfectants, Felicia relied on the foul-smelling ointments that the nurses provided. She balked momentarily at the idea of slathering the mysterious grayish substance on wounds, but again, it wasn't as if she had a choice. These doctors and nurses, her colleagues, she reminded herself, were intelligent and their medicines were as good as she could hope for.

Well, in time, perhaps she could learn to grow and use penicillin, develop anesthetics or work on gaining acceptance for germ theory. But those thoughts were for another day.

She worked in the ward being used for men and boys. Female patients were through a door off the main hallway. A nurse held the men's ward door and two more patients were carried in on what passed for stretchers, wooden planks with cut-out handholds. Four men carried an older man while a boy was carried by two, one at the head and the other at the foot. She caught a glimpse of the boy's face. It was Henry.

He was unconscious and blood covered half his face. Felicia felt her pulse quicken and reminded herself that head wounds tend to bleed copiously, even if they are not severe. She had to remain calm and remove emotion from her evaluation and treatment.

The men moved the stretcher beside an empty bed and the nurses moved Henry off as gently as they could. Felicia had seen the stained wood of the stretchers before as patients had been removed, but Henry's was especially filthy. The men took their stretcher away, and two of the other nurses went to tend the older man, leaving Felicia with one nurse and Henry.

Felicia leaned over the boy, doing a quick examination before the doctor arrived. Blood flowed from his forehead, but slowly. His pulse was steady and strong. His breathing was regular. She didn't have a flashlight, but as she lifted his eyelid, she was fairly sure his pupil contracted properly. His head wound was not too bad and might not even need stitches if they bandaged it well. Felicia hoped to God the poor child would not have to receive stitches without anesthesia. The boy's thigh was still bleeding and the cloth of his trousers stuck to his leg.

"We need to remove his clothing," said Sister Perpetua. The sister had worked on a few patients with Felicia and she was both calm and competent. Felicia was developing a respect for her. Sister Perpetua was willing to listen to Felicia's suggestions and give them thoughtful evaluation. She made decisions quickly and without fuss. And she had not given Felicia any grief about helping out once she saw that she was able and willing. Henry's hat was long gone and Felicia worked at the buttons of his jacket and shirt.

One of the paramedics entered with a violin. "He had this in his shirt," he said. "We took it out, of course."

"Please put it on the table over there," said Felicia, jerking her chin at an empty table. Henry would want his instrument later. The case had been backstage, most likely, but Felicia had watched Henry sprint from the stage, leaving the case behind. The bow seemed to be missing also.

She unfastened Henry's suspenders, or as these people called them, bracers. She managed to get his jacket and shirt off. No injuries to his torso. Good. No broken bones. Also good.

"Now that's a thing you don't see every day," said Sister Perpetua. She had removed Henry's shoes and trousers. A folded sheet covered the boy to his knees, leaving the wound on his thigh exposed. His thin cotton underwear clung close to his body. "This is a girl."

Felicia took a second look. She didn't need to remove the underwear to see that Henry was missing the necessary anatomy to be in the men's ward.

"We should move her next door," said Sister Perpetua. "Her injuries can wait that long."

Felicia was about to protest, wanting Henry to be treated as quickly as possible. But Sister Perpetua was correct. The doctor would be busy for a while with more seriously injured patients. And Felicia could treat Henry herself if left alone for a bit. The sister pulled the sheet up to the girl's neck and ordered her moved to the women's ward.

Fifteen minutes later, Henry, or whatever the child's name was, gave a little sigh and her eyelids fluttered.

"Don't wake just yet," whispered Felicia. "This is going to hurt."

She moved quickly, cleaning and binding the head wound and removing the small amount of wood that had lodged in the skin of Henry's thigh. The thigh wound was not deep and Felicia didn't have to dig much to get the wood splinters out. Henry's bed sat next to the window, and Felicia moved aside to get as much light on the wound as possible. Once it was cleaned as best she could, she bandaged it. She would have to remove the bandage for the doctor to examine the injury, but for now, it would do.

The girl stirred and mumbled something. Then she breathed a heavy sigh and turned her face toward the light. She looked very young and small.

"Who are you, little one? And why were you running?" Felicia whispered.

No other patients arrived, and though she could do no more today, Felicia did not wish to leave. The sisters tidied up and some left for the evening. Felicia located Sister Clare, a tall, sturdy woman who worked in the men's ward.

"Is there anything else I can do to help?" she asked.

Sister Clare looked her over, taking in her splattered apron and dress. Felicia imagined that her hair and face looked just as bad. "We can always use someone to roll bandages," the sister said. She took Felicia to the supply room and showed her the bags of loose cotton cloth.

"Have you heard anything else about the explosion?" Felicia asked.

"Much of what I've heard is conflicting," said the sister, pulling a bag of cotton strips from the shelf and handing it to Felicia. "But everyone is in agreement that someone set explosives somewhere near the stage. But no one understands why anyone would want to harm the players. Some of them were children."

Felicia had an idea of who would do it. The stage had been sponsored by the Mississippi Cotton Collective and The Southern Cargo and Trade Company. The stage itself and the Delphia Queen were the two most potent symbols of Southern economic power and ingenuity at the Steamboat Festival.

"Did the Delphia Queen catch fire? I heard yelling that the engines were overheating," Felicia said.

"One of the other sisters heard that the crew was able

to cool the ship in time. They cancelled the river cruise for all the ships after the explosion, naturally."

"Naturally," Felicia said. She glanced over the shelves until she found the rows of rolled bandages. She grabbed a roll. Sister Clare gave her an inquiring look. "As an example," Felicia said. "So I can make sure I roll them perfectly." She couldn't very well tell the sister that she had never rolled a cloth bandage in her life.

Felicia removed her filthy apron and tossed it into a soiled laundry bin. She took the bag of bandages to Henry's bedside and pulled a chair into the patch of sunlight. After examining the rolled bandage, she was fairly sure she could do a decent job if she concentrated. She began to roll.

She wondered if the commotion about the overheating engine on the Delphia Queen had somehow been planned to drive people toward the stage. Around twenty people had been injured, and it was fortunate that none had died. Would the krewe or the politicians use this as an example of Northern aggression? Could the North convincingly be blamed? With the death of Buchannan on top of the attack at the Steamboat Festival, the South would feel under attack.

Henry regained consciousness a few times, drank a little water and then fell back asleep. At four o'clock in the afternoon, Felicia heard Seamus's voice in the hall. She had not seen him since shortly after the explosion when they split up to assist people. A sister Felicia had not seen before pushed open the door to the women's ward. She had a firm set to her mouth and had the look of someone in an argument.

"The girl is in here, I assure you," the sister said.

Seamus caught sight of Felicia and strode across the ward, sweeping past the sister with a muttered apology.

"I regret that I could not be here sooner," he said. "I was stuck at the police station with Mr. Grey. They wanted to ask about the blasted riverboat. I got here as soon as I could get away."

He stopped when he was close enough to get a good look at Henry.

"She's going to be fine," said Felicia. "The bandage on her head will come off in a day or so, and her thigh has a cut, but not a bad one. She regained consciousness and is now just asleep." The child didn't look too bad, all things considered. "Oh, and it turns out she's a girl."

"Henry is a girl?" he said it slowly, as if trying out the idea.

"She's going to be fine," said Felicia.

"Mr. Grey told me that he got Henry over to the ambulances but they had to keep making return trips to get all the patients to the hospital. He's going to be all right, you said?"

"She. And yes. No permanent damage. Though she might have a good scar on her leg."

He stayed with Felicia for a few more minutes and made her assure him that she would be home before dark. She was also to tell the sisters that Seamus would be back in the morning and would bring the girl home, if she was well enough. The door swung shut behind him, and the room felt quiet and still. The man was a walking whirlwind.

Felicia looked down the length of Henry's body. The sheet rose in two peaks where the girl's feet were and Felicia moved down to look. She glanced up. The only other nurse was on her way out of the ward. Felicia lifted the sheet.

Henry's feet were the right length for a girl of her size. But a thick thumb, or more accurately, a big toe, emerged from the inner ball of her foot. The four other toes were slightly too long, about the length of an infant's fingers. That big toe though, it looked so strange. The whole upper part of the foot was large and almost hand like. But from the arch to the heel, it looked just like Felicia's own foot. The top of the foot was smooth and hairless.

Felicia had seen people with birth defects, and had never felt revulsion. Sometimes she felt pity for the difficulties the person faced. Sometimes she felt a deep dissatisfaction and helplessness in the face of suffering. But she had never felt disgust. She felt none now, only fascination. How had she not seen anyone else's feet today? It appeared to be standard medical practice to cover patients with a sheet, and when she thought about it, she realized that she had not treated anyone below the knee. Or perhaps she had not been paying close attention.

She stroked the sole of the foot with the back of her fingers and then gingerly touched the big toe. She wanted to see how the joints moved. How much range of motion did the digit have? Could Henry pick up objects with her toes? She smiled at the thought of these proper Victorians in their fancy dresses or top hats walking around with apelike feet in their big, boxy shoes.

The big toe twitched, and before Felicia could pull away, Henry's warm toes curled around her hand. Felicia looked up to find Henry watching her.

CHAPTER 23

L ATER, WHEN HAZEL TRIED TO recall her stay at the hospital, she remembered little. She recalled talking to Miss Sanchez, answering questions, but she couldn't remember everything she said or what was asked. Miss Sanchez knew she was a girl, and once Hazel took in her hospital gown and her place in the women's ward, there was no sense in denying it. She remembered telling Miss Sanchez her name, and something else that was a secret, but it was so hard to think straight and to keep her eyes open. Everything seemed far away, as if she was looking at the world through a sheet of fine mesh and listening through wads of cotton.

She drifted in and out of sleep, noting that a sister in a nurse's apron checked on her periodically and made her drink something bitter.

"Where is Miss Sanchez?" Hazel asked after forcing herself to drain the glass.

"She had to go home. But she told me that once you're well, you'll go back home to her and the Professor."

"What happened?"

"What do you mean, love?"

"What happened to me?"

"Miss Sanchez told you, but I suppose you don't remember, do you? The stage at the Steamboat Festival exploded. You were hurt, but not too badly."

Hazel found that once she was sitting up, her head felt clearer. The nurse checked on other patients and left.

A doctor came to examine Hazel and told her that she could go home soon. There was nothing more they could do for her, and Miss Sanchez could change her bandages at home. They needed to free up beds, so those healthy enough to leave would have to do so.

Hazel wondered what time it was. There were no clocks in the ward. The nurse was gone, and she was surrounded by sleeping women. The one closest to her had both arms in splints. Yes, she had been fortunate not to be so badly hurt. Aside from the thick grogginess in her head and the tenderness in her thigh, she felt well enough. She experimented with standing, then walking, and after walking back and forth across the ward a few times, she felt she had regained her balance and mental clarity. Then, she grew restless.

When the nurse returned, Hazel was standing near the window, looking down on the street below.

"We found this for you," said the sister. She carried a cotton dress in an ugly yellow and orange floral pattern. She also held a pair of shoes, bloomers and stockings.

"What time is it?" Hazel asked.

"Eight o'clock at night." The sister set the clothing on Hazel's bed.

"Can I go home now?"

"The doctor said you were well enough, though he thought you'd be here until morning. But someone is here for you now."

Hazel smiled. Miss Sanchez must have come back. She pulled on the dress, bloomers and stockings. "Is Miss Sanchez outside?"

"No, sweetheart. It's your uncle. He was so worried about you."

The last remnants of grogginess in her head cleared in an instant and the ache in her thigh vanished. "Uncle Seamus?" she asked, holding very still, like a rabbit frozen. The title of "uncle" sounded so strange. But perhaps the

Professor had told the sisters that they were related so he could take her home. Maybe.

"Must be," said the sister.

That answer wasn't good enough. Hazel glanced at her violin on the bedside table. The bow and the case were gone, she noted. She looked out the window. She was on the second story of the building, so she couldn't very well leap from the window. The only exit was through the door to the hallway.

"Sister, is it the man who came to see me before?" asked Hazel.

"I just came on shift a bit ago. But I would assume so."

"The Irishman? He's tall and thin with dark hair that sticks up."

"No, that's not him," said the sister. "Are you feeling all right?"

"No. I don't think I am. I can't go with that man. He's not my uncle. My uncle is the tall man."

"Now, Hazel. He is Andrew Dubois. Same last name as yours, and I can see the family resemblance just by looking at you. He says you're a runaway and a troubled young girl. Now get your shoes on."

"I think I need to stay an extra night. I'm feeling dizzy." Hazel leaned heavily on the bed and blinked hard. She rubbed her eye with the heel of her hand.

"Now, that's about enough of that," said the sister. "Your uncle said he and your aunt are worried sick about you and want you to come home immediately. There's no need for you to stay here." The sister knelt and slipped on Hazel's left shoe while Hazel dilly-dallied over the right one. The sister gave her a once-over look. Hazel knew that her hair was too short to ever look becoming on a girl, and the dress was a size too large. It hung on her skinny frame like a sack.

"You look fine," said the sister, as if hearing her thoughts. "Now come along."

Hazel had a moment to grab her violin before the sister pulled her through the women's ward doors, into the hallway and down the stairs. Uncle Andrew leaned against the wall, staring straight ahead. He turned slowly to take her in.

"There you are, angel," he said, moving toward them. "Ready to go home?"

Hazel turned to the sister in one last attempt. She grabbed the sister's wrist and looked up into her face. The woman was young, only in her twenties, and had round cheeks and a kind look about her. She had not raised her voice when Hazel had tried to avoid leaving. Maybe there was hope.

"Please don't make me go," pleaded Hazel. "Call the Professor."

"What Professor?"

"Seamus Connor. He's my uncle. He's the one who I am supposed to go home with."

At her uncle's raised eyebrow, she realized her grave mistake. She had just told him the name of the person who had given her sanctuary. She looked at him then, meeting his eyes, and in them she saw nothing. No malice, no anger, just nothing. He had an expression of mild curiosity, but nothing more.

"Stop that, you're hurting me," said the sister, prying Hazel's hand from her arm. She had been digging her fingers in hard without realizing it.

"He killed my dog. My dog Mandy. He just killed her dead." She wanted to say more, but she couldn't. No one would believe her. Looking at her uncle's concerned and hurt expression, for an instant, she herself wondered if any of it had happened.

"Sister, her dog was old and in pain," said her uncle. "I put the poor animal out of its misery. And Hazel here blamed me for the dog's death. You know how it is with children and animals."

"You liar! You killed her and you know it." Her voice quavered. "Mandy wasn't old or sick."

"Now Hazel," said the sister. "The poor old dog was hurting. She's in heaven now. Do you understand?"

Hazel wanted to slap the sister's round-cheeked face. The idiot woman wasn't listening. The sister put her hand on Hazel's shoulder, and she jerked away.

"Now, what's that you have?" said her uncle. He had moved closer while she was focusing on the sister and he reached for the violin.

"Don't you touch it," Hazel hissed, backing up against the wall.

"You've been living on the streets, posing as a boy. It's not good for you, dear," he said. "Now give it to me."

"Go to hell!"

"Now you just stop it!" said the sister. "You apologize to your uncle this instant."

"I won't. He can't have it. It's mine!"

"I apologize, Sister," said Uncle Andrew. "Living on the street has clearly affected the poor girl's mind. I'll just take her home."

"Of course," said the sister. She opened the door to the front lobby, where large double doors led out to the street. Hazel took a step toward the door, and the violin jerked from her arms. She spun to see her uncle holding it up, examining it. He narrowed his eyes and plucked at a string. The little twang it made was high and short.

"You give that back!" Hazel screamed and leapt to grab it.

Before she knew what had happened, he shoved her away. It wasn't hard enough to make her fall, only enough to make her lose her balance and take a few steps back. He dropped her violin to the floor and set his foot on it. With slow deliberation, he shifted his weight and crushed the place where the neck met the shoulders. Then he placed his foot on the rounded wooden belly and crushed it. The hollow wood splintered with a sickening crunch. The front panel split into pieces, and a huge and irreparable crack bisected it almost completely in half. The broken neck was only connected by loose strings, like tendons.

Hazel stared in horror at her violin. The sister and her uncle were speaking, but she did not hear what they said. She did not crouch to touch the violin pieces. The instrument had been a gift from her father. It was neither fine nor expensive, as her family had not been well-off. But her parents had scrimped for music lessons, and she had played it for both of them many times.

Her uncle took her by the upper arm and led her through the front doors of the hospital. A man at the front desk looked on in approval, and Hazel knew that he thought she was either mad or willful. Maybe he was right. She felt like a feral animal.

Uncle Andrew's grip did not loosen for an instant, and Hazel knew she would have bruises on her upper arm. But the pain was nothing. Her violin was crushed on the hallway floor of the hospital. She could never get another.

Her uncle hailed a coach and it pulled to a stop. The speckled gray horse pulling it tossed its head and shifted its weight. It was livelier than most carriage horses that were grateful for a rest. It was ready to go.

Well, Hazel thought, perhaps I should take a page from the horse's book. When her uncle shoved her into the coach, she saw that like some of its kind, it had one door on the right side, but none on the left. Very well. The door had to open some time. And if she could not get away then, then her uncle couldn't keep her locked up forever. There would be opportunities.

She was wedged between the wall and her uncle's body. His proximity and the scent of him made her feel like she couldn't breathe. He kept hold of her arm until the coach was moving. "You've caused your aunt some great worry," he said. "I fitted your bedroom door with a lock. Your new bedroom that is. It's in the attic. It's larger than your old one, but a little colder, I'm afraid."

Hazel didn't answer. The attic window would be too high to climb from, and she could not break a lock. She wished she had learned how to pick locks from one of the street boys.

"Living like a wild animal on the streets," he shook his head. "If your father ever knew, he'd be so ashamed of you. Thank God he's dead."

"Better if he were alive and you dead. He was worth a hundred of you," said Hazel, so low that she wasn't sure if he heard her. He didn't move or answer, but an instant later he struck her hard across the face. Once she blinked a few times and the interior of the cab became clear again, she noted that he had let go of her arm. Good.

"You are an insolent, unruly, disrespectful, ugly and worthless girl. You are lucky we took you in at all."

"Then why did you come for me? Why not leave me?" She did not raise her hand to the place where he had struck her. She turned to look him in the eye. It was torture to do it, but she forced herself.

"Your aunt and I would never turn away a family member in need. Even one such as you."

"You know, I remember everything." There, she had said it. She looked away as she spoke, and now made herself look at him again.

"I'm not sure what you mean, child. We've given you a home, comforts, even a few luxuries. And you repay us by running off and shaming us. What do you think our neighbors said about that? And your teacher and friends?"

"I don't know what they say, but they don't know how you are. You came to my room at night. You killed Mandy." Her heart was beating so hard that she was sure he must be able to hear it. Her body shook and she felt as tight and tense as an over-stretched catgut string.

"Now, that never happened. Maybe you dreamt it."

His voice was soft and gentle. Almost fatherly. He looked worried for her, as if she had truly lost her mind. "Your dog was old and sick."

"I may be a bad girl. I may be a liar and I may live on the streets. But you know what else I'm not?"

"What's that?" He had a small, patronizing smile.

"I'm not like you."

She jumped up, stomped his foot as hard as she could and scrambled past him, flinging herself against the door. She turned the handle and clung to the door as it swung outward. Then she dropped into the street, falling face-down on the paving stones, scraping her knees and palms. She pushed herself forward, running blindly, turning down streets and into alleys. How many times had she run like this, terrified and disoriented? She was losing count. She would run as long as she could. She would run forever. Her vision blurred with tears, though she felt no sadness. It must be the tears that came with anger. Could one fear and hate someone so much that one would cry?

She spotted a cemetery across the street and hurried toward it. From there, she could hear anyone coming and still be able to hide. She hurried to a place somewhere near the center of the cemetery and listened. Nothing. No people, only the sound of a steam carriage rumbling past, the voices of its occupants raised in raucous laughter. Perhaps they had come from the Steamboat Festival. But no, the festival had ended with the explosion.

She felt nauseated and shaky. A minute of being still, and she thought she would be all right. She leaned her back against a tomb, a small, plain one. She was at the rear of the tomb, so there were no carved names, only a blank white surface. Someone had scratched words into it, but she did not read them.

Alive. She was alive. She could have died in the explosion, but she had not. She could be locked up in her aunt and uncle's attic bedroom, but she was not. She was breathing, if hurt. She touched her face, and felt the skin from her eyebrow to her cheekbone was hot and swollen. It could be worse. Her thigh hurt, but obviously she could still run. She had a bandage on her head, and knew better than to take it off. Miss Sanchez could do that when she got home.

Home. The Professor said that she was to go to his house once she was well enough. Miss Sanchez and the sister had said so. She didn't know what cemetery this was, or in what direction home might be. She looked up and found the big dipper, then the North Star. Her father had shown it to her when she was a little girl. Polaris, it was called. Like a pole, around which the other stars rotated.

Would her father be ashamed of her? She was a street child, filthy, homeless and disobedient. She played violin, not in a proper parlor performance that suited a young lady, but for spare coins on the street. She ran wild. She had been so bad that it caused her uncle to do terrible things to her. If she had only been more obedient, more docile and had angered him and her aunt less, maybe things would have been different.

Polaris twinkled overhead, strong and bright. Hazel said a prayer, not to God, but to her parents. She asked them to show her the way to go to get to the Professor's house. She knew from the catechism that you could pray to saints and ask for their intercession, but you were only supposed to pray to saints that the church had named. Praying to your grandmother or parents would be heathen ancestor worship. Hazel didn't understand the difference. If her parents were in heaven, then they were saints. Seemed simple enough. Besides, she knew she had lied and disobeyed. She had even tried to kill her uncle by leading him to the Delphia Queen. It was the last thing she remembered before waking up in the hospital, though she had a niggling feeling that there was something else she should be remembering. Whatever she had forgotten, she knew that God didn't listen to the prayers of those in a state of mortal sin, and she was sure she was neck-deep in it.

Without waiting to see if her parents answered her prayer, she stepped out onto the street and headed in what she thought was the direction of home.

CHAPTER 24

THE NEXT MORNING, JUST AFTER dawn, Mr. Grey came to call on Seamus. He made Mr. Grey wait while he dressed.

"A bit early for a visit, isn't it?" he asked as he met Mr. Grey at the bottom of the stairs.

"Is Henry all right?"

Seamus told him that Henry was a girl named Hazel, that she had come to the house the previous night and that she was asleep upstairs. Mr. Grey did not seem surprised.

"Good. Good. Now, I need you to come and meet with my colleague," said Mr. Grey.

"On a Sunday? And at this hour?"

"It won't take long, and it's important."

"I still don't know why the engines are exploding. The police are going to be disappointed. I told you I couldn't help."

"Not those colleagues. I work for the police, but only temporarily as a consulting detective. I have another person I work with. And you'll need to come along."

Seamus knew something was wrong. He understood the concept of a consulting detective, especially when a previous police detective had been killed in the line of duty. Seamus hoped that Mr. Grey was being adequately compensated for such hazardous work. But even so, being dragged about to visit Mr. Grey's colleague was taking up his valuable time.

"Tell me, who is it you work for, Mr. Grey? I'm not

exactly in the frame of mind to be talking to one more higher-up who wants answers that I can't give. Without one of those engines, I can't figure anything out."

"I got word that it was urgent and that you should come. Please, Mr. Connor."

Seamus studied him and then made a decision. "Very well. Let's get this over with then."

Mr. Grey hailed a cab and spoke to the driver while Seamus climbed in. Seamus shoved his hands in his pockets and fingered the contents. A rubber stopper, a piece of yarn, three screws of varying sizes.

"It was a bit of a shock to find out she's a girl, wasn't it?" Mr. Grey said. "She's one tough cookie."

"That's a strange way to put it, but yes."

"And you'll take her in, raise her, correct?"

"What concern is she of yours?" Seamus asked. "You don't seem to be taking in every stray off the streets yourself."

"I won't be here long enough to, even if I were so inclined," said Mr. Grey and looked out the window.

Seamus stared out the opposite window and looked over the Steamboat Festival lot as they passed. It was covered in paper wrappers, wax-lined paper cups and pieces of wood and metal from the explosion. A torn red pavilion flapped from one pole, abandoned after the commotion. Something in the distance caught his eye, some kind of movement. It was near the riverbank. No boats were there now, and there were no people about.

He squinted, scanning for movement. There it was, a rippling in space, like the wavering of air on a hot day. But this movement wasn't limited to just the horizon, it seemed to move horizontally, at about the speed of a person walking. It was gone a moment later.

"Something's wrong. Stop the cab," Seamus ordered.

Mr. Grey rapped the roof. Mr. Grey had not waited for him to explain why and Seamus appreciated it. As soon as the cab slowed, Seamus jumped out and ran toward the riverbank, toward the spot where the Delphia Queen had been moored.

The driver shouted behind him, and he glanced over his shoulder to see Mr. Grey turn back from following him and give the driver his pay. Seamus went on without him and then slowed.

"Don't go any closer," said Mr. Grey. Seamus had not heard him run up behind him. The man seemed to be able to move almost silently.

"I'm not soft-headed. I know better than to go near. You saw it too then?"

"No."

"It was a shimmer. It only appeared for a moment. I think we can get a little closer. I think it's safe."

They walked across the empty lot and Seamus kept his eyes forward, scanning the riverbank for another shimmering spot.

"You want to see if we can look through one, don't you?" asked Mr. Grey.

"Do I want to look through a tear in time and space and see the other side? Dear God, yes," said Seamus.

"I do too."

"It is a bit marvelous, isn't it?" Seamus said. "Something about the engines does it. I wish I knew what it was."

"You'll figure it out. I'm sure of it."

"I thank you for your unwavering faith, but I fear it may be misplaced."

"It isn't."

Both men stopped in their tracks at what they saw next. A shimmering spot appeared a few yards into the river. The doorway was only open for a few moments, but through it they saw all the way across the river. A rowboat floated halfway across, but instead of being made of wood, it was made of metal. A man sat at the back, his hand resting on a handle attached to some kind of engine that hung down into the water. He had a strange hat on, a tight cap with a brim only in the front. It was black and gold with what looked like a fleur de lis design on the front. The man and the shimmer disappeared.

"You saw that, didn't you?" asked Seamus.

"Yes." Mr. Grey was looking at him, not at the spot where the man had been.

"That man in that boat was from the future, wouldn't you say?" Seamus asked.

"Yes."

"I wonder how far in the future."

Mr. Grey did not answer.

"Don't talk my ear off, please," said Seamus. "Wouldn't want you to lose your voice."

"I believe you do enough talking for us both."

A pair of boys ran along the riverbank. The taller one knelt to pick something off the ground. He called to the younger boy who trotted over to have a look.

"Street children from the look of them," said Seamus. "They ought not be there. It's dangerous." But he had not finished saying it when Mr. Grey called out to the boys and went to meet them. He pulled something from his pocket and held it up. The boys ran toward him. They took the proffered coin and took off back in the direction from which they had come.

"Told them to stay away for a few days," said Mr. Grey when he returned.

"It wouldn't be good for them to end up going through one of those holes like Miss Sanchez."

"That was my thought also. Now, it's only a few blocks to the place we need to go. We can walk."

"So the engines, these engines can reliably tear holes in time," Seamus said, letting Mr. Grey lead the way.

"I would not say, 'reliably.'"

"Well, perhaps not. But somewhat predictably. And they can open and reopen."

"That's what worries me."

"Have you seen something like this before?" Seamus asked. He glanced sideways to see if he could gather anything from Mr. Grey's reaction. The man's face was as placid as always.

"No," Mr. Grey said.

Seamus tried repeatedly to get more information from him, but Mr. Grey was unmovable.

"The house is just down this street," Mr. Grey said.

They turned down a street of unassuming houses in a solidly middle-class neighborhood. After turning another corner, Mr. Grey indicated a house with a stone path, a few modest flowerbeds and blue and white paint.

"Is this your house?" asked Seamus. It seemed like the sort of place Mr. Grey would live.

"No," he said. He stopped on the front porch and turned to Seamus. "Please try to be polite."

"Why wouldn't I be?"

Mr. Grey didn't answer but knocked on the door. A woman answered, and Seamus thought she must be a servant. She was a black woman in her late fifties or early sixties with a long, sharp face and silver-rimmed spectacles. Her hair was cut as short as a man's and was mostly gray. This neighborhood was a white neighborhood, so although this woman was dressed as a middle-class resident, she surely had to be hired help.

"Ah, you brought Mr. Connor. I'm so glad," she said. She held the door and they entered.

Mr. Grey made introductions. "Miss Wilde, this is Mr. Seamus Connor. Mr. Connor, Miss September Wilde."

Seamus nodded in acknowledgement, wondering why Mr. Grey would swap the order of introductions, as if Seamus were being presented to this Miss Wilde as a social inferior, especially after Mr. Grey's admonition to be polite. Miss Wilde put her hand out sideways in the manner that Miss Sanchez had done upon their first meeting, as if she wanted to shake hands like a man. Seamus took it and bowed over it. Miss Wilde seemed amused. Mr. Grey hung his duster on a coat rack beside the door and Seamus did the same.

"I have some cookies in the kitchen. I'll meet you in there," she said, indicating the front room. The house was modest and would not have a formal sitting room. Mr. Grey and Seamus seated themselves on the sofa and Miss Wilde set a plate of cookies and a stack of cloth napkins on the table in front of them. She then seated herself in the chair opposite, took a cookie and looked inquiringly at Mr. Grey.

"Anything to report?" she asked.

Mr. Grey told her about the shimmering places they saw at the riverbank. Miss Wilde asked for clarification here and there, and listened until Mr. Grey was finished.

"Do you have anything to add to that?" Miss Wilde asked Seamus.

This had gone on long enough, Seamus thought. "When are we going to speak with your colleague?" Seamus asked Mr. Grey.

"I am she," said Miss Wilde.

"I'll thank you for not having me on," Seamus said to Mr. Grey as quietly as he could. He knew that Miss Wilde would overhear, but could do nothing about it.

"Miss Wilde and I work together. We are coworkers."

Coworkers. Miss Sanchez had used the term for her fellow medical students and the doctors and nurses with whom she worked in her hospital in the future. Seamus glanced at Mr. Grey's feet, then at Miss Wilde's, but both had regular shoes on, not the narrow things that Miss Sanchez wore.

Miss Wilde gave an exasperated sigh. "There is no time for this, Mr. Connor. I would ask you to accept the fact that Mr. Grey and I work together for the time being and withhold your reservations for later when you may ponder the oddity of my social placement at your leisure."

Perhaps this was why Mr. Grey so easily listened to Miss Sanchez's theories about Mr. Lincoln and Mr. Buchannan instead of brushing off her ideas as uninformed or silly. He was used to women of that sort. Well, Seamus wasn't raised by an addle-headed ninny himself. His mother and sisters could read, write, do sums and even quote the Bible and Shakespeare. More to the point, they were clever and wouldn't back down an inch for any man. All except Branna, he thought.

"Very well, Miss Wilde," he replied.

"The traveler is secure, for now," said Mr. Grey.

"Good," said Miss Wilde. "Under no circumstances can the traveler be lost."

The way Miss Wilde said the word "lost" held more meaning that Seamus liked.

"I don't intend to lose her," Seamus said. "Miss Sanchez is safe at my house, and there she'll stay until we can find some way to send her home. I won't let anything happen to her."

"Of course you won't," said Miss Wilde fondly. She seemed to have forgiven him for slighting her.

"I need one of those engines," said Seamus. "If I have one, I may be able to learn how it works and find a way to send her back."

"That is the idea. That is why I asked Mr. Grey to bring you here. Two of our agents have managed to get an engine. Huginn volunteered, and Pangur Ban insisted on going with him."

"How did they get inside the manufactory?" asked Mr. Grey.

"I'm not sure, but they are probably the only ones who could."

"From what I understand, the machines are rather large. How did they manage it?"

"They managed," said Miss Wilde, taking another cookie.

"If you could get a machine, why wait until now?" Seamus asked. "Why not days ago?"

"We couldn't do it before now," said Miss Wilde. "We have people watching the McCullen Manufactory, but getting an engine is difficult. So now you have one and can examine it. You can learn why they are exploding. And please, have a cookie. I made them special."

He took one to be polite but did not eat it. "Perhaps you think I am a fool," he said.

"Quite the contrary," said Miss Wilde.

"But I can see that you aren't from here, just as Miss Sanchez is not. Am I correct?"

Miss Wilde just looked at him and patted her mouth with a napkin.

"If you are both from somewhere, somewhen else, then why can't you take Miss Sanchez back to her home the same way you both came here?"

"Is that what you want?" Miss Wilde asked.

"What do you mean? She needs to return home, simple as that."

"True. She does. But we cannot do that," said Miss Wilde

"Why not? Did you walk through one of those shimmering holes also? Are you both trapped here as well? How many of you are there?"

She held up a finger to silence him. "I cannot tell you more, and I am sorry for that. Getting an engine to you is the best we can do. But I am able do something additional for you. Something I think you'll like very much."

She took a clean napkin from the stack and wrapped up the remaining cookies, tying a little knot at the top. As she did so, Mr. Grey went into the hallway and brought back both of their coats.

Miss Wilde handed the tied bundle of cookies to Seamus. "For you and Miss Sanchez and Hazel. I'm sure you'll enjoy them."

CHAPTER 25

"IT IS SUNDAY, AND THE girl will be going to Mass on Sundays for as long as she lives under my roof," said Seamus. Felicia had finished changing Hazel's bandages and stood in front of the girl's bedroom door, glaring up at him. He was being completely impossible and she was having trouble keeping her temper.

"You said she was healthy enough," he said. "She can walk around just fine. She goes."

"She can, but you can't force her to go," Felicia said.

"Like hell I can't."

"Like hell? You talk like that in church too?"

The man was insufferable. He may have been born some time in, what, the 1830s? But forcing a little girl to go to church when she didn't want to seemed too harsh, especially with what Hazel had been through. The child needed peace and quiet, not to be dragged around the city.

"Now listen," said Seamus. "Long after you have gone back you your own heathen world, Hazel will still be here with me. And I will give her a proper upbringing. And that means going to Mass on Sunday mornings."

"No matter what?"

"Well, there are exceptions. If one is deathly ill or incapacitated. But other than that, it's a mortal sin to miss Mass on Sunday."

"And you believe that?" she asked. He gave a half shrug and looked sideways. "I think I see," she said. "Your parents took you, rain or shine, and you want to do right by Hazel."

"That's what I said."

"Let's talk over here," Felicia whispered and pulled Seamus's sleeve. She led him to the landing on the stairs and spoke as quietly as she could. She knew Hazel was listening from inside her bedroom and didn't wish to be overheard. "She's scared. Terrified to go out of the house."

"Because of that man. Well, just let him try to take her back. I saw that bruise on her face. He won't be doing that again, I assure you." His eyes burned and just as in the cathedral attic, he seemed to grow larger. "I'd like to see him try it."

"I have to agree with you there," Felicia said. "And I wouldn't stop you from giving that man a matching bruise on his own face. But understand what she's been through."

"It would do her good to see the filthy blighter bleeding out his nose and lying on the pavement among his own teeth. It would do her a heap of good."

"I think what would do her a heap of good is time to be away from him. When she was delirious in the hospital, I asked her questions. Some of what she said didn't make a lot of sense, but eventually I got the gist. Her uncle didn't just hit her and kill her dog."

"Her dog? He killed a little girl's dog? Was it old or infirm?"

"No, you're missing the point. He killed the dog because it bit him. And it bit him to protect Hazel. Her uncle was doing something."

How could she say the rest? Seamus had seen so much suffering, famine and death. How could she tell him that another helpless person he cared about had been harmed? Seamus said that her world was heathen, but in his time, the concept of sexual abuse was not even acknowledged. Child abuse and spousal abuse weren't either. In a world where slaves could be beaten to death without repercussions, some things were still deemed too scandalous to discuss.

But then, he was a grown man, a former prison inmate. It wasn't as if he would faint from hearing the truth. Seamus was waiting for her to finish.

"He molested her," she said, very softly, unsure if the word "molest" had the right meaning in this time. From the way his face fell and his lips parted, she judged that it had the meaning she intended.

He stood silently for a while. "Get her to tell me where he lives."

"Now stop it. You getting imprisoned for murder isn't going to do her any good either."

"Someone has to do something. You're sure of what she told you?"

"Yes, I had her repeat it, and I asked questions. I don't know if she remembers telling me, but I'm sure. I asked a few more questions, gentle ones, when I was in her room a few minutes ago, and her reaction confirms it. She's terrified to go out."

"I'll be with her."

"It's not that she's afraid he'll do something to her in public. It's just seeing him. Just knowing he's there, or that he might see her. Imagine if he had done that to you."

Seamus snorted. "Not bleeding likely. I wouldn't have allowed it."

"Oh, so you think when you were ten years old you would become some kind of ninja and fight off a man twice your size? Right."

"If these ninja people are able to bloody up wicked bastards, then yes."

Felicia sighed in exasperation. This wasn't the time to argue that Hazel bore no culpability or that a boy being sexually abused by a grown man was not some kind of blight on the boy's masculinity.

"Let her stay home," she said. "She can read a page of the Bible or say a rosary or whatever you like. Just give her a few weeks. I'm sure God will understand and let her off the hook for Mass attendance."

"Are you coming?" Seamus asked.

"A Latin Mass in St. Louis Cathedral in 1857? I wouldn't miss it for the world."

Seamus nodded but looked uncertain. She had intentionally left it ambiguous as to whether she wanted to attend church on its own merits. Her grandmother had been a devout Catholic, though her mother and father had not. For her grandmother's sake, she had been baptized and had her First Communion and Confirmation, but as an adult, she had only attended church for funerals, infant baptisms and weddings. But the chance to see the historic cathedral in all its glory was not to be missed.

"Will Mrs. Washington be home? We can't leave Hazel home alone," said Felicia.

"Why not?"

"She's only eleven." Then she realized the silliness of her statement. The girl had lived on her own for months. A few hours in the house would not pose any danger.

When they arrived home after Mass, a large trunk waited in the kitchen, covered in an oilcloth. Seamus ripped off the sheet with a flourish and tossed it aside.

"That was on the back steps with a note saying to keep it covered," said Mrs. Washington. "Now, Professor, tell me this thing isn't stolen."

"It's a gift," he said.

"From McCullen? The man who had you arrested and who stole your engine design? No, don't tell me. I don't want to know." She left the kitchen and Seamus knelt and opened the trunk.

"Oh you beauty," he murmured to the engine, stroking it. "Look at you. What secrets do you have for me, my sweet little thing?"

"Do you need to have some time alone with it in your laboratory?" Felicia asked. "Sounds like you may need some privacy."

"Quite right." He rushed out to the shed, brought in a hand cart and pulled the engine up the stairs amid thumps and curses. At last, Felicia heard the laboratory door bang closed and she heaved a sigh. Finally, the Professor had what he needed.

She missed her own time. It was noisy and dirty and manners had definitely deteriorated over the intervening years, but it was hers. She missed take-out Chinese food, TV, the public library system, electricity. At least there was indoor plumbing in the house. Seamus had created a water heater for the bathroom, and though you had to light it an hour before your bath, the water was hot.

Her grandmother had been born on a farm in Mexico and had seen segregation, the civil rights movement and modern equality, such as it was. What would she think of her granddaughter's current predicament? And if Felicia was trapped in this time, could she manage? She could neither vote nor own property, have a career or do much of anything besides get married and keep house. She had no idea how to sew or do laundry by hand. Even cooking would be difficult. She couldn't stoke and keep a fire going in the wood-burning stove. And plucking a chicken? Her chicken had always been born in pieces on Styrofoam trays at the supermarket.

At 11:30, Mrs. Washington started making lunch and Felicia assisted her.

There was a crash from upstairs, then muffled swearing. Mrs. Washington shook her head but did not look up. A few minutes later, Mr. Grey knocked on the kitchen door.

"We have more people calling at the back door than at the front," said Mrs. Washington. But when she opened the door, she greeted Mr. Grey warmly. "Would you like to stay for lunch?"

"Thank you, but I must decline," said Mr. Grey. "I came to speak with Mr. Connor and see how he's coming with the engine."

"Oh, was that from you?" asked Mrs. Washington, but in a lightly disinterested tone that did not encourage any further discussion of the topic.

There was another sound upstairs, like the crash of breaking glass. Seamus shouted again.

"I'll go up and speak with him," said Mr. Grey.

"I'll be up in a few minutes," said Felicia.

"I don't think the Professor is any decent company for a woman right now," said Mrs. Washington.

"It's all right, I'm used to it."

"He said you were a nurse or some such. I bet you hear men swear a blue streak in that line of work."

"I've heard my share," said Felicia. She may not ever excel at housekeeping, but one career was open to her. She could become a nurse. Her penicillin mold was growing well upstairs in the laboratory, and though she couldn't make pills from it, she could experiment with ways to treat infections. And if the Civil War was coming, she thought she might be useful as a battlefield nurse. Later, she could find work in a hospital, hopefully in the North. Maybe after the war, she could go to New York, or somewhere where her skin color wouldn't be such a detriment. She remembered learning about Florence Nightingale and the Crimean War. When was that war? Had it happened yet? She wondered if she could somehow serve with Nightingale's nurses even though she wasn't British. Those women were respected and independent and Nightingale formed some sort of formal nursing school, although it was probably in England.

She carried the tray out of the kitchen and was just at the top of the stairs when the grandfather clock finished chiming noon. The door stood ajar and she pushed it open with her foot and found a spot to set the tray.

"Any news?" she asked.

"Oh, plenty," said Seamus. "It didn't take nearly as long as I had feared. There have been a few, er, mishaps.

Small ones. But I have some good information. I amplified the signal on the mapping device just a little, not because I needed to record the results of sonic amplification as previously," he said, waving wildly toward the rolled metal sheet with zigzag scratches on its surface. "No. I amplified it a bit, just enough to cause a reaction. Amplifying the zed waves between thirty and forty percent was enough to do it. Once I managed that, it happened. Do you know what I saw?"

"What?"

"Guess."

"Oh for the love of Pete. Just tell me," said Felicia. Mr. Grey leaned against the desk with his arms folded.

"You'll never be so happy. It was the best thing I've seen all day. And it was right there, and it was—"

"A shimmer," interrupted Mr. Grey.

"I was getting to that," cried Seamus, throwing up his hands. "I was explaining everything. So yes, a shimmer, a door! Anyway, you'll never believe what is being used in addition to the silver as the catalyst for the peroxide engine."

"Please don't make me guess."

"No, we'd be here all day, because there's no way anyone would figure it out, not even a lass as clever as you. Well, no one could except for me, but then I have a certain advantage."

"Okay, Mr. Humble," said Felicia. But she wasn't offended. The Professor paced from one end of the table to the other.

"I wouldn't have thought of it, but for your coming through time. And once I knew that, I was able to figure it out. The catalyst is matter from another universe!" He jabbed a finger into the air.

"What? What do you mean?" Felicia asked.

"Matter from another place is being used as a catalyst. The silver is just there for show. Well, not exactly. The regular engine, the one I created, produces a decent amount of energy, enough to power an apparatus that in turn can puncture one eensy weensy hole in time, to another world, another universe even. I can see how he managed it, but only barely. It's all very strange. Very strange.

"The hole is like a needle hole. That's when McCullen's portion of the engine takes over. Matter, air specifically, is taken in as a catalyst. It has to be air, as that's everywhere. And since nitrogen is the most abundant element in air, he's using that. But it's different than our nitrogen because it's from another world. That's the catalyst that makes the engine able to produce so much power. The better the catalyst, the more energy it can break down which means heat, energy and steam for the machines. This all happens inside the machine, in a secondary part of its very core. That's how that bastard McCullen is able to have an engine that produces more energy than it should."

He stopped and faced Mr. Grey and herself. His eyes were dancing and he was bouncing up and down on the balls of his feet. For an instant, she thought he was going to take a bow, but instead he spun around to grab something from the table.

"So can you get Miss Sanchez home to her own time?" asked Mr. Grey.

"Not yet," said Seamus.

"What does he mean?" asked a voice behind Felicia. She turned to find Hazel behind her. The girl popped the last piece of a butter cookie into her mouth and looked from person to person. She wore the boy's clothing she had gotten a few days previously. But then, she didn't have any dresses except for the one she had worn home from the hospital.

"What does he mean about going home to your own time?" asked Hazel. She caught a glimpse of Mr. Grey, and seemed wary, but he gave Hazel a polite nod and turned to watch the Professor.

"It's all right, Hazel. Come on in," said Seamus. "You

might as well know. Everyone else seems to. Well, close the door behind you. I don't want poor Mrs. Washington getting any more gray hairs than she already has."

Hazel shut the door and circled the disassembled engine. "This is the thing we wanted the plans for at McCullen's house?"

"It is indeed."

"And it can send Miss Sanchez home?"

"It can. With luck," said Seamus.

Felicia saw that Mr. Grey was partially turned away, but she knew he was watching Hazel from the corner of his eye.

"Home being her own time. That's what Mr. Grey said. But that doesn't make any sense," said Hazel.

Mr. Grey looked from Felicia to Seamus, waiting for one of them to answer Hazel. When neither of them did, he looked down at the floor.

"So this machine, you said something about a shimmer," said Hazel.

"How long were you listening?" asked Seamus, but Felicia could tell that wasn't upset with the girl.

"You said this thing can make shimmer doors or some such thing, yeah?"

"Yes. Doors to other times. Miss Sanchez comes from another time. The early twenty-first century, over a hundred sixty years from now," Seamus said. He spoke quickly, presumably assuming that Hazel would keep up. She knew that Hazel was bright, very bright, and she appreciated that Seamus didn't treat the girl any differently than he had when she was a boy.

"Is that why your feet are like that? What, do they cut off your toe there?" Hazel asked, turning to Miss Sanchez.

"No, we're born like this," said Felicia.

Felicia watched Hazel glance at Mr. Grey's feet, and he looked up at her. She looked away quickly. He wore the same type of shoes that everyone else did.

"How's that work then?" Hazel said. "A hundred fifty years and people are missing toes? That's not right. No, there's something else to this." She looked to the adults, and stopped at Felicia. "And you were talking about that Lincoln fellow and Buchannan and how they were supposed to be presidents. Like you knew what was going to happen in the future." Hazel stopped and looked at the Professor. "And you said that the air is pulled into that machine from another world or time or universe."

"That's right," said Seamus.

Hazel turned to Felicia. "So like the air, you're also from some other place or world, then. You got pulled through instead of the air?"

"Ha! That's my girl," said Seamus and mussed her hair. She pulled out of reach and swatted gently at his hand.

"It's not exactly like that. But the doors, rips, whatever you like to call them are impossible to control," said Seamus. "From what I can tell, they'll open and re-open over and over, growing larger and larger."

"That's bad then?" said Hazel.

"Very," said Mr. Grey.

Seamus sighed. "The hole in front of the house appears to have closed on its own. No more shimmers. But the one where the Delphia Queen was docked is still opening and closing. McCullen needs to stop allowing these engines to be used."

"Then someone needs to tell him," said Felicia. She didn't like McCullen, but he seemed to have a strange fascination with her. She might be able to coax him into at least considering not using the engines. He was greedy, but even a greedy man could see the danger in ripping holes in time to power steam engines. "We can go together."

"Not we, Miss Sanchez," said Seamus. "I alone will see him."

"But he seemed to like me. Maybe I could—"

"Out of the question. He is not a man with whom you

would wish to have a better acquaintance, I assure you. On Mondays, he likes to dine at his club, Blanchard's. Women aren't allowed. I will have to go alone."

Felicia bristled at being set aside so easily. Well, if Seamus failed, she could always visit McCullen on her own. There was no law about women hiring coaches and visiting with whomever they pleased.

"And what about you then?" Hazel asked Mr. Grey. "What are you going to do?"

"Anything I can, Miss Dubois."

Mr. Grey excused himself and Hazel ran off to find Mrs. Washington. Felicia moved to stand beside Seamus as he rifled through pages of notes.

"How close are you to being able to send me back?" she asked.

"Not very. I'm sorry, but I cannot see any way to regulate the place or time that the holes lead to."

"But with time, you could figure it out?"

Seamus stopped and turned to her, then turned back to the notes. "I will not lie to you or give you false hope. I cannot promise anything."

"Then I may be trapped here, in this horrible time."

"There now, lass. It's not so bad. You said yourself that slavery will end with the Civil War."

"Yes. There's that. But it's more. There's my nephew. And even if he were healthy, a woman in your time is supposed to keep house, sew and cook. I can't do any of that. And women can't vote or be on juries."

"You want to be on a jury?" Seamus looked puzzled.

"Well, no actually. I always tried to get out of jury duty. But my point is that here, I'm a second-class citizen. Third class, if anyone finds out I'm Mexican-American instead of the supposedly superior Castilian."

"But you're working on your penicillin. And you said there are little things called germs that cause disease. You know about other medicines and treatments. You can help people here," he said.

"But I'm meant to help people back home. And where will I live? It's not as if I can buy a house or rent an apartment, can I?"

"There are boarding houses for female factory workers. You could get housing there. But I have the space. You are welcome to stay here as long as you like. We could tell people we are cousins. There would be no scandal."

She was trapped. The hope of finding a way home was fading, and the hopelessness of her situation enveloped her. Trapped in this time, with this culture, was a horror. The past existence of such suffocating, painful rules of race and sex was bad enough, but that she would have to live out her life forced to abide by them was too much to bear. She turned to him.

"Tell me, why were you playing with that engine? Didn't you consider the consequences? Maybe you didn't know that a person could come through, but you could have blown yourself up, or set the house on fire with Mrs. Washington in it. Didn't you learn anything from blowing up your laboratory? You had to keep screwing around with dangerous machinery, didn't you? When you saw that tube of blue stuff, didn't you stop and think that it could possibly be something beyond your expertise?"

The hurt look on his face told her she had gone too far. "Perhaps my work is not always safe," he said. "And I take a few risks I shouldn't. I am responsible for what happened to you, and I will make it up to you. If that means that I spend years finding out how to send you home, I will not stop working until I discover the answer. And until then, I will ensure that you come to no harm. If you leave, it will be of your own free will. You can stay here as long as you like."

Seamus had taken a step toward her, and she had to tip her head up to look him in the eye. He was sincere, and sad. Her anger dissipated a little.

"I would not wish to stay where I am a burden," she

said. "I'll stay for a while until I get my feet, but then I will strike out on my own. I'm thinking about becoming a nurse. Maybe even the first female doctor."

"Certainly. Yes. That's fine. Whatever you like," he turned back to his pages, though he didn't seem to be focusing on them, just moving them from one stack to another.

"One question though, as we're going to be housemates for a while," Felicia said.

"Yes?"

She hesitated. She didn't want to push him to give her information he did not want to. But she was still angry, and she wanted to know.

"What is your name?"

He paused, but only for a second.

"Seamus Doyle."

CHAPTER 26

AS HIS HIRED CAB PULLED up to the curb, Seamus put on his top hat and took up his walking stick. He had worn his nicer clothing and knew he looked the gentleman from his best top hat to his polished shoes. As long as he didn't allow Oren McCullen to goad him into saying anything hot-headed, he would have no trouble at Blanchard's.

The gentleman's club was on a side street, one door down from a busy avenue filled with upper-class shops. Blanchard's had no shingle hanging overhead, nor did it have painted lettering on the windows to indicate what sort of establishment it might be. Its patrons knew its location, and anyone else who required the knowledge would find out by word of mouth.

Seamus knew from experience that Blanchard's rarely opened its curtains, as the men inside were either engaged in talks about business or politics or they were simply seeking respite from the company of their wives. A woman who came to Blanchard's, even a wealthy matron seeking her husband, would be politely asked to wait just inside the door. She would not be asked into the dining area nor would anyone offer to take her wrap or hat. The club was a haven of masculinity. Even the wait staff was all male.

Seamus only knew a few men who had memberships at Blanchard's. Most of the professors at Tulane did not, although a few of the deans and department chairs did. The professors who did have memberships were seeking advancement, presuming that acting like one of the higher-ups would grant them access to the administrative echelons of the university. Seamus had no such aspirations. He had no desire to be promoted out of his laboratory. He had obtained a membership at McCullen's insistence when they first gained positions at the university. McCullen had insisted that they ensconce themselves in their adopted world, taking full advantage of the new start that their fabricated identities allowed them. But Seamus had only come to Blanchard's on rare occasions, being perfectly content to smoke or read or drink in his own home.

Seamus entered the club and a host took his hat, coat and walking stick. The interior of Blanchard's was clean, if dark, and the air was thick with fragrant tobacco smoke. It was the supper hour, and most of the men were eating in small groups, or chatting and enjoying the fine wines and cigars that the establishment provided.

"I am here to see Mr. Oren McCullen. He is not expecting me," Seamus informed the host. Though he was a member, barging in on another guest during a meal would be rude.

"And your name, sir?"

"Mr. Connor."

"And may I inform him of the nature of your visit?"

"Tell him it is a matter of great importance."

The man dipped his head and went through an archway at the back of the room. A few moments later, he reappeared.

"He is ready to see you," the host said.

Seamus was not surprised in the slightest that McCullen was willing to see him. He either knew Seamus would beg to see an engine, which would gratify his enormous sense of pride in his own genius, or he thought that Seamus truly did have something significant to tell him, and needed to satisfy his curiosity.

McCullen sat at a table at the back of a second room. In front of him stood a crystal glass of claret, an open book and a half-finished plate of herb roasted pork, collard greens and potatoes. How McCullen managed to eat potatoes without all manner of terrible thoughts ruining his meal was beyond Seamus. He could not abide the things.

"Mr. Connor," said McCullen, closing his book. He put a slight emphasis on the name, just enough to remind Seamus that he knew his true name. "Please have a seat." McCullen turned to the host. "Another glass for my friend, if you please."

Once the host was out of earshot, Seamus said, "It's about the engines. They're dangerous. Not just the explosions, but something else."

"Have you eaten? I can ask for another plate to be brought out," said McCullen. The second glass of claret arrived and Seamus took it.

"I'm not hungry, thank you." He sipped the claret and set it down. "We need to talk about the engines."

"A little softer, if you please," said McCullen quietly. "Little pitchers have big ears."

There were a few other men in the room, all of whom were silent. Were they just enjoying the quiet or were they listening in? Seamus supposed that most men of influence did not get where they were by being ignorant of the intrigues and secrets of others.

"Would you like to speak in Gaelic then?" Seamus asked quietly.

"Surely not. That would be even worse."

"Ah yes, a savage tongue for a savage people," Seamus quoted one of their English prison guards who had enjoyed beating prisoners for invented offenses. If people heard McCullen speaking another language, it would make him seem more foreign, and that was precisely why McCullen had done his best to lose his accent.

"Will you be attending the ball I am hosting tomorrow evening?" McCullen asked brightly.

"I don't believe I was invited."

"Your invitation must have been misplaced by my secretary. I insist you come. It's going to be the grandest ball ever hosted in this city." He leaned forward, and in a quieter voice said, "I know you haven't attended many, so you will have to trust me that it will be the grandest."

"Why a ball? Are you looking to meet a pretty debutant to marry?" Seamus had never known McCullen to have much interest in seeking a wife, but then, neither had he. Endangering a woman by enticing her into a marriage using a false identity was unconscionable, especially if one had a criminal past.

McCullen said, "Since acquiring my fortune, I have found myself a subject of interest to matrons hoping to marry off their daughters. But no, it is simply for the public enjoyment."

"But the public aren't invited to your grand ball," said Seamus.

"Of course not. The rabble have their Mardi Gras parade, and those of the upper crust have their ball. It's a very simple solution."

"So it's a ball for Mardi Gras?"

"Isn't that what I said? Yes, on Mardi Gras."

"Why such a fuss over the day? It's not as if you are especially devout." McCullen was Catholic, as were all the Irishmen Seamus knew, in name anyway. But the Tuesday preceding Ash Wednesday and the following forty days of penance that comprised Lent had never been significant for McCullen.

"Well, some friends of mine and I thought it would be great fun. Give the people something to look forward to between Christmas and the warmer summer months. And it's one last hoorah before all that righteous sour-faced prayer and fasting that we have to endure until Easter. Some people don't eat meat for the entire forty days. Can you imagine?"

"They haven't seen what we have," said Seamus. "We've fasted enough for ten lifetimes."

"It's not fasting if you have no choice, but yes. I intend to eat as much as I like while I can." McCullen patted his stomach, which had grown a little bit since their time in Mountjoy Prison. All of the prisoners had been gaunt there. Thankfully, the two of them had gotten out before their teeth loosened and they developed permanent physical afflictions.

McCullen looked down into his glass and then drank the last of his claret. Seamus could tell he was remembering other times, perhaps a family. McCullen refused to ever speak of his past before the prison, other than in the barest detail.

"Tell me about this Krewe Taranis," said Seamus.

"Now, I know you wouldn't be interested in such a group. You are far too happy working in your laboratory and too disinterested in amassing a fortune or any social influence. It's almost endearing. A member of the krewe would never be found mucking about with the clockworks in that cathedral of yours. Speaking of which, I have made a decision. The ball will be having an intermission of sorts just before midnight so all the guests can go and see the automaton display."

"I'm honored." Seamus was surprised that McCullen would allow his guests to stop in the middle of their festivities to watch something that he had created. There was something suspicious about it.

"But back to my ball. It's going to have an Egyptian theme, though I wouldn't expect you to dress the part. Although, seeing your lovely friend Miss Sanchez in a gauzy, sleeveless Egyptian gown would be a feast for the senses."

"You leave her be." Seamus was at attention now. The vapid talk about balls and parades had lulled him into complacency. Seamus had been absently sipping at the claret and was half finished. It wasn't enough to cloud his mind, not hardly. It would take much more to get him drunk. But this was a reminder to stay alert.

"Don't be so tense, Seamus. I told you I am not seeking a wife. Although you seem taken with her."

The men around them had returned to their conversations. Seamus spoke very low, so only the two of them would hear. "I didn't come to talk about Miss Sanchez. I came to talk about the engines. Did you know they are ripping holes in time? In the wall between worlds?"

McCullen motioned a server over to refill their glasses.

"The rips, they're marked by shimmers in the air," said Seamus. "Like mirages. They can open and reopen. I was down near the Steamboat Festival site, and I saw one of them. They've reopened, McCullen. Someone could come through from the past or the future."

"And you know this how?" Now McCullen's look was intense, almost frightened. It confused Seamus. What did McCullen have to fear?

"An educated guess. I've seen through one, and if light can pass through, then it stands to reason that matter can also. Did you know that you were using matter from another world when you made the engines?"

"What do you think? Have I ever done things accidentally?"

"Not once," said Seamus. It was true. McCullen had planned his escape from prison from the day he arrived and had planned their new life in New Orleans as soon as he knew they could get to the city. Seamus would be shoveling horse manure in Tasmania had it not been for McCullen's planning.

"You say that you saw these shimmers near the Steamboat Festival site," said McCullen. "What exactly did you see when you looked through it?"

Seamus told him about the man in the metal boat and McCullen's eyebrows raised. "Fascinating," was all he said.

"The rips are unpredictable," said Seamus. "And they

appear to be getting larger, if my calculations are correct."

"They usually are," said McCullen. Seamus was surprised at the compliment. "But with time, don't you think they could be used as doorways?" asked McCullen.

"Are you mad? Taking people from other worlds?"

"No, no. I mean, us, going to somewhere else."

"The ultimate escape," muttered Seamus. "No thank you. I'm quite happy here."

"I have heard of similar doorways," said McCullen. "At a few places. Old stone circles, some hilltops, places like that. Back home."

"Faerie stories for children," snorted Seamus. "Did your wet nurse tell them to you?"

"Don't mock me. Your description, the mirage, doesn't it sound familiar? People out of their own time? Like the faerie stories from our boyhoods. People go to the fairy circle and vanish for years, or forever. And men lost in the deserts of the Sahara, seeing a mirage, buildings, women, things that aren't there, then returning twenty years later. Holes in time."

"Preposterous," said Seamus, but only halfheartedly.

"And if those stories are true, then these shimmers, these holes, are naturally occurring. And if that's true, then they must close on their own. People return to those stone circles and faerie hilltops and never find the doorway again. So they must close safely."

"We have no scientific evidence that those stories are true," said Seamus. "Drunken people get lost, travelers become disoriented."

McCullen was undeterred. "But if they are naturally occurring and if we can create them, then we could harness them. Just as lightning is untamed electricity, but we can make batteries that generate electrical current, so too we could find out how to use these rips."

"Ripping doorways in time is the work of a madman. Only a fool would think that he could control them. If even one person accidentally came through, it would be terrible."

"You seem terribly concerned with people accidentally falling through. It's not as if we would set up a doorway and then walk away. Besides, these people who fall through the naturally occurring holes, they never get home. People vanish every year, from big cities, from little villages. They just vanish. What if some could find their way home?"

McCullen was watching his reaction too closely. This conversation was getting far too close to reality and Miss Sanchez.

"Just promise me something," said Seamus. "Stop selling more engines until we understand how the time rips work."

"Oh no, I won't do that. Not when we are so close."

"We?"

"You're a countryman, so yes, we."

"Close to what?" asked Seamus.

"The engines create so much energy. I'm working on improving them currently to do even more. Come work with me. Together, we can make weapons that will wipe the English pigs off the map. And if we planned it correctly, our country wouldn't have to fight alone."

"A war?" said Seamus. A war was coming, but was this how it was to start?

"If you like. This country's war would simply be the first act of the play. In addition, we can use our natural advantage over the common man to make ourselves wealthy, influential, whatever we liked. You could go home, see your family. Maybe there is a pretty girl waiting?"

"There is no girl," he said, but a few faces flashed through his mind, girls back in Ireland who he had loved, or liked well enough. They would all be married by now, with gaggles of little ones pulling at their skirts.

"Your Miss Sanchez, then. Wouldn't she like some pretty things? A house even grander than yours? Jewelry?

Servants and a fine carriage? They think it makes them look greedy to admit it, but women desire these things."

"I didn't come for courting advice. Nor am I interested in causing a war or ripping holes in time. Honestly, man, you intend to use your engines for this purpose?"

"Not solely, no," said McCullen. "The engines could do so much for the poor, the working classes. Would your father have liked a self-propelled plow? And would your mother like a machine that washes clothing?"

"A clothes washer with an engine?" Seamus had to stop himself from laughing. "And what, a steam-powered octopus that waves the clothing in the wind to dry?"

"Whatever we could imagine. And I think I could imagine quite a lot."

"You were ever the man with the ideas."

"I need you, Seamus."

"Then perhaps you shouldn't have had me arrested. And refused to share information on the engines."

"How did you figure out the engine? I must know."

"I need to be going. Please consider ceasing engine production. If you do, I may consider working with you again."

"I will consider it, as long as you consider my thoughts on the English."

"Very well," Seamus said. But he knew he would not. He could not use his talents to create weapons. He refused to hurt a man unless it was in self-defense. He and McCullen could arm the Irish. But then, giving arms to his countrymen, in itself, would be an invitation to war. His people would not hesitate to use their advantage to fight against those who had tormented them for so long. No, the weapons could never be made, not with his help. Seamus finished off his claret and stood. McCullen stood as well, and Seamus was mildly surprised at the show of equality.

McCullen offered his hand. "Perhaps next year's ball

and parade will have a Chinese theme. With fireworks."
He smiled a little, contemplating the thought. "Your
Miss Sanchez could come. I've heard that they bind the
feet of women in China, and your Miss Sanchez has the
tiniest feet."

CHAPTER 27

"YOU DIDN'T NEED TO COME with me for this," the Professor said. Hazel didn't know if he was speaking to her or to Miss Sanchez. "You can go home right now if you like."

"We don't mind, right, Miss Sanchez?" Hazel said, glancing at her hopefully.

Miss Sanchez agreed. Hazel knew that it would cost the Professor extra to have their coach wait for them while they visited St. Louis Cathedral, but Hazel felt better staying with both Miss Sanchez and the Professor. The coach was partially filled with parcels of clothing. The Professor had insisted that Hazel get girl's clothing instead of running about in trousers. He also insisted that Miss Sanchez buy a ball gown for some big party the following night. Hazel knew that Miss Sanchez already had a pretty gown, but Seamus had hated it because it was from McCullen.

The Professor hadn't been thrilled to accompany two females on a shopping trip and had spent a good part of the day leaning against the wall with his arms crossed. Occasionally, he had pulled out a notebook and jotted down some equation or idea. Hazel was glad he was there, and she was unspeakably grateful that he had not said anything when he caught her scanning the street for her uncle.

"Are you okay, Hazel?" asked Miss Sanchez as they crossed the square. Hazel had learned what "okay" meant, since Miss Sanchez used the term frequently. "We can go straight home if you like."

"I'm all right. He won't be here. He goes to Mass, but would never set foot in a church any other time." Hazel tugged at her dress. It was soft cotton, in a pale blue shade with minimal ruffles. It was not uncomfortable, but she felt strange in it.

"I'm going to take a look at my wee babbies," said Seamus "They've been neglected." He rushed into the cathedral, perhaps grateful to be away from all the ribbons and frippery. He would be upstairs with Brother Joe while she and Miss Sanchez stayed below.

"What is he looking for?" asked Hazel.

"McCullen is letting all of the people who attend his ball come here to see the midnight automaton show," said Miss Sanchez. "The Professor is suspicious that he's planning something with the cathedral. And the show is tomorrow night, so he has to make sure the machines are all in order. Brother Joe can set them up, but the Professor wants to look them over."

"All this is for Mardi Gras? That's so strange," said Hazel.

"In my world, there is a huge parade with parties and drinking for Mardi Gras."

An infant idea stirred in Hazel's mind, but it did not coalesce. Miss Sanchez pulled open the heavy wooden front door and they entered the dark, cool interior of the cathedral. The church was of the standard shape, with two rows of pews on either side of a tiled aisle. The pews were old and worn from decades of use, but the sisters managed to keep them clean. Hazel scanned the pews and corners for people. They were alone.

Two upper galleries ran along either side of the church with two rows of gilded Corinthian columns supporting them. The outermost halves of each set of pews were under the gallery overhangs. Over the main aisle stretched a long arched ceiling with medallion-shaped paintings of Christ, the apostles and various saints, surrounded by ornate golden frames. Hazel had spent many an hour staring at them or at the stained glass windows. To one side was St. Blanche and St. Cecilia and, of course, various scenes from the life of St. Louis himself. On the other side of the church were scenes from the life of Christ. Miss Sanchez paused before the picture of the sacred fire of the Holy Ghost raining down upon the saints and the Blessed Mother.

"When I was your age, I never understood the whole, 'tongues of flame' thing," Miss Sanchez said. "Such a weird idea."

Hazel didn't know what to say. She had never given it much thought. It was simply another theological mystery to her. Miss Sanchez moved on to get a good look at the Rococo altar and at the retablo, the wall behind it. The retablo was gilded and full of little niches for statues and paintings. Miss Sanchez contemplated the items in silence, her lips pressed tightly together and her eyes narrowed. Hazel turned to look back toward the entrance of the church.

"A few weeks ago, I heard that they were going to be putting in a new steam organ," Hazel whispered. "I haven't heard it played yet. The music is my favorite part of church."

"Do you play the organ?"

"No. I learned a little piano before I found that I liked the violin best."

"Have you asked the Professor for a new one?"

"No, of course not."

"It never even occurred to you, did it?" asked Miss Sanchez, giving her a sidelong look. The idea made Hazel uncomfortable. The Professor's kindness and generosity were already more than she deserved. Asking for anything more would be churlish and the height of selfishness.

"Maybe you shouldn't go home," Hazel said. "You would have a good life with the Professor. He likes you."

"He feels responsibility for me. Like he does with you."

"No. Mrs. Washington said that you're good for him, and I agree with her. He's happier. He swears and drinks less and spends less time in his laboratory."

"That's because he's been running around, getting in trouble on my behalf."

"But you like him. Don't you think he's good looking?"

"What are you asking me that for?" Miss Sanchez's voice had risen and Hazel was glad the church was empty.

"I've heard a few women say as much. And I have eyes in my head. I don't like boys much, yet, but I know what handsome looks like."

"Let's drop it, okay?"

"I hope you don't go home."

"Why would you say something like that?" Miss Sanchez looked hurt.

"Should I lie? I want you to stay. And besides, just because you come from somewhere doesn't mean that it's where you should stay. Maybe God didn't want you in that time anymore." Hazel glanced toward the crucifix.

"I hardly think God had anything to do with it. It was a freak accident of science."

"An accident," muttered Hazel. The same thought tickled in her mind again. She wandered around the church while Miss Sanchez studied the stained glass windows. After a while, Hazel's thoughts formed into something coherent.

"The Professor said you came through to our time in front of his house when there was an omnibus accident."

"That's right."

"So you were just walking and you fell through?"

"No. I was on a bus. A motor bus. Not steam powered, but sort of like the ones you have. And I saw the shimmer in the air, and then there was a man from your time who was thrown from a horse. I wanted to help him. My bus crashed somehow into the omnibus, and I found myself here."

"So your bus was traveling in the same space as the omnibus, but in different worlds?"

"I suppose. Yes. And then two parts of time intersected."
Miss Sanchez's eyes scanned the ceiling.

"And where the Delphia Queen was docked, do you
have ships there?"

"Yes. There are ships there."

"So it happens where things are the same on both sides
of the time rip."

"My God, Hazel." Miss Sanchez looked at her in
astonishment when a door opened at the far front corner
of the church and the Professor stepped out.

"She's figured it out!" said Miss Sanchez, rushing to
him. Hazel watched the Professor's face light up when he
saw Miss Sanchez.

"Figured what out?" he asked.

"Tell him, Hazel."

"In Miss Sanchez's world, the omnibus and her motor
bus were in the same place. And the river has ships in both
times. I think that's why the rips formed in those places."

"Similar things happening on both sides of the doors?"
Seamus muttered. "Could be."

"A synchronicity," said Miss Sanchez.

"What an interesting word," the Professor said. "But
never mind that. If McCullen was right, then those stone
circles and hilltops, they'd have people repeating actions
there through the years. People walking the same paths.
Desert caravan routes also have people moving in repeating
patterns. Yes, synchronicities."

"And Mardi Gras will be the biggest synchronicity of
all," said Miss Sanchez. "People traveling the same streets,
the floats."

"Floats full of McCullen's engines," added Hazel.

"But how would McCullen know about Mardi Gras in
your time?" said the Professor. "Unless he's fooling me.
He's a perfect liar. But he has no reason to open more
rips. There has to be something else."

The Professor headed down the aisle toward the doors

and Felicia and Hazel trailed behind. As she got closer to the front of the church, Hazel looked up and saw the organ.

"Professor? We should look at the organ."

"Why is that?"

"They put in a new one."

"Why would that matter?" asked Miss Sanchez.

"There are engines that run the air pumps," said the Professor. He turned away from her and dashed around to one side, taking the stairs two at a time. Hazel sprang up the stairs behind him and knelt to see what he was looking at underneath the keyboard.

The Professor sent her to fetch Brother Joe and amid the brother's protests, the Professor removed the organ's covers and poked around inside. After taking forever looking through the parts, the Professor collapsed on the bench and sighed.

"There's nothing there."

"Of course there's nothing. And you're not taking my organ apart any more than that with Ash Wednesday coming up," said Brother Joe. "Now help me put this back together."

The Professor grumblingly obeyed and twenty minutes later, he, Miss Sanchez and Hazel were back in their coach. Hazel didn't talk, as both adults were deep in thought.

When they arrived home, supper was nearly ready. Mrs. Washington had prepared a glazed ham with roasted carrots and green beans and a hot loaf of fresh bread with butter.

"Mr. Grey will be coming by after supper," said the Professor to Hazel. "Would you like me to tell him your idea, or would you prefer to?"

So the Professor had noticed that she was uncomfortable around Mr. Grey. There was nothing wrong with the man, only the way he had looked at her the first time they had met still bothered her. It was as if he recognized her. Well, if he had recognized her somehow, it didn't matter now.

Everyone knew her name and that she was a girl. There was something else about him, but again, she felt like her brain wasn't working fully. She couldn't remember something.

"You can tell him," Hazel said. "But I want to stay and listen." She refused to let the Professor coddle her, and she intended to look Mr. Grey straight in the eye. Something about speaking to her uncle in that coach made her less afraid of things. She had faced the devil himself and had spat in his eye. She was still terrified of her uncle, but something in her had changed since then.

For some reason, she remembered the alfalfa seeds her mother had let her plant in a cup and set on the kitchen windowsill. For days, the dark earth had sat there, damp and empty. And then one day after lunch, she leaned over the sink to peek over the edge of the cup and a tiny green point, almost invisible, had appeared. Something had been happening under the soil all along, her mother had told her. But she had not believed it until she had seen the sprout.

"Oh, and Hazel," said the Professor. "I sent a note off to the headmaster of St. Gerard's to see about enrolling you. It's only February, so you'll have a few months to attend before you're out for the summer. The school is only a few blocks away, and you can walk."

Hazel had attended a school across town when she had lived with her aunt and uncle. A new school would mean new teachers and new children who didn't know her and would not ask a lot of questions. Yes, a new school would do.

After the supper dishes were cleared and Mrs. Washington started the coffee, there was a knock at the front door.

"So Mr. Grey is using the front door now," said the Professor, rising. "I may yet run a civilized household." He gave Hazel a wink and went to answer the door.

"Hazel, would you lay these out?" asked Mrs.

Washington. She had a few remaining butter cookies along with a quarter of an almond cake with sugar glaze. Hazel got to work arranging the items on a plate while Miss Sanchez set out the cups. Hazel noticed that she had included one for Mrs. Washington, though she would not be joining them in the front room. Working with the two women was pleasant, even if Miss Sanchez had trouble finding things or was so addle-minded that she didn't know how to make coffee.

Not for the first time, she wondered about the world from which Miss Sanchez had come. Women could be doctors and do anything they liked. They didn't even have to marry if they didn't want to. That sounded good to her. Hazel imagined owning her own little white house with a vegetable garden in back and some pretty gingham curtains in the kitchen. Was that what she wanted? Something about it was unsatisfying.

She jumped when someone knocked at the back kitchen door. Miss Sanchez went to answer it.

"Mr. Grey! I thought you were at the front door," Miss Sanchez said.

"Hazel," said Mrs. Washington. "Would you please take that plate into the front room?"

Hazel took the plate through the kitchen door and was walking down the hall when she heard his voice. Her thoughts snapped into panic. Her uncle. He was here. She stood frozen, the plate of cookies and cake forgotten. She backed up and bumped into Mr. Grey who must have followed her.

"Excuse me. I'm sorry," he said behind her. She spun around and watched his face change when he looked at her. "What's wrong?" he asked. "Are you okay?"

Another thought slammed into her at his last word. The plate was gone from her hands, but she saw that Mr. Grey had taken it. Had she been about to drop it?

"He's at the door," she whispered.

Mr. Grey took off toward the door without a word. Hazel's breath was coming hard and she felt sick to her stomach. Her armpits and palms were wet and cold. She stood in the hallway, straining to hear but couldn't make anything out. The door to the front hallway was closed.

She could run back to the kitchen, back to Mrs. Washington and Miss Sanchez. They would comfort her. Or she could go see what the men were saying. She thought of the little green shoot in the cup and wiped her palms on her dress.

She pushed the door to the front hallway open a crack so she could listen. The door would be partially in her uncle's line of sight, and she hoped he wouldn't look too closely into the depths of the house.

"You need to leave immediately," she heard Mr. Grey say.

"You're threatening me with a plate of cookies in your hand?" said her uncle in a mocking voice.

"Not threatening, no," said Mr. Grey.

"Well, I am threatening," said the Professor. "I'll stuff the cookies down your ugly gullet, shatter the plate on your head and slit your throat with the shards. Now get out."

"A moment, please," said Mr. Grey. His voice was cool and even.

Silence stretched on until Hazel's curiosity was driving her mad. She had not heard the front door close. Did she dare to open the door further and peek out? She counted to three, and then pushed it open, darting sideways around a corner and out of view of the front door. It was light in the front hall and she heard street sounds, which meant the front door was still open. She got down on all fours and peeked around the corner near the ground. She knew from her time sneaking around abandoned buildings that people, adults especially, tended to look right at their eye level for other people. Staying low could mean the difference between discovery and staying hidden.

Out on the front walk, Mr. Grey and her uncle were

speaking. Her uncle looked furious. Mr. Grey had his back to her and still held the plate of cake and cookies. If she hadn't known better, she might have thought they were neighbors, having a chat about a broken fence or a loose pet. The Professor walked back toward the house, scowling. He slammed the door behind him and muttered Gaelic curses.

Hazel got up and stepped out. He caught sight of her.

"So, you listened in? Is this going to become a habit with you?" he asked.

"It was my uncle so I'm allowed to listen. And I didn't hear anything anyway. Only you telling him you'd cut his throat with a cake plate."

"But that I could, lass. But that I could."

The Professor ran his hands through his hair, turned toward the staircase and sat down on the second step. He leaned his head forward into his hands.

"What is it?" asked Hazel.

"Nothing of your concern."

"Yes it is. It has to do with me, so it's my concern."

"You're a fierce little thing, but I can handle this."

"My uncle said something, didn't he? Did he threaten you? He's a lawyer and he said that with grease in the right hands, you can make anything happen."

"I think you mean if you grease the right palms."

"Fine, palms. What did he say to you?"

"Let it be, child," he said. He refused to answer any of her questions and just sat, periodically glancing at the door. Finally, the front door opened and he jumped up.

"He won't come back," Mr. Grey said to both Hazel and the Professor.

"What did you say to him?" she asked.

Mr. Grey didn't answer, but looked down at the plate of cake and cookies. "Where should I put this?"

The Professor waved his hand to indicate that he didn't care where the plate went. "Hazel, you need to go back to the kitchen for a few minutes."

"I will not. I have a right to hear this," said Hazel. She wasn't about to let the adults talk about her situation without her.

"I said, go back to the kitchen." The Professor turned toward her and pointed at the kitchen door. "Now."

"I'm staying."

The Professor took a step toward her, his face dark with anger at being defied, but she knew better than to think he would strike her. He might physically drag her to the kitchen, but she'd take her chances.

"If you live in my house, you will do as I say. And I say that I need to talk to Mr. Grey alone for a minute. You'll go to the kitchen immediately."

"Like hell, Professor."

Mr. Grey was shaking, and when Hazel glanced at him, she saw he was laughing. She had never seen the man smile, and his face was so different. All of a sudden, he looked pleasant and alive. The Professor turned to him.

"Is this humorous to you, Mr. Grey?"

"Leave him be," said Hazel. "It's my fault that my uncle is here. I did something inexcusably stupid. I said your name when he came to get me at the hospital. That's how he found you. It was the stupidest thing I've done."

"No, the stupidest thing is not listening to me. Now give me a moment with Mr. Grey."

The Professor was not going to budge. She decided to try a different tactic.

"Mr. Grey. What time are you from? Somewhere near Miss Sanchez's time?"

Mr. Grey had only just stopped laughing, but for some reason, her words made him laugh again. Even stranger, he looked as if he was proud of her.

CHAPTER 28

T HE NEXT NIGHT, FELICIA LAID her new ball gown across her bedspread and pulled at it until it was straight. The fabric was a rich cream satin with coordinating lace trim. It hadn't been exactly what she had wanted when she went to the shop, but once again, she was rushed to find a dress and she took what the dressmaker was able to finish up on short notice.

Her mobile phone had been sitting dead on her nightstand for days, but she wasn't ready to put it in a drawer just yet. It made her room feel more like home. She could no longer listen to the messages from her mother and sister, nor could she view the pictures she had taken of her family and friends. Everything was gone. All she had left were her memories.

Were her mother and father worried, crying, wondering if their daughter was kidnapped or murdered? Was her nephew getting worse, or was he already dead? The thought took her breath away. The loss of her nephew and her own disappearance would devastate the entire family. She wondered if anyone had called the police yet to report her missing.

She cursed herself. If only she had told someone about the Brazilian doctor's treatments, then someone could put him in touch with Nathan's mother. Or she could have told the doctor her nephew's name and his hospital. But no, she had wanted to protect her family from false hope, and now they would pay the price for her excessive caution.

Her purse lay on the floor beside the bed, and she dug around until she found her makeup. A little black mascara, some powder on her nose and a little rose-colored lipstick and she felt more prepared.

She wished she had paid more attention to history and to Doug and his science fiction movies. She wondered if her old housemate would have any ideas about time travel. She knew that Einstein had an idea about time passing more slowly when you travel near the speed of light, but she had never understood the theory of relativity, even when a friend in class had attempted to explain it to her. The human nervous system, organs and skeletal structures made sense. They were concrete things.

She pulled the dress over her head and left it untied. Then she called for Mrs. Washington to tighten her corset and then fasten the row of tiny white pearl buttons up the back of the dress.

Felicia had learned a lot about the role of servants during her stay, and had noticed how the housekeeper kept to herself and rarely chatted unless Felicia started the conversation. Mrs. Washington was smart, and certainly knew that something strange was going on in the house, but she asked no questions and even seemed to actively remain ignorant by slipping out of the room during spots in the conversation when either Seamus, Hazel or herself said something strange.

"It's a little low, don't you think?" Felicia asked Mrs. Washington after she was laced and fluffed. She tugged at the bodice of the dress which was too low cut for comfort. The corset pushed her breasts up and together, creating some impressive cleavage, but a few inches of her skin were covered with only a thin rectangle of lace. She was technically decent, but the dress seemed racy for this time, she thought. It was racy for her own.

Mrs. Washington moved around to look at Felicia from the front and chewed her lower lip. Felicia knew that she would give her honest opinion, and she was grateful for it.

"It is a tad low, but you'd be surprised what some of these society types wear. If a woman of my station showed that much flesh, we'd be called a name. But let the rich ladies do it, and it's fashionable and daring."

"I don't know if I like it," said Felicia. She tried to push the corset up and wiggle her chest to get more of herself covered.

"No, no leave it. McCullen might like it."

"I'm not interested in impressing McCullen."

"Oh no, I didn't mean that," said Mrs. Washington. "I know he's an odious man. Only, you two aren't going to McCullen's ball for a lark, I know that. I know you are a good girl, but a woman can sometimes use what the good Lord gave her. You know what I mean?"

"I suppose," said Felicia.

"Here, let me fix your hair," said Mrs. Washington.

Felicia had always despised the idea of dressing provocatively to get men to pay attention to her or to manipulate them. But then, if she wore this dress and McCullen was somehow charmed by her, he just might listen to sense and stop selling the engines. Or she could find out what he was up to with the Mardi Gras festivities.

When Mrs. Washington finished, Felicia's hair was held up with a number of pearl-topped pins. A cameo pendant dangled from a cream ribbon and modest pearl earrings hung from her ears. The light dress made her skin look darker in contrast, but then, if she was going for daring, she didn't want to look like all of the fair Southern belles anyway.

She turned, feeling the sway of the heavy skirt as it moved side to side with its own inertia. The bodice of the dress, aside from the lace trim, was relatively plain. The skirt, however, was covered in lace and flounces and had bows held up gathers of material, exposing triangles of the layer of lace lining beneath. Was it meant to look like she was showing her crinolines? She sighed. Since when had she become so modest in her appearance? She had walked down the streets in blue jeans and now worried about the modesty of a floor-length dress.

She went downstairs and found Seamus beside the stairs, kneeling over a leather case, sorting through various mechanical devices.

"Ah Miss Sanchez," he said, looking up. "I uh. I wanted to ask—" He stared at her with embarrassing intensity, and then looked back down at his case. "I er, wanted to make sure you had enough money with you if we happen to be separated."

"Oh, let me grab my purse." She hurried back to her room and grabbed the tiny satin purse that she had bought with the dress. It hung from a ridiculously thin string and a little metal clasp held it closed. It was for formal use only, but even ladies in the past needed to have a few things for a ball. She tossed in her lipstick and compact and headed back downstairs.

Seamus had finished with his little devices, and his closed case rested on the claw-footed entryway table. He stood, and Felicia paused to get a good look at him. He looked pleasantly unfamiliar in his fine clothing. This was more than his Sunday best; this must be the finest clothing he owned. He was in a black tuxedo with a silver cravat tied in some kind of elaborate rectangular design. His coat had tails, and the lean cut of it emphasized the width of his shoulders and his slim hips, as well as his height. Being indoors, he was hatless, and his hair was slicked back with pomade. It still curled up in an unruly fashion along his collar, and Felicia thought that she would have preferred his usual mussed and wild appearance to this formal one. But since when did she have any opinion on the Professor's hair?

"You look very nice," he said, inclining his head slightly and a tad too formally. He handed her a few folded bills and she thanked him and slipped them into her purse. It galled her to take money, like a kept woman, but she had enough sense not to dwell on it.

Mr. Grey pulled a wheeled trunk down the front hall. Hazel trailed behind.

"If you won't tell me what you said to him, at least tell me why you talked to him at all," said Hazel. She was dressed in her boy clothes and Felicia had to admit to herself that the girl looked much more natural and comfortable that way.

"Because I need your help today," said Mr. Grey. "And it wouldn't do to have you shut away in that man's house across town."

"I said I'd help you already, and now you need to do something for me and tell me," Hazel said and then she spied Felicia. "Oh, that reminds me!" The girl rushed off.

"What do you have planned for her?" Felicia asked Mr. Grey. "Nothing dangerous, I hope."

"No. Mr. Connor has given me equipment to set up near the cathedral, and Hazel is going to help me. Better to give her something safe to do. I doubt she'd be able to keep herself in the house if we left her. I'll watch out for her."

Felicia wasn't particularly satisfied with that answer, but he was probably correct. Hazel wanted to see the Professor's midnight clockwork show, and more importantly, she knew something else was likely to happen at the cathedral. Besides, she'd sneak out if they left her home alone.

Hazel came down the hall with a freshly picked stem of sweet Joe Pye weed, presumably from the backyard. It was a sickly sort of lavender color with hundreds of tiny spiky petals, and Hazel walked straight up to Seamus with it.

"For your buttonhole," she said.

To his credit, he did not refuse the ugly plant, but allowed her to slip the stem through his buttonhole. The flower was too large and strange-looking to be a proper decoration for a ball, but Seamus stood up and pulled his coat straight. Hazel nodded in approval.

Hazel and Mr. Grey lugged the wheeled trunk of machinery to the hired carriage and Seamus tossed his leather case onto the seat. He had hired a fancy carriage since the two of them would be appearing at the ball in it. Felicia wondered if the thing was the equivalent of a limousine in her own time. It hardly mattered. What was important was getting to McCullen and finding out what he had planned for Mardi Gras besides the innocent festivities. The formal invitation that had arrived the previous afternoon indicated that the event was to take place at a ballroom in the French Quarter. It would allow the partygoers to walk to Jackson Square for the automaton display and then return to the ball to dance until dawn, drunkenness or exhaustion overtook them.

As the carriage reached the edges of the French Quarter and drove down Dauphine Street, the crowd grew thicker and thicker until the carriage pulled to a full stop. The driver managed to turn around and get away from the crowds, but while trying to move down Burgundy Street, they again were held up by the throngs of people. The driver slid open the little hatch near his seat and leaned down.

"You want me to leave you here? It's that or we drive all the way around and go down Ursulines Avenue. But I don't think I can get to Jackson Square at all."

"Here will do," said Seamus. The four climbed out and Mr. Grey pulled out his wheeled trunk. Seamus paid the driver, who had to get off his seat and lead his mare by her bridle to get her turned around. He jumped back into his seat and cursed at a cart that stopped directly in front of him.

The crowd gathered for the first official Mardi Gras had taken the spirit of celebration to heart. It was full dark now, but the streets were illuminated with gaslights, hanging purple and yellow paper lamps and hand-held lanterns carried by merrymakers. Here and there were carts selling coffee, lemonade, pastries, apple turnovers or toasted sugar almonds served in paper cones. Once they reached Bourbon Street, Hazel stopped at a nearby booth carrying little colored flags and mechanical toys.

"Look," she said and pressed a tiny button on the side of a crocodile. Its mouth opened slowly and then snapped shut while its eyes glowed red. The eyes did not dim while Hazel picked up another, this one a sleek black cat with green eyes. It gave a metallic meow and its paw waved up and down.

"How do the eyes glow?" Felicia asked Seamus.

"A tiny battery generates an electrical signal," he said. But he sounded distracted. The booth was doing a brisk business, and Seamus scooped up a crocodile, a cat and a hawk and paid the proprietor.

Felicia saw Hazel look at him hopefully, thinking he had bought them for her, but he turned aside and led them down a side street. The crowd was thick, but they could stand up against a wall without being elbowed and shoved. Mr. Grey rolled the trunk against the wall and sat on it. Seamus gestured to offer Felicia the other end of the trunk, but it was too low to risk soiling her gown, so she declined.

Seamus dug through his leather case, but didn't find whatever it was he was searching for. Hazel picked up the hawk and was making it screech and flap its wings.

"Don't get too attached to it," Seamus said. "I'm going to disassemble it in a moment."

"But why? I like it, and you have those two," said Hazel.

"Because I have an idea. Now, I need something small and thin, like a needle," he said. He narrowed his eyes and scanned the street, but most of the shops were closed. The only ones open were ones that could sell food or beverages or little strings of beads and trinkets for the parade. "Or a pin!" He jumped up and faced Felicia. "May I?" he asked.

"My pins?" she said. It had taken Mrs. Washington so

long to do her hair. She knew it was silly to resist, but she didn't want her careful hairdo undone. "Fine. But try not to mess it up too much." She untied her bonnet and carefully removed it.

Seamus reached hesitatingly for one pin, then changed his mind and moved to another. "I don't know which to take," he said.

Felicia reached up, grabbed a random pin and pulled. Her hair shifted, and a long tendril fell and curled past her collarbone, the end resting on the top of her breast. From the corner of her eye, she saw Seamus look down and a little thrill went through her. A moment later he had taken the pin and was back on his trunk, bent over the mechanical crocodile.

"I understand!" said Hazel. "These are all Egyptian animals. Is that right?"

"At the far end of that booth, I saw a little gold sarcophagus," said Mr. Grey. "But someone bought it."

"Do you suppose it opened?" said Hazel.

"Got it!" said Seamus. "I knew it!" He held aloft the tiniest glass tube Felicia had ever seen. It was filled with less than a drop of glowing blue fluid.

"A McCullen engine in miniature?" she whispered.

"Thousands of them, and sold so cheaply that even the poorest citizens can purchase one. Can you imagine all the children, the people, pressing these buttons over and over?"

"Even if we managed to stop the floats, all of these tiny engines will still be going."

"That's one third of the question answered then," said Seamus.

"What are the other two thirds of the question?" asked Felicia. But Seamus was tearing apart the tiny cat and wasn't listening.

Mr. Grey waited before saying, "What signal is being transmitted, and to whom?"

It was nine o'clock at night already, which meant the parade was already starting somewhere. It would snake through the French Quarter and end at the cathedral about an hour and a half later. By then, the ball would be in full swing until nearly midnight.

"Look at it while we walk," said Felicia to Seamus. "Or we're going to miss everything."

Felicia and Mr. Grey led the way, parting the crowd so Seamus could examine the tiny devices as he trailed behind. They turned down St. Peter Street and once they reached Jackson Square, they found a spot that wasn't too crowded. Mr. Grey opened the trunk and began working on assembling one of the devices contained within.

"I'm a daft bloody idiot!" Seamus yelled.

Felicia couldn't stop herself from laughing and he looked at her in surprise.

"Energy," the Professor said. "McCullen has always been the idea man. He told me that some day, he wanted to work on a way to send energy from one place to another."

"Like over electrical lines?" asked Miss Sanchez. "We use those. They send electricity through wires. We run them on poles or underground."

"McCullen talked about doing it without wires, sending energy through the air."

"My people can't even do that," said Miss Sanchez.

"There was a man," said Mr. Grey as he worked on the device. "He claimed he could send electricity through the air without harming anyone. He managed to illuminate lamps at the Chicago World Fair without using wires."

"And what year was that?" asked Hazel in a casual tone.

"Eighteen ninety-three," he said, looking her straight in the eye.

She grinned with delight and hopped up and down. "I knew it! Ha! You're from eighteen ninety-three!"

"No," he said. "I wasn't even born yet."

"From after that? From Miss Sanchez's time?"

"Later, Hazel, if you please," said Seamus as he worked on assisting Mr. Grey. "If he's transmitting power, then my tripod sensors will detect it. You should set them up, say, there," he pointed, "there and there." Seamus gave Mr. Grey other instructions and Hazel stood by his side, listening raptly and nodding in unison with the man as if taking the instructions herself. Felicia was glad to see that Hazel seemed to have gotten over any apprehension she had about Mr. Grey, although she herself didn't fully trust the man. He had known she was from another time, yet had kept his own state a secret, forced Seamus to help him and had generally been too secretive to be trustworthy.

The moment Seamus picked up his leather case and offered his arm to Felicia, Hazel started peppering Mr. Grey with questions. Felicia took Seamus's arm, and his proximity was both familiar and a little uncomfortable, but in a pleasant way. Even through his sleeve, he felt warm. He gave her a little smile before they started in the direction of the ball.

Felicia didn't hear Hazel's last question, but she did hear Mr. Grey's answer.

"There are others, yes," he said.

CHAPTER 29

SEAMUS CHECKED ON MISS SANCHEZ as they pushed through the masses of people separating them from the ballroom several streets away. The sidewalks were clogged with all manner of carts and vendors selling food, flowers, paper pinwheels and ribbons on sticks for children to wave. The owners of the carts with the little mechanical animals were selling the creatures as quickly as they could take the money for them.

A group of children leaned over the railing of a home's upper gallery, tossing bits of colored paper over the side. It drifted down like snow onto the people below and clung in their hair. The wrought iron railings themselves were festooned with ribbons and paper banners, and colored glass bottles hung by their necks. They sparkled emerald, ruby and topaz in the lamplight. How had McCullen gotten so many people to take part in his parade? Was it all a matter of funding it, or were the people of New Orleans so starved for some excitement?

When they could no longer walk side-by-side, Seamus took Miss Sanchez's hand and led her along, parting the crowd so she would not be jostled too badly. Her hand, which was so small and delicate, was warm and soft and he found his mind wandering to other parts of her exposed skin that were also warm and soft. He tried to distract himself by focusing on getting them through the crowd.

A shout rose from the people up ahead, and Seamus caught sight of the first float. He turned to point it out to

Miss Sanchez, but she had already seen it. Her skin was lit softly by the glow of the overhead lanterns, and her eyes glowed amber in this light, giving her an otherworldly look, like a dark fae maiden, come to dance in the firelight. Her lips, darkened by a bit of cosmetics, were parted. They were full without being overtly sensual, and they turned up at the corners, just a little. She was listening to a strolling band, enjoying herself. A little glow of warmth filled Seamus at the thought.

Before the float reached them, rows of dancers and acrobats tumbled and whirled into view. Female dancers spun and bobbed while trailing gauzy red and yellow scarves through the air. Male acrobats with bells on their ankles and wrists flipped and cartwheeled, even stopping to make a human pyramid. Drummers and tambourine players beat out a rhythm and the people clapped and whooped. The air pulsed with the sound of drums. Miss Sanchez, much to his disappointment, pulled her hand from his in order to clap along. But after a minute, she slipped it back into his. He stepped closer to her so her shoulder touched his arm.

The first float was in the shape of a giant crocodile, and like the little toy, its mouth gaped open. A willowy young woman sat inside its jaws, dressed all in gossamer greens and pale blues. Seamus thought she looked like a water spirit. She waved and tossed trinkets to the crowd. Gaslight torches flickered on either side of the crocodile's long body, the flames dancing. The engine beneath the float rumbled, and he thought he spied the little window through which the driver must be looking.

Seamus gave a gentle pull on Miss Sanchez's hand. They needed to get to the ball if they were going to have any chance of speaking with McCullen. Miss Sanchez followed, but he felt her pull back a time or two when a particularly interesting float went by. It looked like the little toys were made to be souvenirs of the parade, as a regal black cat and a flower-garlanded ox went by. Later on came a hawk, a jackal and a white bull. All of them were decorated in an Egyptian style.

Half an hour later, Seamus and Miss Sanchez had only progressed a few blocks. A huge float approached, a Nile barge with enormous sails and rows of automated oars swaying back and forth. A man sat on one of two golden thrones on its deck. A scalloped purple and gold canopy held up by four posts hung over the thrones, though there was no sun from which to be shielded. Two men and two women waved giant palm fans and periodically reached into baskets to toss trinkets to the crowd. On either side of the barge, a white staircase led from the barge's deck to street level, and two women in Egyptian costumes descended, waving, and then sashayed slowly back up. All of the women on the float had black plaited wigs with gold headbands and bracelets up their arms. Their dresses were the white, form-fitting sleeveless things that McCullen had said he liked.

"That's him," Seamus said to Miss Sanchez. "It's McCullen."

"Where?" she asked, tiptoeing to catch a glimpse of the distant float. She was not as tall as he was and could not see over the crowd as easily.

McCullen sat on the throne, dressed in purple with a golden crown upon his head. For an imitation crown at a gaudy parade, it was surprisingly modest, as if he somehow wanted to display his humility with it. He was a king of the people, happy to share his largesse.

Miss Sanchez caught sight of him. "He's the king of the Mardi Gras," she said. "And he'll be selecting a queen."

The float stopped before them. The two women who had been climbing up and down the stairs retreated to flank McCullen. He stood and waved slowly to the people on both sides of the street.

"It is time, my good people," McCullen said, pronouncing

each word in a perfect American accent, "to choose my queen. The Queen of the Mardi Gras!" He threw his hands up over his head and the crowd stomped and screamed. He moved down the stairs on Seamus's side of the street. "But there are so many beautiful ladies here tonight. How shall I choose?"

"Choose her!" someone yelled and pointed at a woman nearby. The crowd pulled away from her, and she looked around, her cheeks reddening. A second woman staggered forward, already drunk from the festivities. The crowd roared their approval. She clapped in glee, either oblivious to their mocking or enjoying the attention, Seamus could not tell. Other women came forward or were pushed forward, until eight stood before the float. McCullen took a turn kissing each of their hands and looking deep into their eyes. He displayed the right amount of sincerity to make him look like he enjoyed the task, while the whole display was overdone just enough to excite the crowd.

"There were girls at the mummy party who acted like they'd love to be queen," said Miss Sanchez. "I wonder where they are."

"A girl of good breeding would never be allowed to be part of such a spectacle," Seamus said into her ear. "Her parents would forbid it."

McCullen had not looked at either Seamus or Miss Sanchez, but Seamus knew that he was aware of them. Why else would he have stopped just there and gathered these women just yards from their position?

"As all of the ladies here are of equal beauty and charm, I must find another method of choosing my queen," he said. The crowd was confused. What did he mean? How else could a parade queen be chosen?

"It shall be a contest of wit!" McCullen bellowed.

A few of the women giggled and some looked genuinely afraid.

"You might have to help me," said Miss Sanchez.

"With what?" Seamus said.

But McCullen was waiting for the crowd to be silent so he could administer this contest of wit. The eight women formed a rough line before him, some of them glancing at each other or whispering. The masses finally quieted.

"Please name all of the planets in our solar system," McCullen said.

Seamus was glad that McCullen did not single out any one woman to ask, and thus spared her the humiliation of not knowing the answer. The poor things were looking, one to the other, in dismay.

"I think I know this. There was this little mnemonic device we learned. Something about pizzas," said Miss Sanchez.

It was then that Seamus understood what she was up to. "You can't go with him!" he hissed. "I can't be there to protect you."

"Shush," she waved her hand. "I'm trying to think."

"I will not shush. McCullen is a dangerous man, and he means no good for you. He is far too curious about you."

"That's why I should go. You haven't been able to learn anything, but maybe I can. And I'll be up there in front of everyone, then at the ball. Is he going to slit my throat in front of hundreds of witnesses?"

Seamus could think of no sensible reply. "Well, I forbid it," he said.

The maddening woman actually snorted. "Good luck with that. Wait. I think I remember it. My Very Educated Mother Just Served Us Nine Pizzas."

Seven of the women had already returned to the crowd, presumably after being unable to answer the question correctly. Miss Sanchez stepped forward and stood beside the last woman, but McCullen gave no indication of noticing her. Seamus wanted to leap forward and yank her back, but there were too many people and he would look ridiculous. Why was she being so pig-headed and stubborn? It was a wonder the human race got on at all in the twenty-first century if the women were like her. They had most likely gained the right to vote by being hard-headed and out-stubborning the poor henpecked males.

McCullen stopped in front of Miss Sanchez. He had a little mischievous glint in his eye as he asked her name. Of course, thought Seamus, it wouldn't do for it to appear that she knew him already.

"Felicia Sanchez," she said.

"And can you name the planets in our solar system?"

"I believe I can. Mercury, Venus, Earth, Mars, Jupiter, Saturn, Uranus, Neptune and Pluto. Though we have recently found that Pluto is a dwarf planet, technically." Miss Sanchez was staring unflinchingly into McCullen's face. His eyes widened with a hungry look and Seamus knew in an instant what both Miss Sanchez and McCullen were thinking.

There was no dwarf planet called Pluto. But presumably, in Miss Sanchez's time, one had been discovered. She was too clever not to know that her farthest planet may not have been found in 1857. And her statement that they had "recently found" that Pluto was a dwarf planet must be some kind of code between her and McCullen. That must be recent knowledge in her time. This was insane. She must be thinking McCullen was a traveler in time, like herself, and was finding a way to tell McCullen that she was a traveler and to get him to reveal if he came from a time before or after hers.

The woman was not only stubborn, but foolish as well. But after a few moments, Seamus remembered McCullen's look at the gentleman's club when they had discussed the time rips reopening. McCullen had been so taken with the idea of doorways in time. But then, he had always been able to come up with the most fanciful ideas.

Good God, his ideas. What if his ideas about scientific advancement were not simply the product of a brilliant mind, but were ideas brought from a future time? Of course McCullen knew what was possible. He had seen it himself.

Miss Sanchez was standing straight and tall, her face tipped upward as McCullen spoke to her. Was the woman on to something? McCullen's feet were as normal as his own. There would be no hiding a deformity like Miss Sanchez's in prison, where the men changed in the same room. But then, every time, every alternative world would not be the same. McCullen's world could have people with normal feet.

But it was all too coincidental. Mr. Grey, Miss Sanchez and McCullen had all somehow come into his life and were all travelers in time. Yes, too coincidental by far. But then, they had all come because of McCullen. A coincidental meeting in prison had led to their friendship, and later, the betrayal. McCullen's invention had brought Miss Sanchez to Seamus, and the engines had somehow drawn the attention of Mr. Grey's group. All because of McCullen.

McCullen opened his palm and Miss Sanchez set her hand into it.

"The Queen of the Mardi Gras!" he cried. "Intelligence, beauty and elegance, a queen for the night!"

McCullen kissed the back of her hand, and Miss Sanchez gave a curtsey. It looked practiced and perfect, a far cry from her clumsy attempts when she had first arrived. The pair walked up the steps and stood in front of the thrones, facing the crowd. McCullen said something into her ear, and he reached his hand slowly toward her throat. With the back of his fingers, he stroked the stray tendril that hung down to her bosom. His hand hovered inches from her chest and Miss Sanchez turned her head aside demurely. Though Seamus couldn't see, he imagined her blushing. The crowd clapped and hollered.

A dark rage boiled up within him. He knew Miss Sanchez was trying to play McCullen, but seeing him look

HEATHER BLACKWOOD

at her, touch her, it broke open a new wound. Stealing his engine designs, deceiving him about being from his own time, the man was as much a liar as the devil himself. But this was too much.

And now Miss Sanchez was smiling as one of the Egyptian women presented a small wooden chest to McCullen. He opened the lid and removed a pair of gold hoop earrings. Miss Sanchez worked on removing her own and putting them in while two women tied a thin gold chain around her waist and removed her cameo necklace, replacing it with a gold circlet set with blue stones. These must be the items taken from the mummy. Seamus had not seen them himself, but recognized the items from Miss Sanchez's description. Finally, McCullen placed a gold diadem on her head. It sparkled in her dark hair, and she looked even more like the fae maiden from another world. The diadem was a thinner, more delicate version of McCullen's own crown. He must have had it custom made.

Miss Sanchez stepped to the very front of the barge, McCullen by her side, and she waved to the crowd. She looked perfectly at ease, but Seamus thought that she could not be enjoying the task. She must want to return to her home very badly, he thought with a pang. She would endure this, draw McCullen's attention and place herself in danger, all to go back where he could never see her again.

The engine beneath the float revved up and the float glided forward, carrying the King and Queen of the Mardi Gras toward the cathedral.

CHAPTER 30

FROM THE CORNER OF HER eye, Felicia watched Seamus as the float pulled away. He crossed his arms and scowled. She spared him one glance as they moved away, just to see if he was following the float. She hoped he would go straight to the ball and meet her there, but he might think it his duty to follow and ensure her safety. It was both endearing and exasperating. But the man had melted into the crowd. Even his height and his fine clothing did not help her find him. She was alone with McCullen.

He invited her to sit on the throne beside his, and she accepted. He made little harmless comments about the shops and festivities and waved to the crowds as the parade twisted through the streets. The crowds cheered for them and men waved their hats. At the end of their route, the floats circled the streets around Jackson Square two times. The crowd didn't seem to be tiring of the parade, the music or the drink that flowed. They danced to the sounds of the walking bands or milled in the streets, eating and playing with their little trinkets.

"We will stop shortly," said McCullen. Their float broke off from the rest and drove up St. Anne Street. A shining black carriage with two liveried footmen, both in gold and green, waited for them.

"What about the parade?" asked Felicia. "Is it ending?"

"The floats will travel through the entire French Quarter. And they'll circle Jackson Square again just before midnight."

That was what she had wanted to know. The engines would be running all night, transmitting their energy all the while. She wished she had a watch, but by her estimation, it was about ten o'clock, maybe ten thirty. The huge float engines would be traveling for hours with the cathedral near the center. She didn't have Seamus's mind for mechanics, but that had to be a huge amount of energy.

She accepted McCullen's arm as she descended the float's staircase. It was narrow, and she had to hold her skirt up to keep it from catching on part of the float. McCullen handed her into the carriage and then stood speaking with a man.

"I told him to let the people have the float," McCullen said as he took his seat. His Irish accent was strong now that they were alone. He was making no attempt to hide it. "The people can take turns playing king for a day. It'll give them some amusement."

Of course he would want the float to keep running. It was nothing to him if the crowds destroyed the thrones or canopy, as long as the engine kept running and transmitting energy.

"That's kind of you. The parade was beautiful."

"Better than in your time?" he asked.

"Oh, yes." It was not strictly a lie. She had loved seeing the old-fashioned parade. But compared to the technologically advanced floats of her own time with their sound systems and electric effects, it was not as grand. She knew better than to say so.

"You must tell me more about your time, Miss Sanchez. I am dying to know all about you." He leaned forward a little, and Felicia saw the eagerness in his face. Was it all just curiosity about a time traveler, or was he really curious about her? He was attractive, in a polished and controlled sort of way, but she also had an idea of what lurked beneath.

Their carriage pulled up to the entrance of the ballroom. There were no other carriages, as all of the guests were already inside. Felicia stepped lightly down from the carriage and allowed McCullen to lead her to the entrance where two uniformed servants pulled open the doors. A puff of warm air and the sound of music enveloped her and she stopped just inside the door, shoulder to shoulder with the King of the Mardi Gras.

The ballroom was bustling and crowded. Many of the people inside were sitting and resting, already sweaty and exhausted from dancing. A few souls on the dance floor swayed to a slow song. Seats ringed the dance floor in a horseshoe shape, and the tiny tables were crowded with revelers nibbling at food and sipping drinks.

The ballroom walls were lined in dark wood wainscoting beneath cream and gold patterned wallpaper. Gaslights cast the room in a warm golden light. A high, wood-beamed ceiling soared overhead, the rafters strung with garlands and crepe streamers. A band in green and gold uniforms stood off to one side, just in front of the large polished dance floor.

Behind the band hung an enormous painting of the Nile, all yellow, green and brown in the hot Egyptian sun. The picture covered the entire wall and depicted palm trees, pyramids, camels led by Bedouins and a hieroglyphic-covered temple. Felicia wondered at the accuracy of the image, but it had the proper affect, making the room have the feeling of the desert at noon. It was certainly warm enough.

Off to one side stretched a long refreshment table filled with pastries, tarts, quiches, tiny meat pies and fruit. In the center, on an ornate stand, sat a large round cake topped with multicolored frosting and sprinkled with white sugar. Carafes of wine and pitchers of ice water with lemon slices floating inside stood nearby. Punch cascaded from a three-tiered fountain, and Felicia wondered for an instant how they powered it without electricity. Seamus would know, and she scanned the room for him. He wasn't there.

Within moments of spotting the King and Queen of the Mardi Gras, servants scurried and guests rose from their seats. People formed two lines, leading from the front entrance to the far side of the room. It was a reception line. Felicia had seen them at wedding receptions, but had never walked through one herself.

McCullen shook hands and spoke a few words to various people. Felicia smiled and tried to be poised as the two of them moved slowly down the line, accepting handshakes and kisses on the cheek. By the end of it, Seamus was still nowhere to be seen.

"Shall we have a seat?" asked McCullen once he had spoken to the last person. "I could use a rest." He was speaking with an American accent now that they were in public.

He led Felicia to an empty table and instructed a servant to bring them two glasses of punch. They sipped the cool, sweet drink in silence.

Felicia studied the other women and saw that Mrs. Washington had been correct. Many of the bustlines of the dresses were far more revealing than hers, and on some of the more generously endowed women, the amount of exposed flesh was positively scandalous.

"Now, you must tell me more about yourself," said McCullen.

"What would you like to know?"

"May I be frank? Please tell me when you are from. I am assuming that the business with Pluto was your way of telling me."

"You first," she said. "I know you are a traveler too. How else would you be able to figure out a radio or those other things?"

"Well, genius is as genius does."

A group of guests stopped by the table to compliment

the food, the music and to chat. Two couples even introduced their young daughters to McCullen. The girls couldn't have been older than twenty. Both of them smiled sweetly at McCullen. It turned Felicia's stomach to see the poor things trotted out with the hopes of engaging the attentions of a rich bachelor like McCullen. But then, she thought, would he be such a terrible catch? The man was polite, intelligent, good looking and wealthy. Seamus had said he was a liar and a thief, but he had legitimately improved upon Seamus's original peroxide engine. Technically, he shouldn't have stolen the idea for the original engine, but the time-ripper engine could only be credited to McCullen's own creativity.

Once the guests departed, Felicia turned back to McCullen. "You never answered my question."

"Nor did you reply to mine, my dear. Care to dance?" He rose and offered his hand. A song was just beginning and she could hardly refuse in front of so many people, especially after sitting on the sidelines for a while. He led her to the dance floor and she put one hand in his and the other on his shoulder.

"I hadn't known that Pluto was a dwarf planet," said McCullen as the dance began.

"Has Pluto been discovered yet?" she said. "I wasn't sure."

"No, they haven't discovered it here yet. I wish science was more advanced."

"I could say the same about medicine. No anesthesia, no sanitation. Do they have anesthesia in your time?" she asked.

"Yes, thank the gods."

"And when is that?"

"This is becoming wearysome, so I shall break our impasse," he said. "I was born in 1927 in Omagh, Ireland. I was visiting the site of an old holy place for Epona. She is one of our gods. And just as I suspect you did, I saw a shimmer. It was so close to me, and I had no idea what it was. I was only twenty when I came through."

She pulled her face back enough to look him in the eye. She sensed no trace of deceit, but a little voice reminded her that Seamus had said McCullen was an excellent liar. Even so, she believed him.

"Thank you," she said. "I was born in 1990 in Los Angeles, California. I was living in New Orleans when I came through in 2015."

"So you and I were born only sixty-five years apart, whereas Seamus is more than a century and a half your senior."

"Well, by that reckoning, you are old enough to be my grandfather."

"How inconvenient for us."

"Now, don't be like that. We can only be friends."

"Are we, Miss Sanchez? Friends?"

"Sure, why not? Time travelers have to stick together, I suppose."

She felt his shoulders relax a little, and though they were nearly cheek to cheek, she saw him look far off, past her ear.

"We are extraordinary, we two," he said. "We have knowledge that can change the world. We have seen the holocaust in Germany and Spain, the atomic bomb fall on Tokyo and Kyoto. We know about the wars that are coming, the innovations, the tragedies."

Felicia considered mentioning that in her world, the bombs had been dropped on Hiroshima and Kyoto and that Spain had not been known for its participation in the holocaust. She had wondered when he mentioned multiple gods, but this clinched it. McCullen was from yet another world. Or was he from this world, but in their future?

"And what would you do with your knowledge, Mr. McCullen? You have created marvelous engines, but they are going to tear apart this world, and maybe others."

"I doubt it. As I told Seamus, the rips seem to naturally repair themselves. We have things to do in this world. We have a responsibility to it."

"I don't intend to stay long enough in this world to have a responsibility to it."

Now it was his turn to pull away and look at her. "Do you still think you can return home?" He studied her. "You do." He pulled her cheek to cheek. "Oh, you poor thing. It's quite impossible. I have tried for years and there is simply no way to do it."

"The Professor will figure it out," she said with more certainty than she felt.

"How precious, to think that Seamus Connor can help you. I worked with him for years, and he may have one of the finest minds I have ever encountered, but he cannot discover how to control the time rips. Like me, he can only make more random ones."

"But you invented the machine. Can't you reverse engineer it or something? You and Seamus can put your heads together and figure it out."

"No, it is not possible. I am so sorry." He sounded as if he meant it.

Felicia was shaking now. "I need to sit down," she said and turned from him without giving him a chance to answer. She took a seat and he brought her a glass of ice water.

"The punch is full of sugar and alcohol. This will make you feel better," he said. "I'm sorry for the shock. But I want you to understand our situation. I will not lie to you and give you false hope. We are stranded here."

She drank the water and again looked for Seamus.

"You're looking for him," McCullen said. "But again, he has left you. I won't say anything against him, but he isn't known for his constancy in his affections for women."

"He and I are friends, nothing more."

"No? I had gotten the idea that you were."

"I'm sure he's busy."

"At the cathedral? Oh, don't look surprised, of course I know where he is. He's welcome to stay there all evening if he likes. I am enjoying your company."

A servant offered her a small cup of purple grapes from a tray and she took it. Then, the cake was cut and served. A young man across the room found the tiny golden baby that had been baked inside, and after wiping it off, showed it to anyone who cared to see.

"I want to ask you something," McCullen said. "If you could prevent the holocaust, wouldn't you do it? You say you are not loyal to this world, but if it was the only world you would ever know, would you try to change it?"

"Yes. I would. But I don't see what I could do."

"With my inventions and your knowledge of history beyond 1947, there is so much we could do. Tell me, what else would you stop?"

"Well, there were other dictators that caused the deaths of millions. Other wars. I'd like slavery to end, of course."

"Naturally," he said. "And you know what the British have done to my people, Seamus's people, don't you?"

"Not much. I know Ireland fought for independence for a long time."

"The British have oppressed and tormented my people for generations. They occupy our land, rape our women, murder our men, steal from us, take what we create or destroy it entirely. And I will see to it that they stop. I will not allow another century of it to go by unopposed."

"Seamus said that you hated the British."

"He is correct. They are not fit to rule their own land, let alone colonize others. But I am a fair man, and would only see them have their own country. I would not extinguish them altogether."

"As if you could," she said. He did not answer, and it chilled her. "Why are you telling me this?"

"I would tell you anything, Miss Sanchez. There is a great comfort in finding another traveler."

"Have you met any others?" she asked.

"Never. Not once. I visited the place I came through time and time again, but the wavering air never came again."

Some of the dancers were getting their second wind, or perhaps they had imbibed enough alcohol to feel a new surge of enthusiasm for the ball. A good number of couples danced, and a few women glanced at McCullen with sullen expressions.

"It looks like you are expected to dance with a few of the ladies," she said. "You are the host, unmarried and the King, after all."

"I would rather not, but I suppose I must. I would like to reserve the last place on your dance card, if I may."

Felicia wondered if there had ever been such a thing as a real honest-to-goodness dance card, and she agreed to dance with McCullen last. A thin man of about forty asked her to dance, and he was so nervous and sweet-looking that she agreed. They tried to have a polite conversation, but he was so anxious and she was so preoccupied with her own thoughts that she didn't speak much aside from answering questions about the weather and what foods she had enjoyed that evening.

When the dance ended and she turned toward her seat, a tall, lean figure was leaning back in her chair, a glass of wine in one hand and a smug look on his face.

"Seamus! Where have you been?" she said as she took a seat.

"At the cathedral, of course. I had to make sure the tripod sensors were all set up properly. Mr. Grey is intelligent, but there are some things better done by someone who knows what he's doing."

"Then why did you come back?" she said. She partly wanted him to say he was worried about her, and she scolded herself for being so silly.

"What, and let you have all the fun? How could I miss something like this?" He gestured with his wineglass, encompassing the band, room and the guests. At a fluttering glance from a blonde woman in a sea green dress nearby, he nodded to her and raised his glass. She smiled at him and then looked away. Then she looked at him sideways and blushed. Felicia wondered if the woman practiced flirting at home.

"I'm making good progress with McCullen," Felicia said. To her satisfaction, Seamus looked away from the blonde and fixed his attention on her. "We danced, and he told me he's a time traveler, from 1927. He fell through a shimmering spot at some holy site. It sounds like there are multiple gods he worships, but I didn't ask about religion in his world."

"What about the engines? What is he planning?"

"I still don't know, but he wants to dance the last dance with me. I'll see what I can find out."

Seamus pulled out his pocket watch. "Well, there's a wee bit of time until the last dance. Care to take a turn on the dance floor, Miss Sanchez?"

"I'd be delighted, Mr. Connor," she said.

Felicia had not danced with many men in her life, but she knew from her limited experience and an elective ballroom dance class in college that some men were easier to dance with than others. Seamus was easy. With McCullen, she had needed to pay attention and let him lead so she could follow. It took concentration. With Seamus, she felt him move just an instant before she needed to mirror the move, so it was smooth and, if she admitted it, fun. He had the scent of pipe tobacco and old books, and though her face only came up to the top of his chest, she didn't feel the need to look up into his face while they talked.

"All of my sensors show that the energy from the floats and the little mechanical toys are all collecting at the cathedral," he said. He spoke low and she half heard his voice in his chest. "My automatons run on their own power, and I checked them over and over. His plan has something to do with the organ, but I took that thing apart all the way to the wall and didn't see anything."

"I thought Brother Joe stopped you partway through."

"I saw enough. There's something happening there, and I can't tell what. It's driving me to madness."

"Not a long trip, I'd think," Felicia said tartly.

"Well now, funny woman, you're welcome to do better. I got back into the cathedral with Brother Joe to see the organ, but there's nothing wrong with it. The clockworks are in order. Nothing is amiss. But now I see something interesting. McCullen waiting for you at your table."

At the end of the dance, she sat awhile and took a few sips of ice water before McCullen asked her for the last dance. The band played a lively number to end that part of the ball. The guests, those who were not too tired, would return after the midnight cathedral show for more dancing, chatting and flirting. Felicia imagined that if she were a socialite looking for a husband, she would have to work an event like this for all it was worth.

"Have you had a pleasant evening, Miss Sanchez?" McCullen asked as they danced.

She assured him that she had and allowed him to pull her a little closer. As they turned, she saw Seamus scowling. He gave her a questioning look and behind McCullen's back, she make the okay sign with her fingers. Seamus looked puzzled for an instant before recognizing it and nodding. He glanced around the room, assessing potential dance partners, and then asked the blonde woman. Felicia's time was short. If Seamus brought his partner close to them, McCullen might clam up.

"Mr. McCullen," she said. "I must know, what are you planning at the cathedral?"

"I was wondering when you would come to that. I'd like you to come with me and see."

CHAPTER 31

HAZEL LOOKED AGAIN AT THE clock face on the front of the cathedral. "Where are they? They should be here by now."

"There is time yet," said Mr. Grey.

"But the Professor said he'd be back for the automaton display. And Miss Sanchez should be with him."

Mr. Grey said no more and Hazel fiddled with the little clockwork jackal he had bought for her. It was an odd toy, and when she pressed the little button on the side, it raised its head and lowered it, as if nodding drowsily. Its eyes glowed green. She knew that she should not be pressing the button, as it would add to the power being transmitted to the cathedral, but Mr. Grey said it would not make any difference, and that she could play with it as much as she liked.

She was too old for toys, but she liked the jackal anyway. Once the Professor had gone, Mr. Grey had reached into his pocket and pulled it out. He had bought it on the sly and offered it to her without a word.

The hand of the clock on the cathedral ticked one notch closer to midnight. The crowd was thick, and Hazel was glad that the Professor's mechanical devices were tucked back into their wheeled trunk. Other articles were in the leather case that he had left in their care. The Professor had said that the instruments had provided the information he needed and they could do no more.

A minute later, the Professor ran up. "Have you seen McCullen and Miss Sanchez?" he asked.

Hazel shook her head. The Professor's cheeks were pink, and he was out of breath.

"The King and Queen, where are they?" he asked, turning around in a full circle. "McCullen left the party with Miss Sanchez in a carriage. They were supposed to make an appearance here just before midnight."

"Maybe they got stopped by all the people crowding the streets," Hazel said.

"I don't like this," said the Professor. He turned to Mr. Grey. "If you see her, tell her to meet me at the statue of Jackson." He waved toward the statue of the mounted Jackson in the middle of the square. Then he turned and vanished into the crowd.

The clock hand moved again, trembling as it stopped pointing straight upwards. The church bells rang out twelve times, vibrating the air and making Hazel's ears throb with the sound. The crowd cheered, but their voices quieted as the first door on the cathedral's front cracked down the center and the door swung outward. It was a door on the far left, and Hazel clasped her hands as if in prayer. But she would not pray, she would not close her eyes for even an instant.

A pair of palm trees clattered out, quivering at the end of their track and then moving sideways a few feet to either side, supported by two mechanical arms. Gentle mechanical music began to play from within, like that of an oversized music box. Then a kneeling figure rolled out, leaning face-down on a boulder. This was Christ's agony in the garden of Gethsemane. The figure lifted his face and hands, then returned to his original position. He did this three times and the rock and trees withdrew. The doorway closed.

To the far right, another set of doorways opened. Again, two palm trees slid out and to the sides. Then two figures emerged, dressed as Roman soldiers. They jabbed the air with their spears. An apostle emerged, but Hazel could not remember which one he was supposed to be. He waved a dagger, slicing the air near a soldier's head. She knew that he was supposed to be cutting off the soldier's ear. A standing Christ slid forward and raised his arm to the man's ear, reattaching it. Then the apostle slid back and the two soldiers moved in, arresting Christ. The two soldiers faced the crowd, standing on either side with Christ in the center, his head hanging down in sorrow. As a group, they slid backwards through their door.

The night was cold, but the crush of bodies around Hazel kept her from feeling chilly. The people turned as the third door, this one on the left, opened. The automaton on the simple throne inside wore rich Roman clothing, complete with golden wrist cuffs and a scarlet cape. This must be Pilate, the Roman governor. Christ was brought before him and Pilate rose from his throne. He slid to the end of his track to stand over the people and the music quieted. He raised an arm, as if giving an oration and his mouth moved. No sound came out, but everyone knew what he was supposed to be saying. He was asking if the crowd should release a criminal named Barabbas or release Christ. He stood still, as if waiting for a response, and Hazel understood. Instead of having some sort of mechanical crowd shown in the display, the observers themselves were supposed to play the part of the crowds that condemned Christ. Hazel knew that the crowd was supposed to shout, "Crucify him!" but no one in the crowd did so. Hazel didn't want to say it either. The very idea made her uneasy. Pilate turned back, just as if they had shouted the words, and then made washing gestures over a golden bowl on a stand, absolving himself of the unjust death.

The automatons this year seemed more lifelike than in years past, Hazel thought, and the music was more varied from scene to scene. She had seen previous displays on Christmas, Easter and Palm Sunday. But this year, the movements and the painted expressions were more realistic. The motions of the hands seemed more fine and delicate and someone had repainted the faces of the automatons. Hazel wondered if Brother Joe had done it or if the Professor had some hidden artistic talent. The eyes were large and expressive, and the seams for the mouths were painted in such a way that they hardly showed.

The fourth door showed Christ being scourged. The sorrowful figure had his wrists tied over his head and was nearly hanging by them. His forehead was pressed to the pillar, but turned sideways enough for the crowd to see his closed eyes and contorted mouth. As the torturer raised and lowered his lash, Christ's bare back opened along mechanical seams and thin red ribbons slipped out to signify blood. A murmur of unease ran through the crowd.

The next window showed Christ slumped on a rough wooden stool. The automatons around him bowed, ridiculing him, and one beat him with a reed. Finally, a guard pressed a crown of thorns upon his head. A woman nearby gasped as more blood red ribbons poured from his scalp and lay against his bearded mechanical cheeks.

Now, two doors opened, one on either side of the largest door in the center and the music became slow and rhythmic, like dragging footsteps. A curved track emerged from the left door and circled around until it disappeared into the blackness of the door on the right, forming a long oval. Hazel was vaguely aware of the crowd making sounds of anticipation, as nothing so elaborate had ever been done in an automaton display before. She hoped the Professor was able to hear the sounds of appreciation for his work, but if he was still searching for Miss Sanchez, he would be oblivious. It was a shame, as he had accomplished something so marvelous.

A bent Christ rolled partway out, the cross on his back, and fell for the first time. Hazel knew he would do it twice more, if the order of the Stations of the Cross was being followed. Then, he rose and the Virgin Mary rolled out to face him. She touched his cheek and then covered her face with her hands in grief before sliding backward through the doors. A man took her place. The cross moved to his shoulders, and he and Christ disappeared into the door on the right. That must have been St. Simon, Hazel thought.

Christ appeared again at the left, and a woman came from the right. She held an outstretched cloth and pressed it to his face. She turned to the audience, holding out the cloth which bore the mark of His face, before moving back into darkness. Christ moved a few feet and then fell once more. Three women emerged from the right this time, all carrying little mechanical infants. Christ raised his hand and his mouth moved.

"What's happening now?" said Mr. Grey in Hazel's ear. She had only vaguely been aware of his presence and she jerked in surprise.

"He's speaking to the women of Jerusalem," she said. Everyone knew what was happening, even an impious child like her. But it seemed that Mr. Grey and Miss Sanchez didn't have much religious schooling.

The track emptied of automatons, and moments later, Christ rolled out again from the left. He then fell for the third and final time, and two soldiers came to meet him and take him away. The curved track pulled itself back in and both sets of doors closed. The last door was the largest, the one in the center, just under the clock face. Hazel knew what it would show, and watched the seam in the door, waiting for it to open.

"My God," said a man's voice nearby, but it was not in any kind of prayerful tone. It was a cry of shock and fear. Hazel looked and found the Professor standing on the other side of Mr. Grey. He was not facing the automaton display, but was looking toward the river.

The music changed to a minor key and the largest door on the front of the cathedral opened. In the center, set on a light blue background, hung Christ crucified. The

Blessed Mother knelt at his feet, clinging to the cross. Her mouth was open and her face was twisted in sorrow so complete it was beyond words. Christ raised His face to the sky and his mouth moved. Hazel knew Christ was asking his father why He had forsaken Him.

Hazel looked toward the river, but the people between her and the water were too tall and blocked her view of everything.

"What is it, Professor?" she asked, but he did not answer.

Mr. Grey had turned and looked also, and though he was shorter than the Professor, he apparently could see something. He glanced at the cathedral and looked over the crowd, as if assessing something. "There are river boats," he said to Hazel.

She didn't think that was so strange. Of course, people would hire riverboats to take them for an evening of dancing or drinking, stopping to take in the automaton display. Unless the Delphia Queen was among them, it didn't sound so dangerous. Hadn't the Professor said that only the Delphia Queen had the new McCullen engine?

Hazel turned back to the cathedral. Christ must have died at this point, because an automaton soldier appeared with a spear, and stabbed at the dead man's side. A gash opened and from it poured two thick scarves, one light blue to signify water, and the other deep red. The scarves fluttered to the ground and lay on the cathedral steps a few feet apart. The soldier withdrew, leaving only the dead Christ with his mother kneeling below his pierced and bleeding feet.

The Professor muttered something to Mr. Grey, and Hazel stood on her tiptoes to see what they were looking at, but could not. Then she had an idea and jumped up on top of the wheeled trunk that held the Professor's gear. At first, she saw nothing. Then, among the riverboats, she thought she saw a shimmer.

"Was that what you saw?" she asked the Professor. But he had already gone.

CHAPTER 32

"I THOUGHT WE WERE GOING TO greet the crowds at the front of the cathedral," said Felicia. McCullen led her to a door at the back corner of the cathedral, just outside the fence that enclosed St. Anthony's garden. This door was small and had no handle on the outside, only a lock. McCullen paused with the key in his hand.

"Would you like to greet them?" he said, looking as if he might agree to it for her sake. His Irish accent was back.

"I'm not sure," she said. She didn't want to see any crowds, but she was also aware that McCullen was taking her somewhere unfamiliar, dark and deserted, or nearly so. McCullen unlocked the door and held it for her.

"It's inside," he said.

"What is?"

"Come and see." He had the look of a boy who was about to present a gift that he had made himself.

"No, I think I need to get back to Mr. Connor. He'll be looking for me."

"I would say that you should invite him along, but I need to be getting inside immediately. But as a fellow time traveler, I think you will find this most intriguing."

"Do you have a way to get home?" she asked.

He gave her a sorrowful look and then reached to touch her cheek. The intimacy of the movement made her jerk back.

"I'm sorry," he pulled his hand away.

The church bells rang out twelve times. Midnight.

"Do what you like," he said. "But I would welcome your company." He slipped into the cathedral, leaving the door ajar.

He had given her a choice. Someone bent on harming her would not have done so, would he? And whatever was inside the cathedral was more important to him than doing anything to her. Besides, she had been the one to approach him to become Queen of the Mardi Gras, not the other way around. And he had been nothing if not solicitous and polite all evening. He had told her about his past and seemed so pleased to have discovered another time traveler, even one born decades after he had been. It felt ungrateful to decline his invitation to go inside. He seemed so alone.

She did not sense danger. And she needed to see what McCullen was doing. If Seamus was right and it was something nefarious, she might be able to stop it. But if she went looking for Seamus, then whatever McCullen had planned would proceed unhindered.

She grabbed up her skirts and ran upstairs. McCullen had made it easy for her to follow, as he had left a door open at the top of the stairs and another at the end of a short hall. Another set of steps rose from this floor, old, rickety and narrow. They were also nearly vertical. So the cathedral had an attic. The hatch at the top stood open, and as she poked her head through, McCullen appeared and offered his hand. She took it and he helped her through the hatch and then kicked it closed.

"I'm glad you came," he said. "Now, if you will pardon me."

From the slant of the ceiling, Felicia figured they were just under the roof. The attic held decades of junk and from the level of dust, it looked like the brothers did not come here often. Small screened holes dotted the tops of the walls, just under the line of the ceiling. They ran along the back and sides of the building, but not the front. They must be ventilation holes, screened to keep out rodents and birds.

McCullen hurried to the front wall of the cathedral where a large panel of wood leaned against the wall. He pushed it sideways just enough for them to pass through the opening it concealed. A wide chamber was beyond, spanning the entire width of the cathedral, though it was not very deep. The area was partially lit through the small screened holes under the eaves. The entire front of the attic must have been walled off at some point, and McCullen had made use of the unused space.

The chamber itself was empty, or nearly so, except for six enormous metal beams, each hinged like a knee, one at each corner and two more at the front and back of the room. The beams were thick, perhaps three feet in diameter.

Over their heads, like the body of a squatting spider, rose a hexagonal metal ship of some kind. It was covered in riveted panels of metal that gleamed, even in this low light. She couldn't see the sides of it, but the rounded bottom had a closed hatch.

"What is this? Some kind of space ship?" she asked. The bottom of the thing resembled the bases of some of the early space capsules she had seen in a museum.

McCullen laughed, but then stopped, a question in his expression.

"We put men on the moon in 1969," she said in answer.

He got a pleased and dreamy look. "Magnificent."

"We're right over the organ, aren't we?" Felicia asked.

"Yes," he said, without any hint of surprise. "You figured it out. The new engines allowed a much smaller organ. Just enough space was left over to conceal the legs of my machine."

The crowd outside let out a cheer.

"It sounds like the automaton display has concluded," he said. He shoved a nearby crate up under the hatch, jumped up and unlatched it. The door swung down and a set of steps slid down on a track.

"Ladies first," McCullen said.

"Oh, no. I'm not going in that thing. Is it some kind of walking machine?"

"Yes. That is precisely what it is. But I must insist. If you stay here, you'll be killed."

"What? You're going to kill people with that thing?"

"Of course not! I mean that if you remain in this room, you will certainly be killed."

Without waiting for a response, he climbed up inside. Moments later, yellow light poured from the hatch and the thing gave a low, throbbing hum which rose in pitch and volume until the walls shook.

Felicia turned to run back through the attic, but at that moment, the machine's knee joints straightened a few degrees and the ceiling cracked in several places as the body pressed against it. The walls and ceiling shook and Felicia remembered being in an earthquake when she was a child. It was all jerking movement and a rumble so low and loud that it had drowned out her screams. She had felt sure the whole house would collapse on her. Pieces of the cathedral ceiling crashed down and she leapt to the only sheltered place, directly under the metal belly of the machine.

"Get inside!" yelled McCullen, and the machine gave another mighty push, making the wall that had sealed it from the rest of the attic splinter and collapse in places. The floor around two of the legs gave way, sending pieces of wall and floor spinning to the cathedral floor two stories below.

Felicia climbed the steps and pulled herself into the machine. The inside was extraordinary. Metal-framed window panes were set into the walls, giving plenty of visibility on all sides. The largest set of windows was at the front, but at present she could only see the inside wall of the cathedral. Control panels ran along three of the machine's sides, forming a rough half-circle shape. McCullen sat before the controls in a brown leather chair atop a thick post riveted to the floor. Dotting the control panel and walls were large switches with black wooden handles, copper- and brass-topped knobs and dials with brown ink numbering on the faces beneath their glass covers. Colored glass bulbs were set here and there and pipes and tubing ran overhead and down into each of the six corners where the legs must begin.

"What is this thing?" she yelled.

"Do you like it?" McCullen asked over his shoulder.

"Tell me what it is!"

"You already said it. It's a walker. I call it my hexapod, but it probably needs a better name. Would you like to name it? Oh, and would you mind closing the hatch?"

Of course, the hexapod would have a McCullen engine, she thought. But even with such an efficient engine, the sound of steam rushing from the boilers and the grind of the mechanical parts drowned out all other sound. She pulled the hatch closed and latched it. The noise from outside was muffled.

McCullen glanced backward to ensure that the hatch was closed before he used both hands to pull two levers down simultaneously. The hexapod groaned and shuddered, but only for a few seconds. Then, it gave a mighty heave and there was a crash that made Felicia flinch. She tried to stand, but the floor lurched and McCullen gave a triumphant laugh.

"You have to stop!" she yelled as rubble crashed all around the hexapod, banging into the windows.

"You may want to hang on to something. I didn't build an extra seat for company. I'd offer you mine, but I'm in need of it just now."

Felicia grabbed onto a thick pipe on the wall and held on for dear life as the hexapod lurched free of the cathedral, crashing through stone and wood and pushing its way free. Out the window, the cathedral walls fell away and the night sky swayed.

"Let me straighten her up," said McCullen.

They rose, leveled out and then stopped. They were higher than the buildings, but only barely. Felicia could see for a few blocks. McCullen flipped a few switches, and the area below them flooded with light. He must have built lights into the underside of the machine. Below, people ran in every direction. She couldn't hear anything over the engine, but she imagined them screaming. She craned her neck to look directly below them.

"There are people lying on the ground! You've killed them!"

McCullen looked. "No, those are the automatons."

It was true. She could see now that they were just mechanical people. But the way they lay on the ground, still and twisted, was unsettling.

"What the hell are you doing?" she demanded. "Whatever it is, you have to stop."

"We're taking it for a walk."

"Oren!"

"Oh, are we on a first name basis now?"

"You're insane! You're going to kill people."

"I will do no such thing." He turned in his chair. "I am waiting right here until everyone has cleared away. I have no intention of harming anyone."

"Then why here? Why in the middle of this huge event with all these people?"

"Didn't your Seamus figure it out?"

"The engines and the transfer of energy wirelessly? Yeah, he had you all figured out there."

"Good. I'm proud of him. This machine consumes enormous amounts of power, as you can imagine. I needed to power it, and to get all the people in one place, more or less. These Mardi Gras festivities served my purpose."

"You gathered them to kill them?"

"Good God, Miss Sanchez. I am not going to kill anyone. What has Seamus been telling you about me? We're just going to pay a visit to a few buildings, all empty at midnight, especially when everyone has come to see the automaton display."

The people ran from Jackson Square. A group of brown-robed monks watched from below before they hurried away. Felicia looked for Seamus, Hazel or Mr. Grey. She looked over McCullen's shoulder, toward the river, and something caught her eye, but when she tried to focus on it, it was gone.

CHAPTER 33

SEAMUS TURNED BACK AMID THE panicking herd of people and tried to get out of their way. A man thumped into Seamus's leather case hard, but he managed to keep hold of it. His large trunk must still be back where Mr. Grey and Hazel had watched the automaton display.

The six-legged machine stood still over the rubble of the cathedral, its engines humming and white lights shining down from its undercarriage. Occasionally jets of white steam spurted out from the leg joints. He tried to see the people inside, but couldn't make anything out. The lights underneath were too bright.

Most of the people fled away from the river. He was glad for that. McCullen was inside that machine, there could be no doubt.

"Grey! Hazel!" he shouted as the pair of them ran by. Hazel heard him and grabbed Mr. Grey's arm. Seamus was glad to see that Mr. Grey had kept his promise to keep an eye on the girl. The crowd was thinning as people poured down the various streets.

The three of them moved up against a building, close enough to see the giant machine but far enough away that they were not in immediate danger.

"What is that spider machine?" asked Hazel.

"Some creation of McCullen's. He's in it," said Seamus.

"What do you think he is going to do with it?" said Mr. Grey. "He can't hope to get back to his own time that way."

"I don't think that's what he's planning," said Seamus. "Look at the front of it."

Mr. Grey and Hazel squinted, but even with the bright lights, Seamus was sure they would be able to make it out. At the front, directly under where the driver would sit, was a Union Jack. On the side closest to them was the three-pronged insignia of the East India Company.

"McCullen is helping the British to attack us?" said Hazel. "I thought he hated the British."

"Oh, he does. That's why he's doing this."

The lights on the machine moved, and it took an instant before Seamus realized that the spider machine, as Hazel called it, was starting to walk.

"Isn't it a little obvious?" said Mr. Grey. "Why would the British paint their flag and the East India Company logo on a machine like that for an attack? I don't think people will be fooled into thinking it's really them."

"It's not so strange," said Seamus. "The British aren't much for stealthy warfare. And after the stage explosion at the riverboat festival, Southerners are primed to believe it."

Jackson Square was empty now, and the machine progressed steadily forward. It moved two legs at a time, leaving four on the ground. The body swayed a little with each step, but on the whole, it was stable enough to remain upright. Seamus took a moment to ponder how McCullen had engineered it with legs that seemed to self-coordinate, but paused when he noticed that the two front legs had a different type of foot than the others. The two legs ended in what looked like curled paws, while the back four had large, blunt feet that spread out into wide cones for stability.

The spider turned now. It stomped down Chartres Street until it reached the courthouse. The machine lowered itself a little, its four back legs bending until the body of the machine was just a little higher than the top of the building. The four legs spread wide, one at a time, and once the machine was settled and stable, the two front legs rose, like arms. The front two feet now opened, like stub-fingered claws, and then formed into balls, like fists. They crashed through two windows at far ends of the building. The elbows flexed and pulled inward in a giant embrace, tearing open the front wall.

Then the machine listed sideways and the legs had to scramble to adjust for the change in the center of gravity. It righted itself and paused for a few moments. Then it continued to punch and tear, ripping off half the roof and smashing in the windows. The structure still had three walls standing when the machine turned away and moved further down the street.

Seamus thought he saw the machine lurch again, as if it was not perfectly under control. Good. If McCullen crashed the cursed thing and died, it would do everyone a favor.

"We have to stop it, Professor! It's going to destroy the whole city!" Hazel dug her fingers into his arm. Her brown eyes were round with fear.

"Mr. Grey," Seamus said. "Get my trunk from the square and bring it over to the river. I'll be on the grass just there," he pointed to the grassy strip that ran along the water. "Hazel, you're coming with me."

Mr. Grey ran to retrieve the trunk and Hazel jogged next to Seamus as he ran for the riverbank.

"What do you need me to do?" she asked.

"Nothing. Just stay out of trouble."

"But what about Miss Sanchez?"

"I don't know where she is," Seamus said. "But I hope she is staying clear of that machine. If anyone was hurt by the debris from the cathedral, my bet is she's with them."

He was worried about her, but he wasn't going to let innocent people die just to satisfy a selfish desire to see her safe. She was probably either running in the opposite direction from the spider machine or tending the injured.

The spider machine was mostly out of sight now, but

Seamus could see its top. It stopped and lowered. He knew it was destroying something else, and if his guess on its location was correct, it was the Ursuline Convent. Why would McCullen do that? The sisters would still be inside. It sat there, eerily still for some time, long enough for Mr. Grey to drag the trunk over. They opened it, and Seamus got to work.

Five minutes later, he heard the crashing of the walls of the convent falling. McCullen had waited, giving the sisters time to evacuate the building. Kind of him, Seamus thought bitterly.

"Tell me what you have in mind so I can help," said Mr. Grey.

Seamus held a screwdriver in his mouth and he had to transfer it to one hand before speaking. "He's destroying landmarks, buildings of cultural significance. Remember the stage explosion and the Delphia Queen? Symbols. Steamboats, trade, commerce. Now he's going after civil and religious buildings, but I doubt he'll stop there."

The machine now moved on to a textile factory and had ripped it halfway apart before stomping away and working on the police station.

"So what's this?" asked Mr. Grey, looking over the device that Seamus pulled from his leather case. He was working on the sensors that he had used earlier.

"This is my modified McCullen engine," he pointed to one item. "And this is my signal amplification device. I had to leave my sonic mapping output module at home, but I brought along the important piece which ought to create the desired effect."

Mr. Grey didn't look like he understood, but Seamus did not feel like taking the time to educate the man.

"Tell me something, Mr. Grey," he said as he fit the pieces of the machine together. "If you are a time traveler, why can't you help Miss Sanchez get home?"

"I just can't."

"Can't or won't?" said Seamus.

Mr. Grey had the grace to look away, past Seamus and across the river. At least the man would not tell an outright lie.

"And where is Miss September Wilde? Can't she do anything?" Seamus asked.

"It's complicated. There are things that can and cannot be done. I'm helping you the best I can. I'm doing everything I can without disrupting essential time threads."

The spider machine was now destroying a workhouse where poor women sewed for a pittance. It was one step above walking the streets, and a fire burned in Seamus when he thought of the workers, mothers and young girls who had nowhere else to go to make a living. It wasn't enough to go after buildings owned by factory owners or businessmen. McCullen was destroying the lives of the poor. But then, once word spread that the East India Company was attempting to destroy the South's production and shipping systems, who but the lower class men would serve as foot soldiers in a war? Already, the North and their shipping interests were inextricably linked to England and John Company in the public mind. It was one step further to blame the North for this attack and bring on a war that would kill thousands. He and Miss Sanchez would be unable to prevent the Civil War. And even if it went on, there was no guarantee that the South would lose.

"Hazel, hand me that spanner," said Seamus. She did so without comment. That was one thing he liked about her. When something needed doing, she did it.

"Do you know what's just that way?" Seamus pointed south, down the river.

"No, what?" said Mr. Grey.

"The Port of New Orleans. We have a few riverboats docked up here, but that port is a beautiful target full of ships and cargo. It's the largest port in the entire South.

See how he's moving that machine?" He pointed in turn at each building that had been destroyed. "He's going to head south at some point, toward the port. And I'm going to stop him."

"How will you do that?" Hazel asked.

"By ripping a hole in time."

CHAPTER 34

"**D**ON'T EVEN LET THE THOUGHT cross your mind," growled McCullen. "I haven't hurt a soul. All those nuns were out and safe, and the other buildings were empty."

Felicia leaned against the wall, glaring at the back of McCullen's head. She only tried to forcibly wrest control of the hexapod from him after she had tried to talk him out of his spree of destruction without success. The best she had been able to do was to convince him to wait longer than he had wanted to before destroying each building. It would give people more of a chance to get out. Her attempt to redirect the hexapod had led to McCullen throwing her to the floor. He had not spoken to her in some time and she knew he was furious with her. She returned the sentiment.

"How many are you going to do?" she asked. "Aren't you finished yet?"

"I'll tell you when I'm finished, and it's not yet. There are still a good number to go."

"But how is the South supposed to survive and fight if you destroy so much? You do want them to win the war, don't you?"

"I've thought it through carefully, I assure you. I am not going to be destroying any military facilities, nor will I do anything that would permanently cripple the area. Please, give me some credit. I am not a madman."

"That's debatable."

She looked again toward the river, and again saw a

shimmer. She thought she had seen three so far, though she wasn't sure if her imagination was playing tricks on her.

"Please, Oren. You're ripping more time holes and God only knows what that's going to do. Would you really condemn others to our fate?"

"Seamus told me that the engines rip doorways, but I have yet to see a man-made doorway with my own eyes."

"The shimmers only last a second or two. But the Mardi Gras celebration created too many synchronicities."

"What are you talking about?"

"If the same, or at least a similar thing is happening on either side of the time rip, it allows the shimmer to occur. In my world, and presumably in yours, Mardi Gras had parades and crowds. So it created synchronicities. That's what's allowing the rips to form."

She was about to mention the Delphia Queen and the rips along the riverbank created by the engines and the multitude of ships docked there in other universes, but she saw a shimmer directly below them.

"There, did you see it?" she pointed.

"Yes," his voice was low and quiet.

"See? We could go back home. If you and Seamus worked together instead of arguing all the time, you could do it. But then I suppose you'd want to start a war in some other world."

"I am not a warmonger. I am merely doing what is necessary for the good of this world. Getting the English to cease their colonial ambitions entirely is what must occur. Independence for my homeland would come next. And then independence for other nations who have been under their filthy English thumbs."

"And what about the United States? You'll be throwing them into civil war."

"That's a secondary concern."

"Not to me, it's not. And not to the soldiers and their

families. And not to the people who are slaves. The North has to win, and they won't if you give your engines to the South."

"Miss Sanchez, you are short-sighted. War there must be, and war there shall be. The English will fight on the side of the North, and commit their troops. Then, when the English are away, the Irish and others can be armed and overthrow their colonizers. It's necessary. And it will free so many. But afterward, don't you think we could create planting and harvesting machines? If I can create the engines and this hexapod, I can create other machines. The South wants slavery because it's economically dependent upon it. Once machines take the place of slaves, once machines are cheaper than people, the institution can die a natural death."

"Over how many years?"

"Well, you can make that a personal project of yours. Discover germs, revolutionize medicine, free the slaves and give women the vote. Could you have done so much back in the twenty-first century?"

He almost made it sound appealing, she thought. She glanced back toward the river and saw a man dragging a wheeled trunk. It was Mr. Grey. She looked in the direction he was heading and saw two figures, one a tall man and the other, a boy. Seamus pulled things out of his leather case while talking and gesticulating.

McCullen turned the hexapod down another street to destroy the tobacconist. She had watched him long enough that she had an idea of how to control the machine, but the buttons and levers were unlabeled, and he was the only one who knew exactly what they did. If she was wrong and did the wrong thing, the whole hexapod would crash to the ground, killing them both.

After McCullen tore part of the wall off of a butcher shop and a neighboring market, he leaned over to examine his handiwork below.

"I'm not going to do any more damage. Let them rebuild."

"A surgical strike. How admirable," she said and looked out the side window. McCullen was absorbed in driving the hexapod down the street, and Felicia stood on tiptoe to look toward where she had seen Seamus, Mr. Grey and Hazel. The riverbank came into view for just an instant here and there between the buildings. It looked like Seamus had some kind of machine set up.

Of course, Seamus knew that McCullen was piloting the hexapod, but the rest of the city would not. McCullen had told her that the British and the East India Company, and by extension, the Northern states, would be blamed for the attack. For a while, she had been frightened that the police or military would come tearing out from behind a building, guns blazing. But no such thing had happened. No one had opposed McCullen's march of destruction.

And then there was Seamus, setting up some mad thing on the riverbank that could possibly kill all of them, or at least McCullen and herself. Seamus had no way of knowing she was on board.

McCullen turned the hexapod south, along the riverbank. It stomped along the long, thin strip of grass that separated the riverbank from Jackson Square. In her world, the grassy area was called Woldenberg Park, but she didn't know the name of it here.

Hazel, Seamus and Mr. Grey were all gathered two blocks south of Jackson Square. Their position was just at the place where the land jutted slightly outward into the water. They were at the middle of the grass, directly at the center point between St. Peter Street and the water. Felicia could see why they had chosen it. If McCullen drove the hexapod along the thin strip of Woldenberg Park or if he went straight down St. Peter Street, they could do whatever they had in mind. She knew that there were ways to interrupt electrical signals with magnetism. Maybe Seamus planned to stop the hexapod that way. But no, she had another idea of what he was going to do.

They were far enough away that McCullen wouldn't see them unless he was looking for them. Mr. Grey and Seamus knelt, working on something on the ground. Hazel squatted nearby. Already, several machines stood ready, including the tripod sensors that Seamus had used around the cathedral earlier.

The hexapod stomped up next to the docked ships. McCullen turned the machine and it reached out its terrible arms, ripping railings and cabin walls from a beautiful old riverboat. It was empty, thankfully, but when he was through, it was a wreck.

"I won't sink it," he said. "They can rebuild."

He moved on to the next ship. He seemed to have formed a little running commentary for her benefit, telling her how the damage he was doing was only temporary. It was all strategic.

"You didn't destroy the Café du Monde," she said. It was at the corner of Jackson Square farthest from Seamus, and even though it pained her, if its destruction gave Seamus more time, then it would be worth it. "It's a huge landmark, isn't it? It even survived until my time."

"It's owned by one of the krewe," said McCullen.

She thought of arguing with him on the evils of sparing one's partners in crime from the pain and destruction others would have to face, but it would do no good. Besides, who could say if the owner knew a thing about Krewe Taranis's assassinations and involvement in nefarious political deeds? The owner could just be interested in mummy parties and balls.

"And what about the police? Does the chief belong to the krewe also? Is that why no one is trying to stop you?"

"A police chief would not be in the social class of the other krewe members," he said.

Oh, yes. Of course. But a police chief could be bribed. And asking someone to leave a terrifying machine alone would not be so hard.

She looked out at the river and thought she saw a shimmer, but it vanished. Seamus looked up. He had seen it too. Then he bent back over the machine. McCullen ripped apart the next steamboat.

From this distance, Felicia could get a good look at the cathedral. The entire front wall was ripped off, and the side walls and roof were partially gone. The inside was a mass of fallen beams, shattered plaster and debris. The automatons were still scattered about like corpses and somewhere inside were statues, probably buried or broken. Felicia knew the people would rebuild, and by her time, the landmark would be shining and whole. But to see all the beautiful buildings destroyed was torture.

McCullen was focused on the riverboat and did not see Mr. Grey stand up and speak to Seamus. Hazel did a little spinning dance, jumping in a circle and clapping.

It was going to work. Seamus was going to open up a time rip as she and McCullen were passing by. They would be sent to wherever it led, past or future. They could arrive when no humans other than a few Native Americans were in the area. They would freeze or starve. Or they could come through in prehistoric times. Or maybe in some distant future time where she would be a strange relic, unable to function in the world.

McCullen finished with the steamboats and marched the hexapod down the strip of Woldenberg Park. Seamus crouched down next to his machine. Hazel and Mr. Grey moved off toward the buildings. Of course Seamus would want Hazel away from any time rip. But then, what was he doing so close to it?

Then it came. The shimmer appeared, but it was over the water, not on land. And McCullen was not about to drive the hexapod into the water. That was where the synchronicity must be. All the riverboats through the centuries had traveled that route. Vehicles as large as hexapods driving down St. James Street were much more of a rarity.

Seamus was doing something with the machine, most likely trying to get the rip to appear over land. He turned the machine sideways and then pounded the top with his fist. She would have laughed if she hadn't been so terrified.

"Ah, there's my boy," said McCullen. "I was wondering when he'd show up."

This was Felicia's only chance. McCullen paused to watch Seamus's frantic movements. She was fairly sure she knew which levers to pull to steer the hexapod the forty-five degrees necessary to hit the center of the shimmering time rip. With luck, she could open the bottom hatch and get out. But if not, at least she could spare this world from McCullen's madness and war. She would spare Hazel and Seamus, and even secretive Mr. Grey.

She leapt forward, shoved the levers and then, when McCullen grabbed her from behind, she elbowed him hard in the stomach. She levered her torso forward and when she felt McCullen become unbalanced, she flung her head backward into his face. McCullen's nose make a soft popping sound as her skull cracked into it. His arms released her as he grabbed at his face. Instead of checking to see what he was going to do next, Felicia pushed the levers farther, adjusting them to what she thought was the correct setting.

The hexapod swayed wildly, then staggered in the direction of the water.

"You damned idiot!" screamed McCullen. "You'll kill us both."

He went for the controls and shoved her aside. The front feet of the hexapod stepped into the mud on the riverbank. Felicia pushed McCullen and he as he lost his balance, he grabbed her. The edge of the chair hit him in the back of the knees, sending him backward onto the floor, with her sprawling on top of him.

The hexapod lurched sideways. The floor tipped one way, then the other as the hexapod tried to stabilize itself.

It then slogged forward, pulling its feet out of the mud two by two, its engines roaring with the effort.

"We're in the mud. It will get stuck!" shouted McCullen. He leapt into the chair, so when the floor tipped backwards again, Felicia slid to the back of the compartment while McCullen stayed put. He righted the hexapod for an instant, and through the glass, Felicia saw the air shimmering in front of them. They were now pretty far into the Mississippi River and the water was only about five feet below the base of the hexapod's body. The hexapod swayed sickeningly and Felicia saw shimmers on either side of the hexapod, just a few feet from the side windows. It was just like on her bus back home. The shimmers seemed to be all around them.

McCullen worked at the lever and cursed in Gaelic, but it wasn't the lilting and amusing way that Seamus cursed at his machinery. McCullen just sounded ugly. The hexapod's feet had a harder and harder time pulling free of the mud. It leaned forward for another step, the feet straining to find purchase. But it was too late. Brown and white crashed outside the windows as the body of the hexapod splashed down into the river. Then dark water covered the front windows.

Felicia grabbed onto a pipe as the hexapod floated on its side, some of its feet still stuck in the mud. Water poured in through the cracks between the window panes. Moments later, something broke free in the mud below, and there was a different sort of movement, gentle and undulating. The current was carrying them. The hexapod was floating directly into the shimmering time rip.

CHAPTER 35

SEAMUS WATCHED THE HEXAPOD SPLASH down into the water. A few of the lights on the underside of the machine flickered and blinked off, but enough were still on to give plenty of light. It seemed like there was somehow too much light. The body of the machine was half-submerged and he saw a figure inside.

A few people were gathered on the riverbank. They had been hiding inside the shops and down side streets and now that the machine was crippled, they ventured out to watch its death. Seamus thought that the gigantic contraption would have been magnificent, if only it had not been used as an instrument of destruction. Then he imagined hordes of the machines, stomping through Atlanta or Memphis, Philadelphia or New York. Would McCullen stack the war in the South's favor, or sell machines to both sides? The monsters could tear through London, through Dublin. The world was hardly at peace, but machines like these would tip whatever fragile balance currently existed. The thing had to be destroyed. Or better yet, removed entirely from this world so no one could ever learn from it or create another.

But what if the rip sent it to the past? It could change the entire course of history. But then, if that were the case, then history would already have been changed. Did that mean that the rip was to the future?

"Professor!" screamed Hazel and pointed at the machine. "I see white inside!"

It took a moment for Seamus to know what she meant, but by the time he understood, the hatch on the bottom of the machine banged open. Out came a foot, a slim foot clad in a purple canvas and white rubber shoe.

He ran toward the water. He was a God damned idiot. He tore off his coat and cursed himself with all the viciousness brought on by his ice cold fear. Miss Sanchez was with McCullen. Of course. She had been with him when Seamus had left her. And she would have wanted to learn what McCullen was up to. But how had she ended up in the machine? Had McCullen forced her inside?

When he was waist-deep in the water, Seamus turned and made eye contact with Mr. Grey. "Turn it off!" he yelled. "Shut it down!"

Mr. Grey yelled something back, but Seamus had already leapt into the water and was swimming toward the machine. It was only ten yards away from the shimmering doorway. The water was so cold that it took his breath away, but he didn't need to breathe. He just needed to get to Felicia. Stubborn, mad Felicia who had allowed herself to be taken by McCullen as Mardi Gras Queen. He understood now. She would have gone with McCullen to try to stop him. That was why the machine had taken a sudden turn toward the time rip. That was why it had lurched earlier, as if the driver had lost control. It had been Felicia.

He kicked off his shoes underwater and swam hard, trying desperately to close the distance between them before she was pulled through the rip. The air burned in his lungs and his limbs ached and protested, but he did not slow.

Seamus now understood why there was so much light. Sunlight shone through the time rip. It was daylight there.

It didn't matter. Another light on the bottom of the hexapod dimmed and flickered out, but Seamus could still see Felicia clinging to one of the legs. She was submerged to the neck and her arms kept grasping at the thick metal leg and sliding off. She was struggling to keep her head above water. Couldn't she swim?

Then he understood. Her dress was made of yards and yards of heavy fabric, and once it was wet, it would weigh so much that it would easily drag her to the bottom of the river. Even a strong swimmer could not overcome such weight.

A dark shape in the water approached Felicia. It was McCullen and he pushed her up onto the leg of the machine. She climbed and lay sprawled on it, dragging her lower body out of the water with effort. She sat up and started tearing at her underskirts, kicking them off. She was getting rid of some weight. Good girl. Tear them off and swim to safety, he thought.

The spider machine was caught in the current and moving swiftly now. It was floating toward the rip faster than he could swim.

McCullen was beside Felicia now on the machine's leg. Though she was still in that dress, he pulled her arms around his neck from behind, as if he were about to give her a piggyback ride. Then they leapt into the water together. McCullen had not left her and swam to safety alone. He intended to tow Felicia to shore. He was trying to save her.

But it was already too late. A moment later, the shimmering time rip swallowed Felicia, the spider machine and McCullen. The river went black as the daylight from the rip and the machine's lights disappeared.

Seamus swam on, then slowed, then stopped. He treaded water, looking at the place where the rip had been. There was nothing there now but black water with little sparks of light where the moonlight reflected on its surface. The doorway was closed.

It took a few moments for a clear thought to register. Felicia's nephew would die, she would be trapped in a new time, and it was all his fault.

People on the shore were shouting. They were jubilant. They were safe. The danger was gone. The terrible machine was no more.

"Seamus!" a voice shouted close by. Behind him, Mr. Grey rowed an old dingy. He must have found it near the shore.

When he got close enough, Seamus said, "I thought I told you to close the rip!"

"We did," said Mr. Grey, pulling up alongside him. "But it stayed open."

Mr. Grey helped haul Seamus into the dingy and Seamus was vaguely aware that he was cold. His teeth chattered and his clothes clung like icy skin to his body. It made no difference. As suddenly and as strangely as she had come into his world, Felicia had gone.

CHAPTER 36

S HE WAS IN A HOSPITAL room. Felicia knew that much. It was clean and modern. Well, mostly modern. It wasn't what she was used to, but it wasn't the hospital from Seamus's time either. There was no TV and the bed seemed to move up and down with levers and cranks instead of the electric push-buttons of her time.

She knew she had been here a while, as she had fuzzy memories of nurses and a doctor. She remembered looking out the window, but her room was too high up to see anything but the sides of the nearby buildings. They were made of glass and smooth concrete.

An IV pole stood beside her bed with a tube snaking to the needle taped to the back of her hand. There was a moment when she wanted to tear it out, but that was foolishness. It was only fear that would make her act so rashly. She could take the IV out properly. But not yet.

She swung her legs over the side of the bed and noticed that her feet and legs were bare and uninjured. Her arms and hands looked fine as well. She was wearing only a flimsy hospital gown and the cool, recirculated air made her backside feel chilly. She pulled the gown closed.

She needed to see the street below. If she could see cars or look at people's clothing, she could make a guess as to what era she was in. She grabbed the IV pole and rolled it across the cold linoleum floor to the window. Down below, there were cars. Not horses or carriages or steam-powered mechanical contraptions. Just cars. They looked like the cars from photos of her parents' childhood. And there were people on the sidewalks. Men wore suits, which didn't give her much of a clue. The women were more helpful. They wore either dresses or skirt and jacket sets, pantyhose and heels or flats. There wasn't a sneaker or flip-flop in sight. It looked like the late 1950s or early 1960s.

Either way, a hundred years had passed. Seamus would be dead by now, as would Hazel. Felicia's own parents would just be children, if they were in this world at all. And here she was, naked but for a thin hospital gown with nothing more to her name than insane tales of time travel. They would lock her away in an asylum if she ever spoke of it.

"Oh, you're up," said a woman behind her. It was a nurse. Her auburn hair was styled in a modest bouffant and she wore a crisp white uniform with a skirt that came to just below the knee.

"What's the date?" asked Felicia.

"June fifteenth. Would you like to sit down? You look a little woozy."

"I'm fine," she said. And though she was indeed dizzy, it wasn't the terrible sickening feeling she had experienced when she had come through into Seamus's time. "How long have I been here?"

"Eight days. Do you remember the accident?"

Felicia did. She remembered it all: the darkness of the water, the light coming through the rip, the weight of her dress pulling her under and the terror that she would drown.

"No, I don't remember," she said. "What happened to me?"

"Come on and sit down. I'll be back in a minute to take your blood pressure." The nurse left and came back a minute later. "I notified the front desk and I had Dr. Fairfax paged. He has been very concerned about you."

Felicia sat on the bed and the nurse fastened on the

blood pressure cuff and pumped the bulb. Felicia let her do the mental countdown without bothering her.

"Can you tell me what happened to me?" Felicia asked when she was through.

"You had a boating accident and you almost drowned."

"There was a man with me. Oren McCullen. What happened to him?"

"He was discharged a few days ago. But he sent you those," she indicated a dying bouquet of flowers beside the bed. Felicia had not noticed them before. "He's fine. Is he a friend of yours?"

Felicia nodded, but only because she could hardly say that he was an enemy. He was back in his own time, approximately where he should be after going missing in 1947. He had told her he was born in Omagh, Ireland. She wondered if he would head home, assuming this was his home world.

"Someone at the desk will call your aunt," said the nurse. "Ah, there he is."

The doctor entered. "May I have a moment with my patient?" he asked.

Something about the shape of his eyes and jaw was familiar to Felicia. The nurse nodded and left.

"Felicia Sanchez," he said, flipping through a chart. "It's good to see you up and awake."

"Where am I?"

"LSU Medical Center, New Orleans. June fifteenth, 1961."

She had only asked the location, not the date. He looked at her unflinchingly, watching her reaction. He knew. She was sure of it. She glanced at his feet. The toes of the shoes were big and blocky. Seamus's universe then. In 1961.

"What's this about an aunt? And how do you know my name?"

"You told us your name, though you probably don't remember. As for your aunt, she has been visiting every day. A nurse called her and let her know that you are awake. She says she's your only living relative."

Dr. Fairfax was silent as he examined her. She noticed that he did not put on rubber gloves.

"What happened to me in the water?" she asked.

"The paramedics reported that you and a gentleman friend had a boating accident. You almost drowned. It was touch and go there for a while, but you pulled through."

"What about the machine? The thing we were in?"

"I don't know about the boat. You could ask the police. I only treat the patients who are brought in."

"Am I allowed to leave?"

"I want you here for a while for observation, but then yes, you can leave. I can release you to your aunt."

Felicia hesitated. She wanted to know who this person was who claimed to be her aunt. But asking something like that would make her seem brain damaged. It was sure to get her placed under observation for another day or two.

"Doctor, I have a question," she said. "Have you ever seen feet like mine before?"

He paused. "Once, when I was younger."

"My shoes, where are they?"

"I think they were lost in the river, or maybe after. You didn't have any personal belongings registered."

Well, her fancy ball dress was gone for good. That was not as bad as losing her shoes.

"What about my jewelry?" She had no personal affection for the Egyptian antiquities, but they might fetch her a little money if she sold them.

Dr. Fairfax flipped a sheet on his clipboard. "We had no belongings registered to you."

A nurse came with a stack of clothing. The items must have been abandoned, or perhaps they belonged to the dead. There was a wool skirt and cotton blouse, a camisole, shoes, clean panties and a bra in something close to her size. There was also a sealed plastic bag with a comb and a toothbrush. Felicia went to the bathroom to get dressed and clean herself up. She looked in the mirror. There were dark marks under her eyes and her lips were pale and sickly. Well, a week in bed will do that to you. That, and falling through a time rip twice in as many weeks. Her hair looked terrible and her skin felt like it was covered in a grimy film. She showered, shampooed, combed her hair and got dressed.

When she left the bathroom, a woman in her sixties stood looking out the window. She had gray streaked through her mouse brown hair and wore a gaudy paisley shirt in a blue and green print with some kind of loose trousers tucked into soft leather boots. The woman turned, and though age had changed her face, her eyes were the same. They were brown with an impish spark that the years had not touched. Then, she smiled, and there was no doubt left.

"Hey, Miss Sanchez."

CHAPTER 37

"**I**'VE COME TO SAY GOOD-BYE," said Mr. Grey.

Hazel stood in the entryway of the Professor's house, her house, but she could not speak. She just hung onto the door and stared at Mr. Grey. She had seen him coming up the walk from her bedroom window and had run downstairs, glad to see him. And now here he was, holding a large paper sack and telling her good-bye.

"Where have you been?" Hazel asked. "It has been a week since the spider machine."

"I had business to conclude with the police. Please tell the Professor that with McCullen gone, they have been able to confiscate a few of the engines. Some have been surrendered by owners who now understand the danger they pose. There are still some being used, but the police think that they can use the legal clause that makes the machines revert to the McCullen manufactory if they malfunction. If they are accident prone, then they are classified as defective. Then the matter is simply forcing the manufactory to surrender or destroy them. Without McCullen pulling strings with the krewe, the police can act without fear of repercussions. McCullen was very secretive about the designs, and the second in command at the manufactory is now more concerned with keeping his fortune and avoiding prison than in making more engines."

"I'll tell him. Why do you have to go? And where are you going? Why can't you just stay?" She knew she sounded whiny and childish, but she didn't care.

"I have to. I came to do a job, and I'm done."

"Well, you failed at it." He looked startled, and Hazel felt an evil satisfaction. "Miss Sanchez is gone, the Professor is miserable and McCullen is with Miss Sanchez, wherever that may be. If your job was to do nothing while terrible things happened, then you did it. You're a terrible time traveler. And that's a fact."

"And what should a good time traveler have done?"

"Well, he should have helped people. And saved people. And fixed things, not just let them get worse and then leave."

"Is that what you would do?"

"Darn right," she said, not caring if she didn't sound polite or ladylike. Mr. Grey wasn't the sort of man who thought that little girls should be sunshine and smiles all the time. "I'd save all the people who needed saving. I'd have saved Miss Sanchez."

"How?" he asked in a way that meant he really wanted her opinion and wasn't just asking to rile her up.

"Well, I don't know," she admitted after thinking for a few moments.

"Neither do I. But I did accomplish some things. I kept the Professor from being detained for days by the police for rummaging around McCullen's study. And my partners got the Professor an engine." He looked as if he really wanted her to understand what he had done. "And I can tell you this. Things will work out in the end. You're in the midst of the worst part just now."

"Yeah, and it's always darkest before the dawn. I'm too old for that load of rubbish. And hey, there's one more thing. How are you leaving if you don't have a way to rip a hole in time? Are you going to walk back to Miss Sanchez's time?"

He didn't answer. Hazel had learned that Mr. Grey would not tell direct lies. At least, she thought she knew that about him.

"You do have a way to rip holes, don't you?" she asked. He looked at her with that expression that was part surprise and part pride in her. "You awful man! You have a way and you didn't save Miss Sanchez and now the Professor is in a terrible state. He's up in his laboratory all the time. He only comes out to teach his classes or eat supper. He barely sleeps and I think he's drinking again. I hear him rattling around in there at all hours, working on the machine. He curses and yells and he's just miserable."

"He'll be fine. He'll figure it out."

Hazel glared at him and then a thought clicked into place. "He's going to do it? He'll get the machine to work? Are you sure?" At his little shrug, she gave a little jump. "Ha! Of course you're sure. You're using his machine!"

"Now pipe down. You can't go saying that. I never said anything about using his machine. You can't say a word."

"Yeah, yeah. I'll keep my mouth shut. Promise." She traced an X over her heart with her finger.

"There's something else," he said. "Did you see the newspaper?"

"Mrs. Washington says it's not proper for a little girl to read the papers." Hazel was rarely limited by propriety, but she was trying to be an obedient child to please the Professor and Mrs. Washington.

"And I know you'd never do anything improper. Here." He pulled a folded newspaper from his inner jacket pocket and opened it. He pointed to a short paragraph at the back of the business page.

Hazel read. It said that for the last eight weeks, Mr. Andrew Dubois had been under investigation for corruption in connection with local land ownership disputes. Families had been driven bankrupt and had lost their homes and farms. He had made many enemies. Legal circles stated that his disbarment was inevitable. But the night before last, he boarded a train for New York. He was found dead in his sleeper car, apparently of heart failure. The police and coroner were not performing an autopsy and there would be no investigation of foul play.

"Something about this isn't right," said Hazel, handing the paper back to Mr. Grey. He stuck it in the large paper sack he was carrying.

"Nothing about this is right," he said.

She thought of something, a terrible thing. She almost didn't say it, but she had to know.

"Where were you that night?" she asked. He had promised that her uncle would not bother her again, and now it was true. Without Miss Sanchez to restrain him, she could imagine the Professor doing violence to her uncle. But not Mr. Grey. He was so composed.

"I was here, in New Orleans," he said.

"Word of honor?"

"Word of honor."

"I still don't believe that he just died on a train. It sounds like someone killed him." She bit her lower lip in thought.

"He had many enemies. There were all of those people he cheated. Though it says there was no evidence of foul play."

"Even so," she said. She was trying to think it through, but she could find no satisfactory answer. How could someone disguise a murder as heart failure? And how could her uncle die just after he had found her and Mr. Grey had spoken to him on the front lawn?

Then another thought came. Mr. Grey had friends, fellow time travelers. The Professor had mentioned a woman named September Wilde, and there were others as well. But then, none of those people had any cause to harm Uncle Andrew. The explanation that made the most sense was that one of the people he had cheated had come for him. But then how would they disguise a killing? Perhaps, he had truly died of natural causes.

"What did you say to him outside?" Hazel said. "You have to tell me."

"I told him that extradition from the state of New York to Louisiana was difficult. I suggested he leave town."

It still wasn't right. Someone had killed her uncle. Or perhaps, her parents, or even God himself had answered her prayer.

But Mr. Grey was standing on the front step now, and he wouldn't be there much longer. She could think about it later.

"The Professor says that there is still going to be a war," she said. "The papers are printing inflammatory articles and Breckinridge is saying that he's opposing slavery when he takes office in a few weeks. I don't know what will happen."

"No one does."

"You should have stayed with us instead of leaving that night. The Professor and I spent two days going around and closing the time rips. He got what he calls 'extraordinary data' from the tripod sensors when the rip over the river closed. And then he figured out how to close the rips. At least, we think so."

"I knew he would."

"You're leaving for good then?" she asked.

"I'll come back and visit you, but not for a while yet," Mr. Grey said.

"When?"

"I'll see you on January 8th, 1864."

"That's on my birthday. But it's not for years. That's so long."

"Your birthday? Is that right?" he said. "Then this will have to be for all the birthdays between now and then." He opened the paper sack and brought out a long box wrapped in white paper with a light blue ribbon. Hazel stared at it until he said, "Well, take it."

Hazel took the box and stood looking at it.

"Aren't you going to open it?" he asked.

"Not at the front door. You should come in," she said

and they walked to the front parlor. She unwrapped the box, pulled out the tissue paper and stood, staring at the violin case lying inside. It was shiny black, new and beautiful. She remained there, looking at it until she made herself lift out the case and set it on the table. The latches flipped back smoothly with a small, perfect click. The case was lined in royal blue velvet and the violin itself was a fine, chestnut red color. She lifted it out and set it in her lap, then unwrapped a soft cloth at the bottom of the case and found a brand new cake of fragrant rosin. She took up the violin and set it under her chin. The beautiful scent of new wood and fresh varnish surrounded her. She picked up the bow. It was beautiful, and she turned it this way and that, but did not touch it to the strings.

"Don't cry, Hazel, it's only a violin."

She shook her head, though she wasn't denying what he had said. It was just too much for him to give her. She had tried not to think of her dashed hopes of going to a Northern conservatory or of playing in any sort of professional capacity. She had a home with the Professor and Mrs. Washington and she could go to school. To ask for more would be selfish, though she had considered asking the Professor for a violin at Christmastime. To receive this from someone who barely knew her was more kindness than she could bear.

"I'll treasure it always," she said.

"I know you will."

CHAPTER 38

"**Y**OU SHOULD BE OVER A hundred years old, and you look half that," said Felicia.

"Half? Really? You flatter me."

"But you're Hazel Dubois, right? Not her daughter?"

"I'm Hazel."

Hazel turned her 1959 Buick Electra onto St. Charles Avenue and stopped at a light. The Electra was a huge car complete with fins, pointed conical taillights and a thin, spindly steering wheel. It was painted in a metallic lavender shade with white upholstery. Hazel clearly loved the thing. Felicia thought it was a fascinating relic. It being June, Hazel had the top down and had wrapped her hair in a patchwork scarf. Felicia's hair blew loose.

"I live in the Professor's old house," said Hazel. "At least for now. There's something waiting there for you."

They drove on and Hazel made a U-turn and pulled the car to a stop along the curb in front of Seamus's old house. Felicia stood on the sidewalk and studied the house. The intervening century had changed the building and the yard. The shutters were no longer green, but were painted a crisp white and matched rest of the house. The structure of the house was the same, but the trim was different and the railing on the upper gallery had been replaced with one with less elaborate iron scrollwork.

Two huge live oaks shaded the yard and a wooden swing hung from one. Felicia wondered what children had played on it. Or did Hazel go for a swing now and then on a balmy summer night? Yellow jacobinia and heavenly bamboo had taken the place of the star magnolias and oakleaf hydrangea bushes on the edges of the yard.

Hazel closed the car and the two of them walked up the path. It was no longer brick, but was now concrete. They passed under a wooden arbor hung with lush clumps of purple wisteria. The front door had been replaced by one with less glass and the mail slot and door knocker were made of a lighter metal. Hazel let them inside.

"I'm glad you saw the place in its glory days," said Hazel, tracing her hand along the banister. "We try to keep it up, but it's not always easy." The house not only looked older, it had the smell of age. It wasn't just dust or stale air, it was the scent of ancient plaster, aging wood and a century of furniture polish.

"Who else lives with you? Is the Professor here?"

"No."

"And are you going to explain to me how you're here?"

"No, I can't."

"You sound like Mr. Grey."

Hazel laughed as if she had heard as much said to her before. She led Felicia up the stairs and down the hall, toward the laboratory. Felicia almost didn't want to go. If Seamus wasn't there, then the room would be changed. Without his creative chaos, it would be dead. She didn't want to see.

"He left something for you," said Hazel, stopping in the hallway. "It's a good thing. You'll want to see it."

Hazel opened the laboratory door and the room was indeed changed. The dusty space was filled with the relics and castoffs of a century. A set of paintings, all stacked one upon the other, sat atop a trunk. Nearby stood a plaster bust, staring into space. Boxes were stacked haphazardly and a ladder that was missing a rung lay along the baseboard. And there was Seamus's old desk. But instead of being covered in papers, it was lost under a stack of yellowing newspapers, a rusting cast iron stock pot, an old jewelry box and drip-covered paint cans and drop cloths.

At the center of the room rose an object. From the look of the dust on the floor around it, Hazel had dragged it out recently. It was waist-high, rounded on top and covered in a sheet. Felicia pulled it off without asking. This was what Seamus had left her.

The thing seemed larger once it was out from under its sheet, as if it was somehow alive and waking up. It was a machine. The top of it was domed and covered in shining brass, held together with tiny rivets. There were a few knobs on the cover, and it looked like pieces of the dome slid away to expose something beneath.

A row of dials and knobs set into a large rectangle of polished rosewood ran along the base of the dome. Just as with McCullen's hexapod, the faces of the dials were hand-lettered, but these were in a familiar hand. At the end of the row of dials was an on/off switch, sitting under a hinged glass cover, presumably to keep it from accidentally being flipped. The control panel was edged in swirls of metal scrollwork. It was Seamus's little artistic touch.

The base of the machine was long and rectangular, almost like a box stood on its end. It looked like it had once been a trunk, and perhaps it had, with metal latches on one side and hinges on the other.

She studied the dials, but knew better than to touch the knobs beneath them without knowing what she was doing. Under the panel with the dials and knobs was a sliding latch, and now that Felicia looked more closely, there were two hinges about eight inches down from it. It was a small door that spanned the width of the trunk. She slid open the latch and the door fell open and banged flat as two metal hinges snapped open to hold it in place. It was like a little desk, she thought, a little writing surface with a compartment in which to keep things. There was a long, shallow indentation for a pencil, and tipped against the back of the machine, a handmade book. It was not a book, properly speaking, but was a sheaf of papers that had been hand bound with thread. The leather cover was blank.

Felicia turned to look for Hazel, but she must have gone downstairs. Felicia thought of calling to her, but something made her want to be alone. This was Seamus's creation, his life's work, and though he could not give it to her in his own time, he had left it for her.

She laid the book flat on the little desk and turned the pages. It was filled with lists and numbers, which must correspond to the dials. There was some kind of rating system as well, with words like "well-explored," "dangerous" and "do not attempt."

She looked for dates, and saw that there was no rhyme or reason to the order listed in the book. Aside from the rating system on a time's safety were other notes. It looked like a code of letters and numbers.

She flipped through the pages and stopped at a thin envelope nestled between two of the pages. It was just large enough for a half sheet of paper and had one word written upon it: Felicia. She slid out the paper inside.

Dearest Miss Sanchez,

I hope my letter finds you in good health. I regret that I cannot be there to assist you, but I have no doubt you will be successful. I have enclosed coordinates. I know you will be brilliant.

Yours ever,

Seamus Doyle

There was a set of numbers at the bottom and a diagram of the dome of the machine with arrows and positioning notes. Hazel had returned and was standing just outside the laboratory door, watching her.

"What time is it?" Felicia asked.

Hazel glanced at her watch. "Four minutes to noon."

"Then we'll need to pull this into the hall."

Hazel helped Felicia drag the machine into the hallway. Felicia set the dials to the coordinates and moved the panels on the dome as indicated in Seamus's note. Then, she grabbed the laboratory door and pulled it closed.

Hazel moved away until she was all the way down the hall, watching from a distance.

"Aren't you coming?" asked Felicia.

"I'm already there."

Of course, Felicia thought. She lifted the glass cover and flipped the machine's power switch. The hum of the machine was so low that it made the floor vibrate. Then came a second note that started low but grew in pitch, higher and higher until it was inaudible. Felicia wanted to back away from the machine. Every part of her said that it was dangerous, unpredictable and that she should flee. But she stood firm. Her future was waiting. The air shimmered.

In another world, a man would be in front of a tack board covered in papers full of notes and diagrams and equations. His hair would be sticking up at all angles as he paced amid the chaos of wires and tubing and mechanical joints.

And then at noon precisely, when it was time for lunch, there would be a knock at the laboratory door.

THE END

AUTHOR'S NOTE

I love hearing from my readers. To drop me a note or to learn about my other books, please visit www.heatherblackwood.com.

If you enjoyed this book, please post a review on the retail site where you purchased it.

www.ingramcontent.com/pod-product-compliance
Lightning Source LLC
Chambersburg PA
CBHW021321250626

47155CB00002B/575